KISSING CARRION

KISSING CARRION

Gemma Files

PRIME BOOKS
Canton, Ohio

Kissing Carrion

Copyright © 2003 by Gemma Files.
Introduction copyright © 2003 by Caitlin R. Kiernan.
Cover art copyright © 2003 by Dale L. Sproule.
Cover design copyright © 2003 by Juha Lindroos.

All rights reserved. No part of this publication may be reproduced or transmitted in any form or by any means, electronic or mechanical, including photocopy, recording, or any information storage and retrieval system now known or invented, without permission in writing from the publisher, except by a reviewer who wishes to quote brief passages in connection with a review written for inclusion in a magazine, newspaper, broadcast, etc.

Published in the United States by Prime Books, Inc.
P.O. Box 36503, Canton, OH 44735
www.primebooks.net

ISBN: 1-894815-63-7

Gemma Files would like to thank:

Elva Mai Hoover and Gary Files
Stephen J. Barringer
Everyone who considers themselves my friend.
Everyone who's happy to have been my student.
Everyone who's ever published any of my work, fictional or non-.
Everyone who ever went to see a film on the basis of one of my reviews, especially if they kept on wanting to read my reviews even if they didn't agree with my opinion about the film, or
films, they ended up seeing on my recommendation.
Everyone who's even thinking about reading this book right now.

CONTENTS

9.	Introduction by Caitlin R. Kiernan
13.	Kissing Carrion
30.	Keepsake
46.	Rose-Sick
54.	Blood Makes Noise
68.	Skeleton Bitch
76.	Folly
85.	Mouthful Of Pins
91.	Pretend That We're Dead
96.	No Darkness But Ours
115.	Job 37
115.	Bear-Shirt
134.	Hidebound
151.	Skin City
162.	Seen
170.	Torch Song
186.	The Diarist
192.	Dead Bodies Possessed By Furious Motion
213.	Afterword

Introduction

By Caitlin R. Kiernan

People ask me all the time, but the truth is, I don't know why I write dark fiction. The best reply I've ever been able to muster is that it's all I have to say, or all I have to say that's worth saying. It's the way I see and, sooner or later, all clouds become demons in my view. Once upon a time, I kept it all to myself, tangled up inside my soul like loops of thorns and razor wire and blind, squirming things. The images, which always came without my having to call for them, were mine and they were mine alone. And then, at some point, I began to put them down on paper.

I was a slow starter.

I took ages to break down the high, white barriers that I'd erected, or that others had taken the liberty of erecting for me. Years to work through the layers of inhibition, the solidifying strata of guilt arising from my own visions.

And in the beginning, there was a terrible, electric thrill in the simple speaking of the unspeakable. Something more immediate than sex, because it was more than flesh could ever be. Something more honest than confession, because it would never compromise itself in apology. Something as alive as alive can ever be, because it never tried to look away from death. But as the years came and went, and the stories and novels piled up about me, I began to realize that some of that thrill had begun to diminish. Or, rather, that first hot rush of words and raw, dizzying imagery had been spent and something else was growing in its place, something with virtues all it's own, sure, but something that lacked the undeniable urgency I'd felt back at the start. A sort of psychic scar tissue, perhaps, and all the endless conceits of art, filtering what had once escaped me unfiltered, pure and untainted by second-guessing games.

Which brings me, finally, in my own rambling, self-absorbed way, to the matter at hand, which isn't my writing at all, but the writing of Gemma Files, collected here in this volume entitled *Kissing Carrion*. I don't write many introductions, because, truthfully, I don't read very much contemporary dark fiction. Most of it bores me silly. So, when I was asked to introduce this book, I almost said no, because I almost always say no (the particular questions are immaterial). After all, I'd never even read anything by Gemma Files, though I did recognize her name from *Dark Terrors 6*, *The Mammoth Book of Vampire Stories by Women*, and *Queer Fear*, because I'd also had stories printed in those books. I rarely get around to reading the anthologies that I'm published in, though sometimes I do take time to browse through their tables of contents, noting the names of the other authors. Oh, and I also recalled that Gemma Files had won an International Horror Guild award for best short fiction.

Moreover, there's always the imminent danger of misinterpreting the author in an attempt to flatter. I can think of few things more embarrassing, and more annoying to the author being flatteringly misunderstood. Of course, some would say that all interpretations of a given work are valid, in some sense, and therefore such a danger is actually a paper tiger. But those people are fools.

Anyway, I agreed to have a look at the manuscript, but didn't commit to writing the introduction. At the time, I was in the middle of a move from Birmingham to Atlanta and trying to deal with all the chaos that invariably attends a move, and also trying to meet a number of deadlines. One morning early in January, the manuscript for *Kissing Carrion* arrived at my door and a few days later I read the first piece, from which the collection takes its title. I was at once surprised, because the story *didn't* bore me silly and because I liked it even though it was written in first person (a practice that annoys me no end and which I've spent years condemning) and so, the next day, I read "Keepsake," and then "Rose-Sick," and, finally, "Blood Makes Noise." Two of these were also written in first person, and, worse yet, one—"Rose-Sick"—was written in *second*-person, which, if you ask me, is as deadly a sin as any to which an author can ever aspire. Even so, I began to feel that old familiar *charge* again. The electric-bright sizzle in a very dark place. The fleeting spark in an Antarctic night. White fire from abyssal blackness, like the gleaming, ancient creature aboard the doomed submarine from "Blood Makes Noise;"

something whispering in the gloom, whispering with a voice that made me want to listen.

This happens so infrequently that I stopped expecting it a long time back. Very few living authors can find that particular chord in me and still fewer can ever strike it more than once or twice. Fewer still write dark fiction. Kathe Koja. Thomas Ligotti. Ramsey Campbell. Peter Straub. Perhaps one or two others. It's a short list. But, first- and second-person narratives aside, I discovered that Gemma Files *was* doing it, again and again and again. Whatever doubts I might still have had about doing the introduction were dismissed by the next story, "Skeleton Bitch," which left me breathless and wanting more and angry that I hadn't written it myself. That's the highest compliment any author can ever pay another, I think, that envy, that wish that you could make another's words your own.

And I kept reading.

And I kept finding that electric sizzle, those white-out sparks, the fire and whispering fossil voices.

Having done so, I will say this, by way of introduction:

Boldly, brazenly, Gemma Files pushes her hands deep into the red and seeping unconscious places and finds the bits of treasure worth pulling back out into the light. The damned things, forbidden, forgotten, unwanted, feared and loathed, and "Here," these stories say to us. "Look what I found. But look quick, before it's gone again."

Unlike the "splatterpunks" of the eighties and early nineties, and unlike the current self-proclaimed authors of "extreme horror," who were and are rarely more than tiresome and never more than idiot jesters of excess and gore and exploitation, Gemma Files seems to grasp the weight and consequence, the inherent *severity*, of her fictive transgressions. And so her stories do not disintegrate, do not dissolve into accidental comedies of the grotesque. They do not degrade her characters, who are what characters must be, inhabitants of an imagination we're being allowed to share, however indirectly, inhabitants gifted with souls and hearts, strength and failure, hope and hopelessness. Horrible things befall them, time and again, but never merely for our amusement.

This is no Roman circus, no peepshow.

I think Gemma Files has grasped the fine and crucial line between pornography and a *true* literature of the extreme. At least, I hope that she has. *Something* is keeping her voice hung just high enough above the pit that we can hear it clearly without tumbling in and drowning. In the end, if we are wise enough to pay attention, we find she's made us look *away* from the pit, up, towards the stars overhead and probably out of reach.

At her best, in pieces like "Skeleton Bitch," "Keepsake," "Skin City" and "Mouthful of Pins," Gemma Files transcends mere storytelling and her prose approaches the poetic, a prose poetry of terror and awe, ruin and pain and horror and constant sorrow. Here are words placed just so, precisely employed in an artistic economy that few writers ever bother to learn.

Here is passion, which must be more sacred to an author than her own life, and here is mystery, which must always obscure the path before us.

It's not about a good, clean scare, a dark theatre you can leave behind after the credits roll, a carnival ride or a Halloween spookhouse. There are plenty of writers of dark fiction who aim for nothing more than such playful, ephemeral frights, and readers beyond counting who want nothing more. I suspect both groups would be unhappy with the seventeen stories that comprise *Kissing Carrion*.

Because these aren't casual undertakings.

These are the things that make us who we would not be, and what we can't help but become.

Sex. Blood. Death.

Secrets and transformations.

Appetite, and loss, and love beyond any explanation.

But I've said enough, surely. More than enough. These stories, and their author, speak for themselves and have no need of anyone else to speak for them. They know themselves well enough without me.

Now, turn the page . . .

> Caitlín R. Kiernan
> Atlanta, Georgia
> 17 January 2003

KISSING CARRION

Q: Are we living in a land where sex and horror are the new Gods?
A: Yeah.
                    —Frankie Goes To Hollywood.

I am persecuted by angels, huge and silent—marble-white, rigid-winged, one in every corner. Only their vast eyes speak, staring mildly at me from under their painful halos, arc-weld white crowns of blank. They say: *Lie down.* They say: *Forgive, forget. Sleep.*

Forget, lie down. Drift away into death's dream. Make your . . . final . . . peace.

But being dead is nothing peaceful—as they must know, those God-splinter-sized liars. It's more like a temporal haematoma, time pooling under the skin of reality like sequestered blood. Memory looping inward, turning black, starting to stink.

A lidless eye, still struggling to close. An intense and burning contempt for everything you have, mixed up tight with an absolute—and absolutely justified—terror of losing it all.

Yet here I am, still. Watching the angels hover in the ill-set corners of Pat Calavera's Annex basement apartment, watching me watch *her* wash her green-streaked hair under the kitchen sink's lime-crusted tap. And thinking one more time how funny it is I can see them, when she can't: They're far more "here" than I am, one way or another, especially in my current discorporant state—an eddying tide of discontent adding one more vague chill to the moldy air around her, stirring the fly-strips as I pass. Pat's roommate hoards trash, breeding a durable sub-race of insects who endure through hot, cold and humid weather alike; he keeps the bathtub full of dirty dishes and the air full of stink, reducing Pat's supposed bedroom to a mere way-stop between gigs, an (in)convenient place to park her equipment 'till the next time she needs to use it.

Days, she teaches socks to talk cute as a trainee intern on *Ding Dong The Derry-O*, the world-famous Hendricks Family Conglomerate's longest-running preschool puppet-show. Nights, she spins extra cash and underground performance art out of playing with her Bone Machine, getting black market-fresh cadavers to parade back and forth on strings for the edification of bored ultra-fetishists. "Carrionettes", that's what she usually calls them whenever she's making them dance, play cards or screw some guy named Ray, a volunteer post-mortem porn-star whose general necrophiliac bent seems to be fast narrowing to one particular corpse, and one alone . . . mine, to be exact.

Pat can't see the angels, though—can't even sense their presence like an oblique, falling touch, a Seraph's pinion-feather trailed quick and light along the back of my dead soul. And really, when you think about it, that's probably just as well.

I mean, they're not here for *her*.

Outside, life continues, just like always: Jobs, traffic, weather. It's February. To the south of Toronto there's a general occlusion forming, a pale and misty bee-swarm wall vorticing aimlessly back and forth across the city while a pearly, semi-permeable lace of nothingness hangs above. Soft snow to the ankles, and rising. Snow falling all night, muffling the world's dim lines, half-choking the city's constant hum.

Inside, Pat turns the tap off, rubs her head hard with a towel and leans forward, frowning at her own reflection in the sink's chipped back-mirror. Her breath mists the glass. Behind her, I float unseen over her left shoulder, not breathing at all.

But not leaving, either. Not as yet.

And: *Sleep*, the angels tell me, silently. And: *Make me*, I reply. Equally silent. To which they say nothing.

I know a lot about this woman, Pat Calavera—more than she'd want me to, if she only knew I knew. How there are days she hates every person she meets for not being part of her own restless consciousness, for making her feel small and useless, inappropriate and frightened. How, since she makes it a habit to always tell the truth about things that don't matter, she can lie about the really important things under almost any circumstances—drunk, high, sober, sobbing.

And the puppets, I know about them too: How Pat's always liked being able to move things around to her own satisfaction, to make things jump—or not—with a flick of her finger, from Barbie and Ken on up. To pull the strings on *something*, even if it's just a dead man with bolts screwed into his bones and wires fed along his tendons.

Because she can. Because it's an art with only one artist. Because she's an extremist, and there's nothing more extreme. Because who's going to stop her, anyway?

Well. Me, I guess. If I can.

(Which I probably can't.)

A quick glance at the angels, who nod in unison: No, not likely.

Predictable, the same way so much of the rest of this—experience of mine's been, thus far; pretty much exactly like all the tabloids say, barring some minor deviations here and there. First the tunnel, then the light—you rise up, lift out of your shell, hovering moth-like just at the very teasing edge of its stinging sweetness. After which, at the last, most wrenching possible moment—you finally catch and stutter, take on weight, dip groundwards. Go down.

Further and further, then further still. Down where there's a Bridge of Sighs, a Bridge of Dread, a fire that burns you to the bone. Down where there's a crocodile with a human face, ready and waiting to weigh and eat your heart. Down where there's a room full of dust where blind things sit forever, wings trailing, mouths too full to speak.

I have no name now, not that I can remember, since they take our names first of all—name, then face, then everything else, piece by piece by piece. No matter that you've come down so fast and hard, fighting it every step; for all that we like to think we can conquer death through sheer force of personality, our mere descent alone strips away so much of who we were, who we *thought* we were, that when at last we've gotten where we're going, most of us can't even remember why we didn't want to get there in the first place.

The truism's true: It's a one-way trip. And giving everything we have away in order to make it, up to and including ourselves, is just the price—the going rate, if you will—of the ticket.

Last stop, everybody off; elevator to . . . not Hell, no. Not exactly . . .

. . . goin' down.

Why would I belong in Hell, anyway, even if it did exist? Sifting through what's left of me, I still know I was average, if that: Not too good, not too bad, like Little Bear's porridge. I mean, I never *killed* anybody, except myself. And that—

—that was only the once.

Three years back, and counting: An easy call at the time, with none of the usual hysterics involved. But one day, I simply came home knowing I didn't ever want to wake up the next morning, to have to go to work, and talk to people, and do my job, and act as though nothing were wrong—to see, or know, or worry about anything, ever again. The mere thought of killing myself had become a pure relief, sleep after exhaustion, a sure cure after a long and disgusting illness.

I even had the pills already—for depression, naturally; thank you, Doctor. So I cooked myself a meal elaborate enough to use up everything in my fridge, finally broke open that dusty bottle of good white wine someone had once given me as a graduation present and washed my last, best hope for oblivion down with it, a handful at a time.

When I woke up I had a tube down my throat, and I was in too much pain to even cry about my failure. Dehydration had shrunk my brain to a screaming point, a shaken bag of poison jellyfish. I knew I'd missed my chance, my precious window of opportunity, and that it would never come again. I felt like I'd been lied to. Like I'd lied to myself.

So, with a heavy heart, I resigned myself once more—reluctantly—to the dirty business of living. I walked out the hospital's front doors, slipped back into my little slot, served out my time. Until last week, when I keeled over while reaching for my notebook at yet one more Professional Development Retreat lecture on stress management in the post-Millennial workplace: Hit the floor like a sack of salt with a needle in my chest, throat narrowing—everything there, then gone, irised inward like some silent movie's Vaseline-smeared final dissolve. Dead at 29 of irreparable heart failure, without even enough warning to be afraid of what—

—or who, in my case—

—came next.

Am I the injured party here? I hover, watching, inside and out; I can hear people's thoughts, but that doesn't mean I can judge their motives. My only real option, at this point, is just what the angels keep telling me it is: Move on, move on, move on. But I'm not ready to do that, yet.

There were five of us in the morgue, after all, but the body snatchers only took two for her to choose from. And of those two . . .

... Pat chose me.

* * *

Lyle turns up at one, punctual as ever, while Pat's still dripping. She opens the door for him, then drops towel and stalks nearly naked back to her room, rooting through her bed's topmost layers in search of some clean underwear; though he's obviously seen it all before, neither of them show any interest in extending this bodily intimacy beyond the realm of the purely familial.

Which only makes sense, now I think about it. In Pat's mind—the only place I've ever encountered Lyle, up 'till now—their relationship rarely goes any further than strictly business. He's her prime "artistic" pimp, shopping the act she and Ray have been working so hard to perfect to a truly high-class clientele: One time only, supposedly. Though by Lyle's general demeanor, I get the feeling he may already be developing his own ideas about that part.

Pat discards a Pixies concert T with what looks like mold-stains all over the back in favor of her Reg Hartt's Sex And Violence Cartoon Festival one, and returns to find Lyle grimacing over a cup of coffee that's been simmering since at least eight.

"Jesus Corpse, Pats. You could clean cars with this shit."

"Machine's on a timer, I'm not." Then, grabbing a comb, bending over, worrying through those last few knots: "Tonight all set up, or what?"

He shrugs. "Or what." She shoots him a glance, drawing a grin. "Look, I told you it was gonna be one of two places, right? So on we go to Plan B, 'sall. The rest's still pretty much as wrote."

"'Pretty much.'"

"Pretty, baby. Just like you."

And: Is she? I suppose so. Black hair and deep, dark eyes—a certain eccentric symmetry of line and feature, a clever mind, a blind and ruthless will. Any and all of which would've certainly been enough to pull *me* in, back when I was still alive enough to want pulling.

The angels tell me I'm bound for something better now, though. Some form of love precious far beyond the bodily, indescribable to anyone who hasn't tasted it at least once before. Which means there's no earthly way I can possibly know if I *want* to 'till I'm already there and drinking my fill, already immersed soul-deep in restorative, White Light-infused glory ...

Convenient, that. As *Saturday Night Live*'s Church Lady so often used to say.

Oh—and "earthly", ha; didn't even catch that one, first time 'round. Look, angels! The corpse just made a funny.

(I said, *look*.)

But they don't.

Pat tops her shirt with a sweater, and starts in filling the many pockets of army pants with all the various Bone Machine performance necessities: Duct tape, soldering wire, extra batteries. Lyle, meanwhile, drifts away to the video rack, where he amuses himself scanning spines.

"This that first tape he sent you?" he demands suddenly, yanking one.

"Who?"

He waggles it, grinning. "Your boyfriend. *Ray*-mond."

A shrug. "Pop it and see."

"Pass." Which seems to remind him: "So, Patty—realize you two are sorta tight and this comes sorta late, but exactly how much you research you actually do on this freak-o before you signed him up for the program?"

Pat's bent over now, hauling her semi-expensive boots up with both mittened hands. "Enough to know he'll fuck dead bodies if I ask him to," she says, shortly.

"'Cause he *wants* to."

A short, sharp smile, orthodontic-straight except for that one canine her wisdom teeth pushed out of line, coming in. "Best way to get anyone to do anything, baby. As you should know."

Of course, Pat's hardly objective. Seeing how she's in lust with Ray ... love, maybe, albeit of a perversely limited sort. Much the same way *he* is, truth be told—

—with "me".

But Lyle, obviously, doesn't feel he can argue the point. So he just returns her smile, talk show bland and throat-slitting bright, as she reaches for the door-handle: Lets them both out, side by side, into a world of gathering cold. All bundled up like Donner Party refugees, and twice as hungry.

And: *Don't follow*, the angels advise me, uselessly. *Don't watch. Don't care.*

But the fact is, I . . . don't. I really don't. Don't feel, or know what I don't feel. Let alone what I do.

D-E-A-D, but way too much still left of me. I'm *dead*, so let me lie. Let me *lie*. Please.

Pat and Lyle, struggling up the alley and down to the nearest curb. Ray, his obtrusively unobtrusive car—the Rich Pervertmobile itself, far too clean and anonymous to be used for anything but life's dirtiest little detours—already there to meet them, pluming steam.

And somewhere, awaiting its cue, the reluctant third party in this little triangle cum foursome: My body, a water-clock full of blood and other fluids, forever counting down to an explosion that's already happened. A psychic plague-bomb oozing excess pain, a hive for flies, all slick, lily-waxen and faintly bruised in the wake of rigor mortis' ebb, even before Ray's hot mouthings gave birth to that starburst of pale lavender hickeys around what used to be my trachea.

It's not *me*, not in any way that counts—but it's not *not* me, either. And I just, I just . . .

. . . don't . . .

. . . want . . .

. . . them *touching* it anymore.

Either of them.

* * *

Going back—as far back as he can, at least—Ray tells Pat that he thinks the first time he really began to understand the true nature of his personal . . . distinction . . . must have been when his parents insisted he visit his beloved grandfather's freshly-dead body at the local hospital: Washed, laid out, neatly johnny-clad. His parents had already forewarned him it would look like a mannequin, like something made of plaster, an empty husk. But it wasn't like that, not even vaguely. It looked oddly magnetic, oddly tactile; nothing rotten, or gross, or potentially contagious—soothing, like an old friend. And its only smell was the familiar odor of shed human skin.

He wanted to lie down with his head on its sternum, breathe deep and let it cool his fever, this constant ceaseless hammering in his head and heart. To free him, for once and for all, of the febrile hum and spark of his own life.

Since then, Ray's never been able to decide what arouses him more: The concept itself, or the sheer impossibility of its execution. Because anyone can fuck the dead, if they only try hard enough—but the dead, by their very nature, can never fuck *back*. Which is why it has to be guys, though he himself is—in every other way than this—"straight". If that term even applies, under these circumstances.

Their superiority. Their otherness. To him, it's only natural: The dead know more, and knowledge is power. And power, as that old politician once boasted . . . is sexy.

So: Fucked in slaughterhouses, under the hanging racks of meat. Fucked with decay smeared all over them both, in graveyards, animal cemeteries; sure, buddy—just gimme my cut, you freak, and bend on over. Fucked in mortuaries, the "other" corpses watching impassively. Corpses taking part in his own taking, silent voyeurs, sad puppets in countless sweaty menages a mort. Fucked by guys wearing corpses' skins—and wow, was *that* expensive, mainly because it went against so many kinds of weird sanitation strictures; public health, and all that. Same reason you can't just drop your Grandad in the garden if he happens to croak at your house—or die at home at all, these days, for that matter.

Fucked by the dying—guys so far gone, so far in the financial hole, they'd do anything to make their next medical bill. A charge, but not quite the same; not the same, and never enough. And finally, back to the morgue alone with condoms and trocar in hand—here's an extra hundred to leave the door ajar, I'll lock up as I leave. No worries.

Money's no problem; Ray *has* money. Too much, some might say—too much free time, and a bit too little to do with except obsess, jerk off, plan. The idle rich are hard to entertain, Vinnie . . .

Things do keep on escalating, though, often and always. And escalation can bring a bad reputation, especially in some quarters.

Which made it all the more lucky Ray and Pat happened to find each other, I suppose—for them both.

And for Lyle, of course, albeit from a very different point of view . . . Lyle, to whom falls the onerous yet lucrative task of facilitating this gender switched post-Millennial Death And The Maiden tableau they've played out every day this week, given or take; same one that would surely re-run itself constantly behind my eyelids if only I still had either eyes to see with, or lids to close on what I didn't want to see. Same one you might well already have seen already, if you're just hip and sick enough to have paid Lyle's "finder's fee" up front—or bought the bootleg DV8 tapes he peddles over the Internet, thus far unbeknownst to either of his silent partners.

Like Lyle, I never saw that original "audition" tape on Pat's shelf, either. But as the run-down above should prove, I've certainly heard its precis often enough: *Why I Like To Get Screwed By Dead Bodies For The Amusement Of Total Strangers Even When The Money Involved's My Own, In Fifty Thousand Words Or More*. Ray's confession/manifesto, re-spilled at intervals—after various post-post-mortem Bone Machine-aided orgies, usually—over binges of beer and weed which sometimes culminate in fumbling, gratitude- and guilt-ridden, mutually unsatisfying attempts at "normal" sex. Pat lying slack beneath a sweating, huffing Ray, trying to will her internal temperature down far enough to maintain his shamed half-erection even as her own orgasm builds, inexorably. Cursing the demeaning depths this idiot hunger for him can make her sink to, while simultaneously feeling her fingers literally itch to seize the Machine's controls again and do the whole damn thing over *right*.

Part of me wonders exactly how much detail I need—or care—to go into here, vis a vis Pat's "art" and my rather uncomfortable place in its embrace. But then again, close as "I" may get to it in flesh, most of the Bone Machine's complex structural workings will probably always remain a mystery to me. Bolts screwed directly into bones, wires strung like tendons, electrical impulses jumping from brain to finger to keypad to central animatronic switchboard...

Pat pulls the strings here, as in all else. When my dead body's making "love" to him, it's her moves, her ideas, her smoothing, gentle touch translated through my flesh, which keeps Ray coming back time and time again; I'm just the medium for her message, a clammy six-foot dildo powered by rods and pistons. A deadweight sex-aid soaked in scented lube to hide the growing spoiled-meat smell, the inevitable wear and tear of Ray's increasingly desperate affections.

But Ray, like any true fetishist, ignores whatever doesn't contribute directly to the fulfillment of his motivating fantasy. He knows our time together's on a (necessarily) tight schedule, so he tries to wring every extra ounce of pleasure he can out of the experience while Pat watches and fumes, trapped behind her rows of switches. He loves the mask, not the face; the made, not the maker. Decay's his groom, and he doesn't want even the shadow of anything else getting in the way of this so-devoutly desired consummation, this last great graveyard gasp.

It'd be sort of tragic, if it wasn't so—mordantly—funny. Together, Pat and Ray have all the requisite common interests and obsessions, plus a heaping helping of that brain-to-groin combustive spark which so many other relationships are made from; if she was dead (or had the right equipment required to rock his world), they'd be perfect for each other. But her hole just doesn't fit his socket, or vice versa. So the only way she can touch him... and make him *want* her to, at least...

...is with *my* hands.

And more and more, that very fact is already making her dream happy dreams of someday taking a bone-saw to "my" wrists. Of burning them in some Haz-Mat crematorium's fire, like plague-infected monster grasshoppers.

Ray told Pat he was literally up for her ultimate piece of performance art, to bravely go where none of her other co-conspirators were ever willing to, not even with three condoms' worth of protection. She told Lyle, who instantly cheered her on, visions of Ben Franklin dancing in his money-colored eyes; he paged his pals down at the M.E.'s office, and the deal was struck—cash for flesh, tickets at the door and a fresh new co-star every week, after the old one finally started to rot.

And so it went, a neat little cycle, a perverse new rhythm method. Pat called the shots, Ray did the dance, Lyle racked up the take; they soon got into the habit of partying later, while Lyle was on his way to the bank. Pat, using Ray's addiction to feed her own, like any pusher trading "free" product for not-so-free favors, while Ray replays his own earlier performance for both their benefits.

It was, and is, a match made in Gomorrah, or maybe Gehenna: Pimp meets girl meets boy meets corpse(s). And everybody's happy.

Everybody alive enough to count, that is.

All that changed once Pat and Lyle fixed Ray up with my mortal coil, though, and he "fell for" it . . . telling her, ferverishly, and repeatedly, how this hunk of otherwise nondescript white male meat which just happened to come with my restless spirit attached was the end of his search, the literal em*bodi*ment of all his most cadaver-centric daydreams. Suddenly, his fetish had narrowed and shifted to allow for only this one particular corpse or nothing at all.

And: "You know tomorrow night's gonna have to be curtains for Mr Stinky, right?" She asked him, briskly, after yesterday's post-show *pas-de-deux*.

Ray, frowning: "How so?"

Pat reclipped her bra, sponged sweat from her cleavage; I saw the angels' halos reflected in her throat's shiny hollow, a wet white crackle of phantom jewelry. "'Cause he's starting to fall apart, same as the others. Already had to re-wire his joints twice just to get him limber enough to limbo—and his scalp's starting to peel, too. Now it's just a matter of time."

"But if you're keeping him refrigerated . . . "

"Yeah, sure. But there's only so far that goes, Ray. No freezer in the world's totally fly-tight; nature of the beast, man."

A pause. Ray stood silent as Pat wriggled back into her jeans, then shot him the raised eyebrow: You comin', or what? Shook his head. And replied, finally—

"Then I guess we're looking at goodbye for me too, Pat."

At that, Pat turned fully, *both* eyebrows up. "You're kidding."

"No."

Because . . . this is the *one*. Remember? The one and only. No substitutes need apply, not even—

(well, *you*, sweetheart)

Ahhhh, true love.

He feels like he's having a dialogue with it, that's what he's always told her. Like he's finally being privileged, through this nightly series of gag-makingly contortionate sex show antics, to vicariously experience the ecstatic transformation my corpse is already undergoing—the transition from flesh to fleshlessness, an all-expenses-paid tour through time's metaphorical flensing chamber. To share in the experience as it sloughs the residue of its own mortality off like a scab, revealing some clean, invisible new form lurking beneath.

My body, my husk. My shucked, slimy former skin.

It's not *pure*, though, for fuck's sweet sake. It's not *perfected*. It has no "secret wisdom" to impart. And as for powerful, well . . .

If it really *was* powerful—if I was—then we wouldn't be here, would we?

Any of us.

The argument went on for some time, back and forth: Pat's voice soaring snappishly while Ray stayed quiet but firm, unshakable. There was an element of betrayal to her mounting disbelief, as both of them well knew. Suffice to say, Lyle probably wouldn't have been too happy to find out his star attraction had decided to retire either. Not that Pat even seemed to be thinking of things from that particular angle.

"It's just a fucking *corpse*, Ray. You've done fifty of 'em already, most of 'em long before you ever met me—"

Ray nodded. "Because I was looking for the *right* one."

"And this is it?"

"In my opinion."

She stared, snorted.

"Lyle won't like it."

"Fuck Lyle."

A sigh: "Been there."

The unsaid implication—goodbye to it, to this, the nightly grind. To Lyle's meal-ticket. And, by extension, goodbye . . .

(to me?)

Me meaning her. As well as me meaning "me".

Before, whenever Ray's beaux got too pooped to preserve, the routine took over. Lyle got on the pager again, handing out more of Ray's money; the bodies made their exit, stage wherever. Parts in a dump, an acid-soaked tub-ring, concrete at the bottom of a lake, with all trace of Ray's touch, or Pat's—or Lyle's, for that matter, not that Lyle ever *touches* the Bone Machine's prey—salved away in disposal.

Which should be enough, surely: Enough to wash this lingering wisp of me clean and let me rise. Sponge the fingerprints from my soul, and all that good, metaphorical stuff. But—

(but)

At first I just hovered above, horrified, longing for the angels to cover my see-through face with their equally see-through wings. So grotesquely helpless to do anything but watch, and wait, and watch some more. Wait some more. watch some more. Repeat, repeat, repeat.

But then, slowly . . . through sheer, profane will alone, one assumes, while my constant companions loomed ever closer in (literally) holier-than-thou disapproval . . .

Don't look.

But I have to.

Move on.

But—I *can't*.

(Not yet.)

. . . I found myself starting to be able to feel it once more, from the inside out. The ghost of a ghost of a ghost of a sensation. Ray's mouth on "mine", sucking at my cold tongue like a formaldehyde-flavored lollipop. "My" muscles on his, bunching like poisoned tapeworms.

Taking shaky repossession part by part; hacking back into my own former nervous system synapse by painful synapse, my shot neural net fizzing at cross-purposes like that eviscerated eight-track we used to have in the student lounge back at my old high school—the one you could only make change tapes by reaching inside and touching two stripped wires together, teeth gritted against the inevitable shock.

Pat sends her commands and I . . . resist, just a fraction of a micro-inch; she's off put, suspects that her calibrations aren't quite as exact as she'd thought. But even as she reworks them, Ray strains towards me and I . . . strain back. Rise to meet him, halfway. I know he sees what I'm doing, if only on a subconscious level. Her too.

Because: It's like cheating, isn't it? Always is, when love's involved. And lovers *always* know.

"I want to do it," he told her in the car, on the way home. "I want to be the one, this time."

"The one to do what?"

"You know. Finish it."

Pat narrowed her dark, dark eyes. "Finish it," she repeated. "Like—get rid of it? Destroy it yourself?"

Rip it apart, tear it limb from limb, eat it (un)alive. If he couldn't have it . . .

Dark eyes, with green sliding to meet them: Money-colored too, in a far more vivid way. Because it's not that Ray's unattractive, that he couldn't possibly indulge himself any other way. In fact, if you look at it too closely—closer than he probably wants you to, or wants to himself—you'd have to conclude that the *indulgence* is doing things the way he's chosen to.

"You're worried about what Lyle'd think?"

She shrugged. "His customers, maybe."

"Should be a hell of a show, though."

. . . should be.

Another cool look, another pause—silence between them, smooth as a stone. All that frustrated longing, that self-bemused *ache*; enough to power a city, to set both their carefully-constructed internal worlds on fire.

The angels ruffle their pinions, disapprovingly. But I was human once, just flawed and impermanent enough to understand.

I mean, we just want what we want, don't we? Even when it's impossible, perverse, ridiculous, we want just what WE want. And nothing else will do.

Move ON.

Be at PEACE.

But: I can't, can't. Won't. Because I want . . . what I want. Nothing else.

(Nothing.)

"You're the last of the red-hot Romantics, Ray," Pat told him, eventually, knowing what she was agreeing to, but not caring. Or thinking she knew, at least. But knowing only the half of it.

She's had her dance, after all, like Ray's had his: Now I'll have mine, and be done with it. Change partners mid-song; no harm in that. And if there is . . .

. . . if there *is*, well—it's not like anyone'll be complaining.

* * *

And now it's past midnight, the zero hour. Showtime. Lyle's customers file in as he sets up the cameras, trance-silent with anticipation: Stoned suburbanites, jaded superfan ultra-scenesters, unsocialized Western *otaku* with bad B.O. and worse fashion sense. Teens who followed the wrong set of memes and ended up somewhere way too cool for school, let alone anywhere else. Many seem breathless, barely able to sit still. Some—few, thankfully—have actually brought dates, rummaging absently between each other's thighs as they lick their lips, eyes firmly on the prize: The Bone Machine itself, a slumped mantis of hooks and cords; Pat, strapping "my" body in for its final run around Ray's block, suturing it fast with duct tape. Slipping the requisite genital prosthetic mini-bladder tube up the corpse's urethral tract and pumping it erect before condoming the whole package shut once more . . .

The Machine—model number five, re-built on site by Pat herself, due to be broken down to component parts and blueprints when the spectacle's dollar-value finally wears itself thin—occupies a discontinued butchering lab somewhere in the Hospitality area of a shut-down community college campus': Ray's coin bought a deal with security guards who let them in at night after the campus manager goes home, as well as access to a walk-in fridge/freezer just big enough to keep their mutual "carrionette" pliant. It's a vast, slick cave of a place whose dark-toned walls are hung with 1960's charts of cartoon pigs and cows tattooed with dotted "cut here" lines, whose sloping concrete floor still sports drains and runnels to catch blood already congealed into forty years' worth of collective grease-stink. Under the heat of Lyle's lights the air is hot and close, smell thick enough to cut: Meat, sweat, anticipation.

Transgression a-comin'. That all-purpose po/mo word poseurs of every description love so well. But there are all kinds of transgressions, aren't there? Transgression against society's standards, the laws of God and man, against others, against yourself . . .

Here's Pat, gearing up—eyes intent, face studiously deadpan. Here's Lyle, all sleaze and charm, spinning his strip-club barker's spiel. Here's "me", slug-pale and seeping slightly, yet already beginning to stir as the connections flare, the cables pull, the hip-pistons give a tentative little preliminary thrust and grind. And—

—here's Ray, nude, gleaming with antibacterial gel. Right on cue.

See the man, see the corpse. See the man see the corpse. See the man? See the *corpse*?

Okay, then.

. . . let's get this party started, shall we?

Jolt forward, pixilate, zoom in—not much foreplay, at this stage of the game. Just wind and wipe into Ray bent l-shaped and hooking his heels in the small of my jouncing avatar's back, clawing passion-sharp down its slack sides. Pat puppets the Machine's load forward, digging deep, straining for that magic buried trigger; Ray scissors himself and "me" together even harder, so hard I hear something crack. And blood comes welling: Fluid, anyway, tinged darker with decay. Blood already starbursting the cilia of "my" upturned eyes, broken vessels knit in a pinky-red wash of old petecchial hemorrhaging—

Ray groaning, teeth bared. Lyle leaning in for the all-important E.C.U. Pat, bent to the board, her hair lank and damp across her frowning forehead.

Ray, grabbing at "my" hair, feeling its mooring slip and slide like rotten chicken-skin. Taking a big, biting tug at "my" bile-soaked lower lip, swapping far more than spit, before rearing back again for a genuine chomp. Starting to—*chew*.

Pat gags: *Ewwww*, rubbery. You kiss your girlfriend with that mouth?

(Not any more, I guess.)

First the bottom lip, then the upper. A bit of "my" cheek. Sticky cuspids and canines like stars in a gum-pink evening sky. Ray's tearing at "my" sides, "my" chest, "my" throat, as the audience coos and gasps; Lyle's still filming. And Pat's twisting knobs like a maniac, trying to match Ray's growing frenzy, fighting with all her might to keep the show's regularly scheduled action on track: Destruction, ingestion, transgression with a capital "T". Fighting *Ray*, really, as he guides "my" exposed jaws to his own neck again and again, like he's daring "me" to—somehow—bite in, bite down, pop his jugular and give all his fans the ultimate perverted thrill of their collective lives.

Because: Ray feels himself going now, in the Japanese sense. Knows just how late it's getting, how soon the high from this last wrench and spurt will fade. Knows that no possible climax to this drama will ever seem good enough, *climactic* enough, no matter *what* he does to "me". I can see it in his eyes. I can—

(*see* it)

See it. "I" can. And "I", I, I . . .

I feel myself. Feel *myself*. Coming, too.

Feel myself *there*. At last.

Feel Ray hug me to him and hug him back, arms contracting floppily—feel that pin Pat put in my shoulder last time snap as the joint finally pulls free, and tighten my grip with the other before Ray can start to slip. Feel my clotty lashes bat, a wet cough in my dry throat; the sudden gasp of breath comes out like a sneeze, spraying his face with reddish-brown gunk. See Ray goggle up at me, as Lyle gives a girly little scream: Cry to God and Pat's full name, reduced to panicked consonants. HolyshitPahtriSHA*FUCK*!

Pat's head comes up fast, hair flipping. Eyes so wide they seem square.

My tongue creaks and Ray hasn't left me much lip to shape words with, but I know we understand each other. Like I said, I can *see* it.

Gotta go, Ray. You want to come with me?

Well, do you?

And Ray . . . nods.

And I . . .

 . . . I give him. What he wants.

And oh, but the angels are screaming at me now like a Balkan choir massacre, all at once—glorious, polyphonic, chanting chains of scream: Sing *No*, sing *stop*, sing *thou shalt thou shalt thou shalt NOT*. Their halos flare like sunspots, making the whole room pulse—hiss and pop, paparazzi flashbulb storm, a million-sparkler overdrip curtain of angry white light.

(Sorry, guys. Looks like revenge comes before redemption, this time 'round.)

Ray pulls me close, spasming, as my front teeth find his Adam's apple. Blood jets up. The audience shrieks, almost in unison.

I look over Ray's shoulder at Pat, frozen, her board so hot it's starting to smoke. And I smile, with Ray's blood all over my mouth.

So hook *him* up to the Bone Machine now, Pats—make a movie, while you're at it. Take a picture, it'll last longer. Take your turn. Take your time.

But this is how it breaks down: He's gone, long gone, like I'm gone, too. Like *we're* gone, together. Gone.

Gone to lie down.

Gone to forgive, to forget.

Gone, gone, finally—

—to sleep.

* * *

Aaaaaah, *yes*.

The sheep look up, the angels down. And I'm done, at long, long last—blown far, far away, the last of my shredded self trailing behind like skin, like wings, a plastic bag blowing.

Done, and I'm out: Forgiven, forgotten, sleeping. Loving nothing. Being nothing. Feeling none of your pain, fearing none of your anger, craving none of your—anything. Anymore.

Down here where things settle, down below the bridge, the weighing-room, the House of Dust itself—down here, where our faces fall away, where we lose our names, where we no longer care what brought us here, or why . . . I don't care, finally, because (finally) I don't have to. And in this way, I'm just the same as every other dead person—thank that God I've never met, and probably never will: No longer mere trembling meaty prey for the thousand natural shocks that flesh is heir to; no longer cursed to live with death breathing down my neck, metaphoric or literal.

Which only makes the predicament of people like Ray—or like Pat, for that matter—seem all the crueller, in context. Since the weakness of the living is their enduring need to still love us, and to feel we still love them in return; to believe that we are still the same people who were once capable of loving them back. Even though we're, simply . . .

. . . not.

Down here, down here: The psychic sponge-bed, the hole at the world's heart, that well of poison loneliness every cemetery elm knows with its great tap-root. Here's where we float, my fellow dead and I—one of whom might *be* Ray, not that he or I would recognize each other now.

The keenest irony of all being that I suppose Ray killed himself for *me*, in a way—killed himself, by letting me kill him. Even though . . . until that very last moment we shared together . . . we'd never really even met.

Come with me, I said. Not caring if he could, but suspecting—

(rightly, it turns out)

—I'd probably never know, in the final analysis, if he actually did.

Down here, where we float in a comforting soup of nondescription—charred and eyeless, Creation's joke. Big Bang detritus bought with Jesus' blood.

Ash, drifting free, from an eternally burning heaven.

KEEPSAKE

*There is no such thing as evil, just the gradual
removal of good until nothing is left.*
—St. Augustine

It's funny how the hardest moral questions only ever occur to you long after you've lost the power to answer them. Or to put it another way:

How many times have I asked myself what it is with some people, but not given much of a fuck either way? Because the plain fact is, nobody can cure themselves of someone else's disease. The world's full of dying parasites; you can't hold them all, wipe their eyes and their asses, change the channel and tell them one more time how they're going to a better place. Sure, we all talk a good game—but no one actually has the time for that kind of love, let alone the strength.

And I only ever really loved one other person on this whole rotten planet, anyways, aside from my own stupid self.

Now it's long past five in the morning, and I'm still crouched out here in a nest of long grass, halfway into the junk-choked sump that passes for a yard between the Tar Baby dance club—heavy metal and formative rock cover bands all night, every night—and its nearest neighbor, Calypso Heaven. Sitting back on my heels with Jos' second-best gun in my hands, last night's frozen mud already seeping through the seat of my jeans. Sitting here listening to the distant cries of my little brother Loren, as they seep up through those six-plus feet of dirt I piled on top of him last night—after I dragged his limp, rug-wrapped body down all three flights of rusty fire escape from our former mutual home, and rolled him ass-up into a shallow grave.

Thinking about how he's already been dead for a year and a half, and the only difference now is he'll finally have to start acting like it.

* * *

Around twelve-fifteen last Thursday, I jerked abruptly awake at my usual table in the Caf Shack on the corner, and for a good minute and a half, I couldn't remember what I'd come there for in the first place. There was a cup of half-price latte in front of me (Steamy Thursdays, Get It While It's Hot) and a half-smoked cigarette in my right hand, burnt down almost to filter—a shaky column of ash, poised and ready to gild the tattoo winding across my Mound of Venus and up around my thumb with grey. A snake, a triangle, two moons and a line of star-pointed Coptic crosses, all based on some Moroccan wedding designs I found in this old issue of *National Geographic* Rennie stole from my last social worker's office: The kind of shit they usually do with henna on the big day, then leave on until you wear 'em off playing unpaid workhorse for your hubby's family, long after the roast lamb's all been eaten and the band's gone home to sleep.

I remember how the tattoo artist laughed when I showed him the ripped-out page I wanted him to copy them from. Smirking:

"Guess you can kiss your day-job ambitions pretty much goodbye with this one, huh?"

And I just smiled back, ever so slightly. Thinking:

Yeah, that idea would probably scare me too, if I'd ever actually had a day job.

Outside the Caf Shack window, it was just another post-ozone-depletion February in Toronto—equal parts frigid and uncertain, pedestrians eddying to and fro outside like ghosts beneath a livid, par-boiled sky. Streets slick with yesterday's slush, already turned to ice.

Then I let my attention focus back inside the window frame, and realized the guy who'd been cruising me for the last few minutes—so overtly, he could've been wearing a big neon pink sign on his forehead—was actually somebody I knew, or used to. One of Jos' regulars, back in the days; back when I was one glam, Iced-up little Goth girl and Jos was my main squeeze, Mr. Trent Reznor Superfly, all black eyeliner and free drugs to anybody who shared his musical tastes. Before Rennie finally followed my example, broke and ran from that pit we once both laughingly called "home", turned up knocking at Jos' and my apartment door, and we let him crash in that little room next to the iguana tank—the one with no shades on the window, no lock on the door, and nobody left unstoned enough to check who was going in and out, especially during one of our legendary three-day parties.

Before Rennie got sick. And Jos went to jail.

And I ended up in this limbo I've been living, every day-for-night since.

I nodded at the chair next to me, and took another leisurely gander out the window—more than long enough for the guy to take the hint, and slide his skinny junkie ass down in it.

"Hey, Ro," he said, in a tone he probably thought passed for cheerful. "Long time, man." Then, small talk over: "You holding?"

I tapped the ash. "Not here, I'm not."

He nodded, sniffed, coughed; a long, phlegmatic rattle. Shot me a begging glance from under his flip of barely-successful white-boy dreads.

I sighed, and chugged the rest of my latte, letting the caffeine stretch me standing—an unseen chemical noose, just tight enough to make sure I didn't shake.

"My place," I told him. "Tag along, we'll see what I can do. But don't be obvious."

He nodded again. I paid, and left.

As I crossed the street, he was already ten steps behind, like some gender-confused geisha. Trying to follow my advice, and failing miserably.

* * *

So: Back around the Tar Baby, through the sump, down the alley and up three flights of rusty metal steps, brain on automatic as I filtered out the ever-present hash reek from Number Two, the teeth-rattling Techno blast from Number Three-A. Key in the door, and into a former dance studio's worth of dark, square space, lit only by the TV's thin blue glare and an uncertain thread of light, seeping under three layers of Honest Ed's thickest curtaining. A half-sprung La-Z-Boy with a remote on its arm—rescued one drunken night from somebody's Annex curbside—sat angled near enough to the TV to cause serious optic damage. The only other furniture was Jos' futon, a stained mattress lying half-made in the middle of the floor, its red knot of sheets rumpled like an open heart.

I paused in front of the bathroom mirror to light some incense, the stick's red tip writing faint haiku on my reflection, just before I blew it out. A rush of smoke wreathed my hair with fragrance.

No movement in the big room. Just *Quincy M.E.* on A&E's Daytime Detectives, mouthing righteous ire. *If you say it's almost impossible, then that means it's at least possible!*

"Rennie," I called, softly.

Silence.

"Hey, Loren Gault. You here, or what?"

Still no answer.

Then I heard the guy push the door open, addict-cautious—and hit the flush before starting to move around the bathroom, making noises like I was looking for my stash.

"Uh . . . Ro?"

Opening and shutting a drawer, I called back: "I'm in the john." Slammed up the toilet-bowl lid, rummaging inside. "Be out in a sec. Sit anywhere."

Anywhere meaning the bed, the La-Z-Boy being currently adjusted—courtesy of the apparently absent Rennie—to a level somewhat inaccessible for those of us not six-foot-four.

In the drug world, two truths stand so evident they're almost Biblical: Hunger stirs hunger—and where one hunger calls, another answers.

When I came out, he was grinning up at me, sure he'd got his figurative foot in my figurative door. Firmly believing, with every possible section of his body but his brain, that I was obviously so hard up for action we could cut some kind of non-monetary deal—and assuming, probably wishfully, that the length of time elapsed since his last score had rendered him once more capable of getting it up far enough to deliver on his end of the bargain.

"You're lookin' good, Rohise," he said. "I tell you that?"

"No," I replied. Slipping off my shirt.

We fell back on the futon together, kissing like cats—all gesture and hot air, with most of the effort put into sounding interested. Amazingly, he actually did have an erection; anticipation does odd things, especially in a trained animal.

"Oh, Ro," he moaned, with heartfelt sincerity. "Oh, yeah, baby, yeah, baby—yeah, baby, yeah."

I could barely keep a straight face—but lucky for me, his eyes stayed closed. And so we rolled over, and rolled over yet again, and would have probably just kept on rolling over forever—except that we finally hit something firm looming up through all those sheets, something which felt (at first touch) like another, slightly thicker length of mattress, left there by some unknown helping hand, to keep oversexed drug dealers and their fake-enthusiastic customers from dry-humping themselves right off the side of the bed.

But it wasn't.

Then a flap of sheet fell over, like the topmost curl of an unraveling chrysalis, and I saw Rennie's eyes come open in the humid red darkness beneath: Narrow, yellow-touched, under a flaring ridge of brow. Each part, as it revealed itself, successively extrapolating the whole. His elaborate bad-ass 'do, with its improbable Sonny Chiba sideburns, long since bedheaded into oblivion; his pale fingers grabbing handfuls of air, their nails half-slicked with a choice selection of my unused polishes; his mouth, with its sketchy rim of adolescent moustache, packed full of pointy little teeth. Rennie, hitherto burrowed deep as a tick in the bed's rucked flesh, roused now by the mingled smell of sex and desperation—the nearby stink of prey. A gangly trap-door spider rising up from under the covers, arms and lips spread wide.

He met my glance, and grinned.

I grinned back, gave my junkie suitor one last kiss for luck, and pushed him—without a single second's regret—into my little brother's ravenous embrace. At whose touch the guy's eyes snapped back open, finally, wide and appalled.

"Hey, *shit*—" he began.

Then choked off, as Rennie bit deep into the nape of his neck, wrapped his long legs around the guy's hips from behind and squeezed, neatly snapping his drug-soaked spine in half.

* * *

In the back of the studio, under a set of steps leading up to our unused skylight—the same one I spent two days painting black after we first moved in, as Rennie writhed and whined inside a double weight of sleeping bag below—there's a narrow, plywood-lined crawlspace, originally meant for insulation. That's where I used to put them, afterwards. Armed with a set of Ginsu steak-knives I lifted from my former best friend's baby shower, along with a much-renewed supply of green plastic garbage bags, I used the bathroom tub to cut them up in—much to the annoyance of our downstairs neighbors, who complained about the smell. Which is where the incense came in handy.

That was always the one thing Rennie never bitched about, oddly enough. Like the untameable slaughterhouse stink of the bed, I think it kind of turned him on.

Guts in one bag, jointed, washed limbs in another, wrapped tight with gaffer's tape. The latter went under the stairs, the former into my backpack, to be dumped later on into one of the local butcher's tripe-stuffed rubbish cans. It didn't seem particularly risky at the time, though I guess it probably was. But then, getting caught was never really something I'd ever worried about too much.

Quite the opposite, actually.

By the time I'd pulled the plug on the bath, flipped the futon's mattress and stripped off its sheets—stuffing them haphazardly into a well-worn laundry bag, made from two tea-towels sewn together—Rennie was already in full post-kill ecstasy mode, sacked out in the La-Z-Boy, naked and bloody, channel-hopping between *The Equalizer* and *Sailor Moon*. I snapped my fingers against the back of his head as I went by, demanding:

"So what was the deal, slug-boy, back when I came in? You asleep, or what?"

"Sorta."

"You awake now?"

" . . . sorta."

I snorted. "Yeah, well, you better get in the tub under your own speed, cause I ain't about to drag you."

He yawned, widely, and squinted around the room. "Where's my robe?" he asked.

"Dirty clothes."

"What for?"

"'Cause it's *dirty*, you jerk."

Levering himself upright with a regretful sigh, he picked through the pile in question, found said robe, and took a long whiff. "Seems okay to me," he announced.

"Fine, then wear it." I slipped my jacket back on, going through my pockets for laundry Loons. From the bathroom, I heard him hum as he turned the water back on, reacting as he tested its temperature. The slap and splash of flesh against liquid, as he slid inside.

"You love me, Ro?" he called, suddenly anxious, just as I opened the door.

"Like a rock," I called back.

"Good." A pause. "Me too."

* * *

Ice is a hell of a drug, all told; do enough of it, for enough time, and it'll cook you from the inside out. I met Jos when I was twenty-two, having just dropped out of Ryerson (Hospitality program, half a semester's worth), and became one of his preferred customers shortly thereafter. When he told me I could be getting his services for free, I jumped at the chance. Not because of desire—sex never meant too much to me, and I know who I have to thank for that. But when all you know about life is based on the barter principle, selling yourself can look an awful lot like buying your way to freedom.

By the time an unlimited supply of Jos' Ice had me fucked up enough to leave home, I was way too fucked up to take Rennie with me. I couldn't handle it. I could barely handle myself.

And so I left him there, for five more years. With Mom.

And with Dad.

The morning after that last party, I heard Rennie throwing up as I passed his room—a slow, lethargic retching, like he was doing it in his sleep. His face was red, hair up on end. The back of his neck was covered with fresh scabs. And he just lay there, coughing vomit all down the front of his pyjamas and over the side of the bed—thin, bright yellow vomit, linoleum-hued, intermittently laced with liquescent kernels of blood.

I wanted to take him to the hospital, but Jos wasn't having any of that. He said it would be fine, I'd see. He said he'd make us some Ichi-Ban Chicken Noodle and buy Rennie some Tylenol on his way home, and just not to freak out, cause it was a busy day ahead for him, and he didn't need any of my bullshit bringing him down.

Then he took off, leaving us entwined. Rennie still puking. Me sober and already a little shaky, gone hard, the way I'd so often found it better to go—more efficient. More effective.

Caught in the grip of some red dream, whimpering in my arms, Rennie seemed to sweat the rest of his pubescence out along with his humanity, while I slowly got straight for the first time in at least two years. Like his sickness had cured me, somehow, of mine.

And whenever it got almost too bad to bear, all I had to do was hug him tighter, hearing him husk:

Ro, it hurts, it feels like I'm dyin'. Oh, Ro, it hurrrts. Ro, man, what's happening to me?

At which point I'd whisper back:

I'm here, baby. I'm here, I'll never leave. I'll always take care of you, Rennie. Always.

But always, as it since turns out, is one long Goddamn time.

* * *

I put the sheets in to soak, turned one of the Loons back into quarters and made some calls from the back of the Laundromat, doing a little business. Scouted out some of Jos' erstwhile friends, trying to line up future meals for Rennie; paid our overdue cable bill, using my Interac card and the Canada Trust Bankline. It was the second week of the month, and I had all the classic signs of impending menstruation: No appetite, lousy skin, a PMS headache that'd been building at the base of my skull since the very early morning, finally coming to full, pulsing bloom whenever I closed my eyes. It was like a sparkler going off behind my lids—open them again, and for a split second or two, the whole world rained light.

Then it was an hour later, and I looked up from folding to find Leo in the doorway, already headed my way.

"Rohise!"

Yeah, yeah, yeah.

Leo Curran, burly ex-con Street Outreach worker-cum-superhero in his own private comic book—*Leo the Lionheart, Understanding Guy*, maybe; or: *How I Saved the World, One Reluctant Convert at a Time!*

He pulled out a nearby chair, settled his bulk into it. Looked at me over the rims of his sunglasses, all easy frankness—let's you and me just have ourselves a little heart-to-heart and get our differences squared away right now, 'kay?

"Nice to see you, Leo," I said, rolling the sheets back into a conveniently baggable size. "Like always."

You big fuckin' freak.

"I knocked at your door, a little while back," he said. "Your brother sent me over."

"Oh yeah."

"He wouldn't let me in. Sounded like he was still in bed."

I shrugged. "He's sick."

Leo just smiled, and shook his head in a sad, slight way, clearly meant to imply: Well, of course you'd say that—but we both know better, now, don't we?

"Sick?" he repeated. "When people are sick, Rohise, they get better. Somebody's been sick for eighteen months straight, what you do is you take em to the hospital—because there's obviously something genuinely wrong with 'em—and you find out what the story really is. Or you cut 'em loose."

"Uh huh." I slung the bag over my shoulder. "Well, gotta go. Rennie'll be waiting."

"If he's awake."

I paused, squinting against the light. "Meaning?"

"Stop me if I'm wrong," he said. "But if your brother wasn't sick, you could go back to school, right? Get a job. Have a life."

"True. But since he *is* sick—who cares?"

"I do."

He was a nice guy, Leo. Meant well. But I had neither the time nor the energy, just right now, to fully appreciate his good intentions.

Not to mention that my head now felt as though it were rapidly approaching the point of cranial meltdown.

"You deserve better."

"I'm doing fine, thanks anyways."

"Playing fake dealer? Rolling addicts for extra cash?"

"Prove it," I snapped. "Or get the fuck out of my face."

We looked at each other. My eyes pounded.

All of a sudden, my backpack felt almost unbearably heavy.

"I just worry about you, Rohise," Leo said, finally. "You can take care of yourself, I know that. You always have. You always will."

Damn straight, fat boy.

Adding, after a pause: "But at the end of the day, I still find myself worrying about you. A lot."

I opened the door. Quick tic pulling my smile up on one side, lop-angled, like the reaction to some psychic stink.

"So don't," I told him. And left.

* * *

I still don't know who did this to Rennie. Anyone could've—I mean, it's not like I was watching; I don't even really know what was done.

You see your little brother sweating, tossing and turning. Hissing like an unfixed cat under every blanket you have. He can't eat, can't get out of bed, can't get near a window, or the pain makes him cry tears of blood. A week ago, he was just another lanky teen geek, so obsessed over movie shit like whether or not Antonio Banderas does his own stunts that he'd wave his hands in the air and start to stutter. Now he looks brutish, full-grown and all filled out, big enough to frighten.

And you sit there and wonder why all of this would have to happen to him, not you—you, who are responsible for his whole sad, sick semblance of a life, and always have been.

Sometimes, early on, I would get these abrupt moments of clarity, and I'd think: *He's just crazy, and I'm making him even crazier by acting like I can solve his problems. 'Cause after all, living on Queen West don't mean the world is actually full of vampires.*

But get this:

On the first day, his gums started to bleed.

The second day, he puked up most of his teeth.

On the third day, new ones started coming in, calcium whiteness slicing up through puffy pink flesh. Serrated, triangular, packed in double rows. Like a shark's.

And I can still see the look on that plainclothes pig's face when Rennie took out his voicebox with a single, juicy bite, like he was eating a peach. Came by the morning of Day Number Four to hit Jos up for money; he wasn't there, but I was. So down came Officer Friendly's fly, and down I went with it—'til Rennie came padding up behind in that filthy bathrobe of his, so quiet the guy almost didn't notice what was happening. Except that it hurt too much to ignore.

His feet drumming on the tiles, flopping in Rennie's hug, screaming soundlessly. His shirt turning red.

And Rennie sighing, satisfied at last—like he'd just popped his cherry, and couldn't wait to do it again at the earliest possible opportunity.

Jos went to jail for what happened in his kitchenette that day, and I never said a thing about it. Premeditated murder, twenty-five to life. Which I guess seems pretty cold, on my part.

I know this much, though: He wouldn't have been a damn bit of help to either of us, and Rennie would probably just have ended up killing him too. So in a way, he got off easy.

Easier than me, that's for sure.

* * *

By the time I got home, my scalp was crawling. I felt like I could've fried eggs on the top of my head. The TV was still on, strangely enough; Rennie, even more strangely, lay jumped in on himself before it—pungently robed, freshly-dried and sleepy-eyed, half-submerged by his own long limbs. I threw my keys in the corner, turning the bag of bed sheets inside out all over him. He made a noise that might have indicated protest, had it only been a little more conscious.

"Move over, Rennie," I said, flopping down on the futon's edge. Methodically shucking and chucking jacket, boots, jeans, bra. Then, still receiving no reply: "Move the fuck *over*, Rennie. Now, not later."

He squirmed lengthwise, as if scalded. I kicked enough of the rest of him out of my way (lightly, gently) to slide in beside him, pull the sheets as far up as they could possibly go and curl of there in the red dark, breathing slowly, holding my head. Hoping the next thought I had wouldn't be the one to finally make it shatter.

A minute or so of blessed silence. Then, tentatively: "You okay?"

"No."

"Oh." A pause. "Your head hurt?"

I sighed. "Yes."

Another pause. A few more breaths, staggered and stretched. Heartbeat and aftershock matched pulse for pulse, lighting my skull's fault-lines up like a neon map.

"Want me to get you anything?"

Oh, just the last five years to do over. And another whole life before that, while you're at it.

"I'm tired, Ren. All I want is to sleep."

"Sure," he said, like he understood. Adding: "Man, you know I know the feeling."

* * *

I slept through most of Friday, part of Saturday. I needed it. Something had run out in me without warning, like an emptied engine, leaving nothing but fumes; as far as I could see, there wasn't much worth waking up for. I heard Rennie moving around, flipping channels, snickering to himself as he mimicked the cast of *Law & Order*. Once, somebody knocked at the door—maybe Leo, maybe our legendary landlord. But neither of us answered, so they went away again.

Later on, when the credits of *Neon Rider* were just starting to blare, Rennie called: "Hey, speak of the devil—Leo catch you, at the Laundromat?"

"I saw him."

If you've been in really bad pain for a long time, its absence becomes almost good enough to qualify as pleasure. That's where I was now, caught in languorous inertia, barely listening while Rennie rattled on.

"That guy's a serious perv. I mean it, Ro—he wants your body."

"Uh huh."

I could feel his tension mounting. I knew what I had to do, but I couldn't get myself awake enough to care. Maybe I just wanted to see what would happen, the longer I let it slide.

And would it have killed him to do it himself, just this once?

3:00 AM. Global went out in a whine of test-pattern, and Rennie slipped back into bed.

"I'm cold," he complained.

I turned on my side, fetus-curled away from his desperation. "You're always cold," I muttered.

"Rohise, I'm cold. I'm hungry."

"I'll get you something."

"When?"

"Soon."

With no TV, the apartment seemed twice as empty as it actually was—like some semi-permanent party had all just decided to go out for pizza. Rennie touched my shoulder, his hands chill with need. Asked, hesitantly:

"Hold me, Ro?"

"'Kay," I said, rolled back the other way, and drew him to me.

* * *

There's something about a sibling, either having one or being one—less intimate than twindom, less escapable than marriage, so much more chancy than any other relationship. Jos saw Rennie like a bad Xerox of me, unfuckable and uninteresting. Our Dad saw us like owned things, principalities in the familial city-state. Mom saw us so rarely, between trips to the Clarke, it was kind of like she never saw us at all.

I looked at Rennie and saw myself, echoed but not reproduced, hero-worshiped into a flesh reflection at least twice my natural size. An addictive image.

But just like anything else addictive, it's hard to go cold turkey.

* * *

I slept, I dreamed. Warm, pulling threads of sexual abandonment, hooking deep and cracking me apart. Sticky heat on my thighs. A mouth on either breast, wet and insistent, sucking hard on nipples gone tender as rudimentary clitori. Fragrance rising like incense smoke. A mouth between my legs, lips on lips, latched into me like a leech. Digging for buried treasure.

I woke up on the blind edge of climax, riding somebody's face, my feet already starting to cramp. My hands in their hair, on their working jaw. That big, familiar head, slick from chin to moustache with dark, sweet menstrual mess.

I wanted to scream. I wanted to tear his tongue out by the roots.

I wanted to come, so bad I wanted to vomit.

Aroused and revolted in the extreme, I snarled, breathless:

"Loren Gault, get the fuck *away* from me!"

I kicked, pushed, slapped. He wouldn't let go. Moaning curdled nonsense syllables. I felt them vibrate up inside me. I slugged him across the face, hard—and he *snapped* at me, little son of a bitch, with those sharp red teeth. Panting, hands spanning my hips, bruising me. Sweating blood. Holding me down—til I kneed him in the nose, scrabbled back, and fell ass-first against the floor, already twisting up onto my feet.

From whence I fled to the john and slammed the door behind me, barely making the sink in time.

Jos always used to keep his second-best gun wrapped in a plastic bag, taped up under the toilet-tank lid. After he got arrested, I took it with me, and did the same; in such matters, I never saw much point in not following Jos' example.

Out in the room, I heard the TV snap back on.

I caught my breath, spat bile. Rinsed out my mouth.

Stepped back out of the bathroom, carefully—gun trained, at a classic gangsta angle, on that sheeted blur slumped in front of *The 700 Club*.

"You ever do that again," I said. "Ever. And I swear to Christ I'll kill you in your fucking *sleep*."

Rennie, lost in the redemptive power of the cathode image. Not turning. Even to ask:

"Do what?"

And him still licking his pussy moustache for the very last of my blood.

I nodded, slightly.

"Fuck you, Rennie," I said. And shot out the screen.

* * *

Dressing on the fly, jacket and jeans, barely time for underwear—just a wadded-up pair of panties in the crotch of my jeans, to staunch the flow. I got my boots on, toed up one of the floorboards and grabbed the last dead junkie's roll from our designated "escape stash," with Rennie all the while keeping step, gesturing and pleading—at a safe distance, after I'd showed him the gun again.

"Ro, hold up, calm down. I mean, Jeez, Ro—seriously, I don't even know what you're talking about. How could I, man? I was asleep."

"Yeah, you were asleep, you were dreamin'. You didn't know what you were doing, right? Fuck you, Rennie, I've had enough of your crap."

"Fuck me? Fuck *you*, man. I was asleep. I mean, I'm sorry for whatever you think I did—"

I snorted, zipping up. "Yeah, you sound it."

"—but whatever it was, I did *not* do it on purpose. I'm sick. You *know* that."

"You're sick, all right."

That stopped him right in his tracks, amazed. Staring at me with those *I just can't believe what I'm hearing* eyes—all insulted and kind of hurt, like I'd accused him of cheating on the big test, or something. Mr. Teen Angst Dracula himself.

If I stayed there a minute longer, I'd end up as nutsoid as he was.

"I need not to see you for a while, Rennie," I said. Calmly. Clearly. "I need to be alone. I need to be the fuck away from you."

"Ro," he said, as I opened the apartment door. Then: "Ro, wait up!"

But I didn't.

Didn't look back, either.

* * *

I never figured it out, not until they told me. Twelve years old and six months gone, and I thought I was just getting fat. I actually used to worry about shit like that—back before I discovered how easy it was to lose weight, as long as you kept yourself too high to have an appetite.

Oh, Rennie, my baby. My big baby boy. Too self-obsessed ever to ask why they would've waited so long between kids, or how that second kid could even have been conceived, seeing how Mom was doing a month for contempt of court at the time.

You were the one thing our Dad ever gave me that I wanted to keep. And if you were still above ground, maybe I could tell you how it felt when they pulled you out of me—that mind-numbing full-body spasm, that inadequate wishbone snap. How half of me wants to fold you deep inside my ribcage, to hold you tight and never let you go, but the other half of me wants a written guarantee you'll never try to crawl back up in there again.

Love me, Ro?

Like a rock.

. . . me too.

I smiled to myself, mirthlessly, as the Bay Street crosswind drew tears that froze on contact.

Because that's the way it's always been between us, little brother mine. That I love you, more than I love my own heart, my eyes, my life. And you love me too, as much as you can love anybody—which is to say, almost as much as you love yourself.

* * *

I came back Sunday night, to find Leo had already been by sometime late Sunday afternoon. Was still there, in fact.

All over.

Rennie looked up as I came in, covering his mouth with blood-gloved hands.

"Oh, Ro, I fucked up."

A definite understatement.

"You fucked up," I repeated, tonelessly. "That's right, Rennie. And I fucked up. By letting you fuck up."

He crawled towards me, away from that thing on the bed. The big red thing that now amount of laundry was ever gonna get rid of, this time around.

I dropped to my knees, taking his face in both hands, aiming it up at mine. Looked into corpse-yellow eyes dim with tears of fear and self-pity. Heard him whine, plaintive:

"I'm sorry, Ro, I'm sorry, I'm so fuckin' *sorry*."

"I know."

"You went away. I was upset. I . . . got excited."

"I know, Rennie."

He moaned and dug his head into my shoulder, leaving a stain. I just hugged him, letting the rest of his body print my clothes with streaky crimson.

"Just don't leave me, okay?" he asked. "Don't ever leave me again, okay?"

"Oh, Ren," I told him. "Oh, baby. I'll never leave you, baby, don't you know that by now? I'll always take care of you."

Stroking his hair. Slipping Jos' gun out of my waistband.

"I'll take care of you," I told him.

And then I shot him through the back of the head, twice, right where his topmost vertebra met the base of his skull.

* * *

I buried him upside down, so he'd dig himself deeper. Mud in his big mouth, mud on his traitor tongue. Two days now, and I can still hear him screaming. He's getting weaker, maybe figuring out what I've done—but by now it's just too late to turn around. He hasn't got the strength to start over. Playing sick so convincingly, for all those weeks and months—all that year and a half, give or take a few days—maybe he even convinced himself he'd always been that way: The innocent victim, the helpless child.

I should've done it a long time ago; I guess I must have always known that, on some level. I sure as hell know it now.

When he's quiet, I'll go. I can't do anything more. I'll wait until he's quiet and then I'll go.

But I am Goddamned, I am God-damned, if I know where.

ROSE-SICK

I wanted you. And I was looking for you. But I couldn't find you.
    —Laurie Anderson

O rose, thou art sick.
    —William Blake

Love bleeds, like any other wound. And though I believe it can be cauterized, I know I've yet to find anything hot enough to do the job.

Prolonged bleeding makes you weak. It tastes like sucking a quarter, but sweeter—the sour-sweetness of your own waste. A fermented-sugar high. Everything goes limp, languid. Dreams float through, breaking up just as they reach visibility: Static on an empty channel. Then the sweetness fades, and you start to ache—because, without either the sweetness or the dreams it spins to distract you, you're finally awake enough to realize just how empty you've already become.

I want you, baby. I want your hands, your hot touch. I want you to lay them on. I want you to sear me clean again.

* * *

There's a Laundromat of fairly recent mintage up on Yonge Street, the Spin Cycle, where a currently unemployed teacher of English (Romantic poets and Gothic novels a speciality) can load clothes and coin alike unhindered, then retire to the next room and sit comfortably back with the caffeinated beverage of his choice. You go there often, especially so since Lisa hit the highway; in fact, you're there right now. The Spin Cycle is open all night, clean and quiet, free of memory or temptation. Few people to hit on, or hit back—and those who do turn up with their hands out (i.e., the bums who beg on the pavement just outside) rarely have sex on their minds.

She's sitting by the window as you come out of the laundry section, having just separated and rebagged your clothing, and slide into place at the end of the bar for a final installment of liquid insomnia. A brief flash of downcast pupil as she notes—and measures—your proximity. Pale smudge of pale hair against the front window's base-lit glass, indistinct shadow of full mouth under a short, straight hint of nose. Her skin is fair enough to show veins.

Under the lashes, her eyes catch the light: Cloudy blue. Arctic fathoms of lakewater, glimpsed through ice. Matching neon rims her lips, bleaching them cyanose.

Cappuccino's here. You pay, then sip, tensing against the jolt. Count off a shaky string of seconds before you risk a quick glance of your own.

Yes, she's still looking.

You *know* you don't know her. But she's definitely acting like she knows you—like she knows you intimately, and your failure to acknowledge her is just a part of some kinky game you always play. A dominance thing. (People are into that, these days, or so you've heard.) Like she's waiting for you to take control, to get up and go over, take her arm without a wasted word, and lead her off to some black leather Fantasy Island.

Padded cuffs. Paddles. Cigarettes pressed lightly to the fleshy underside of buttock or breast, right at the juncture, where the sweat'll make it rub, and really start to smart.

These are freak closet thoughts, dumbed-down revenge fantasies—Lisa's face hovering disembodied over an EveryCentrefold body, waiting for you to wipe away her sneer. Prospects you would never consider, if you didn't have the very clear idea that this woman would like you to. That she'd *want* you.

And here's the really pitiful part: They're turning you on.

The foreshadowing of a smile hovers at the corner of that uneven, enticing mouth. She shifts her legs beneath the table, deliberately undeliberate: One smooth motion, pure skin on skin, no apparent panty chaser. Her eyes are lightless, inverse mirrors, archaic camera lenses; there's someone caught in each of them, a negative reflection on the scrim of her cornea, doubled and reduced to his barest essence, filling her world entirely. And it's not you, not yet—but for the simple price of a little white lie, it could be. All you have to do is let her recognize you, to be whoever she wants.

Secrecy and decay, Lisa's voice tells you (giving you back your own words, the ones you once bewitched her with, back in your shared undergraduate days), the key elements of any good Gothic. Your life's gone rotten, it literally stinks—so much so you spend all your off-time washing *clothes*, for Christ's sake—so you want to trade up, identity-wise. Maybe even trade down. To see just how far you can get away from you, from your stupor of loss and hatred, your multifoliated ache of thwarted desire.

But needs must, when the penis drives. So you snag your laundry and get up, unsteadily, cross towards her, brush by her. Open the door, hold it a half-breath longer than you need to. Waiting.

And she gets up—smile finally blooming, white-ripe; a fleshy desert flower—and follows.

* * *

Toronto, the fliptop city—grey and gelatinous as a mad scientist's exposed brain, overlaid with a distant hum of thought. Faint memory fog erasing the horizon's skyscrapers from Floor 13 up. And the two of you, drifting through.

More Ann Radcliffe influences: The rain has accentuated Chinatown's usual crab season reek and moved it steadily northward; all up and down the road, the pavement is bracketed by crates of exposed underbellies and weakly waving claws. Her place turns out to be a shutter-heavy house just off of Nassau Street, incongruously squatting in the shadow of a hospital smokestack, its roof wreathed in a cannibal fog of incinerated body parts. You pause, glance up. The moon hangs caught between tree-branches—a lost balloon, half-wilted.

Then you're inside, upstairs, in a room up under the eaves, barely bigger than your bachelor apartment's closet, with a naked mattress on the floor, and a dusty, shrink-wrapped poster of a rose hanging on the far wall, a string of light bleeding from underneath to frame it with a square halo; placed over a small window, maybe, to block the room off from exterior distraction. Water-stains darken the ceiling. It smells stale, with a sickly hint of floral-scented moisturizer. Not exactly enticing.

When you turn around, however, you see she's already unbuttoned the top of her dress and let it slip down around her hips, loosing a pair of snub-nosed breasts with aureolae like cataracts. The light-thread slips along her side, taking the rest of her dress with it, writing hieroglyphs over her emergent stretchmarked hips. Old bruises gild her thighs.

"I found you," she says, the first thing you've heard out of her so far. Her voice is scratchy. A twitch of guilt raises goosesweat; yeah, I guess you did. But it doesn't seem to reach your face—not enough to stop her talking, at least.

"Want me," she tells you.

And then she sucks your lips inside of hers and bites down, knocking you back as your clothes peel apart. On the poster above you, the rose yawns, faded and labial, like a cheesy Grade Twelve creative writing exercise metaphor. But your groin—which jumps and pulses against the smooth weight of her inner thighs, the loose and shaven flesh of her pubis—is no literary critic.

"I found you," she repeats, coming up for air. Then again, with a weird little crack in the words' sandpaper surface: "Want me?"

Yes, yes, yes.

Her blue-rimmed talons, her blue-toned mouth. Her hands scrabble down, points out—the date-rape rosary, reversed: Nipples, navel, pelvis, sac. Incongruous, the contrast; how selected parts of her strike you with such an exaggerated force of detail, while other aspects slide away on contact, impossible to describe. The nape of her bent neck, small-pored and finely furred with a blush of colorless hair—as she glides down along your torso, tongue out—versus the blur of her profile. Halogen skin, almost grotesquely lambent; a stained white radiance, like the kind that spills from lanterns made of human skin. You can count every link of her spine. One hand shelling you with a single twist, a grate of zipper teeth, and slipping to cup your testicles as the other grips you firmly, skins you back. Her breath touches the exposed tip of your penis with condensation.

Then you arch, unable to control you own response, as she takes you to the hilt: A cold scrape of uneven bottom teeth along the underside, a liquid plunge. Back and forth, lips pulling like mist. Nothing to hold onto. And you're so hard now, your cock feels like it's gone numb.

Things are coming to a head, obviously; but it's too soon. You rear up, pull her up as well, arms hooked under hers. (She comes easily, light and frail, a sex-doll stuffed with milkweed down.) Kiss her breasts as they go by, sucking hard, but provoking no visible response, not even the barest stippling of arousal along the inside of her cleavage. Nothing blooms in this garden—stone roses only, petals turned forever inward.

Then you lie back, ready to return the favor.

For a beat, she gazes down at you from this weird Picasso angle, cut off at the knees, the wishbone triangle of legs and pelvis bound together by that pale pubic knot. Seashell furls, secretively overlapped: Put your ear down there, mister, and see what you can hear. Sunken bells? A blood-beat tide, raw and roaring?

Time to find out.

Gently, you pry her apart with both hands—spread her wide. She doesn't stop you.

(But what *would* she stop you doing?)

If her body has limits, she's posted no signs to indicate them. So you stare up into her mystery, put out a hesitant tongue. Taste it. She's waxy and redolent with some indefinite, interior scent: Liquorice, filtered through a watercress base. Narcotized. Her juices sting, slightly.

Again, no visible response. No blush of mere physical pleasure to dampen that detached glow of hers. So you bite deeper, determined to prove you can make her come. All things being equal rights-oriented, they give prizes for that, don't they? The Orgasm Cup. Best Multiple In A Given Session. It's a matter of pride now, because this is beginning to remind you of Lisa—her way of absenting herself, without a spoken word or visible sign: Sure, I'll play along, but this is your business, buddy, not mine. Just hurry up, finish up, shit or get off the pot.

Fuck you, baby.

Oh no, fuck *you*.

"That's enough," she says. Sliding back. And screws herself down onto you with a swiftness that seems to surprise you both equally. You hiss, in unison. Because she's *tight*, hurtfully so. And dry, not slick—all friction, with a vague, talcum-powder stickiness. She churns her hips, frantically, digging around inside herself, trying to find the right button. At which point, part of you rebels.

(I mean, whose fantasy *is* this, anyways?)

So you heave yourself over, taking her with you, forcing yourself securely back in the saddle—sheet-wrapped, one of her knees jammed up against your ribcage. Deeper than you'd thought possible. She hums approval; you can feel it through your sternum, an interior caress. The sheets erase a different view of her face with every thrust. Grasping for her elusive wrists, you wind up just getting still more ells of fabric, looping yourself ever further inward: Bed of lies, bed of nails, bed of quicksand.

"Call me," she says, with barely a catch, between the bellows-rush of your own panting. "Like you used to. Call me—"

"Honey—"

"Slut."

A feather-touch at either palm, steering them inward. Another ripple of speech, intimate and infected, rising up your arms like an arthritic seizure.

"Now hold me like you used to, baby."

As she makes a choker of your hands, centering your thumbs on her larynx.

"Hold me. Hard. Hold me. Tight."

(That black-lettered yellow streak of plastic banner drooping, snapped, by one side of the front door. That front hall carpeted with dead insects. The distinct lack of footprints, other than your own, in the dust beneath you as you mounted the rickety stairs.)

And what's that term? Off of Oprah's newest rival, one afternoon when you cut class to surprise Lisa with a quickie. And she wasn't there, of course; it's not like she could read your *mind*, after all. Any more.

So you flip on the tube, and it's a panel of parents, crying, talking about walking in on their sons in various states of undress, belts and cords looped around their necks. Slumped. Slack. Porno mags nearby. Most do it alone, and die. Some do it like any other contact sport, using a spotter, somebody who loves them enough to let go once they black out. The high as your throat closes off, the luxuriant gasp of climax, as you come like your life depends on it.

Auto-erotic. I mean, erotic. Asphyxiation.

You stare down at her, with eyes abruptly narrow enough to be clear, and see—for the first time—how she waxes and wanes with the ebb of your urges. Her face, seen full-on, is a flicker; something meant to be intuited, meant to be glimpsed from the corner of an eye rather than studied closely. A white darkness in every line of her, slumberous haze of toxic dreams. She arches against your grip like a domesticated animal, flexed and lithe, trained into desperation for human contact of any kind: Love, love me do. Kiss me, kick me.

Kill me.

You see her, suddenly, like a blow to the face, as wholly as one can see any ghost. And she, just as abruptly—

—sees you too.

Both speaking at once:

"You're not—"

"—not. *You.*"

Cloudy blue, Arctic depths, glaring upward. Crystallizing. As the shared delusion of her physicality, punctured by this double recognition, begins—slowly, steadily—to come apart under pressure.

(The moment of truth from that old Japanese movie you saw with Lisa one birthday, not too long back at all. The girl with the long black hair, the morning after; the willing skeleton bride.)

Oh, I'm going, I'm going.

As she melts, becomes ether. Seeps inside you like a novocaine kiss, *penetrating* you to pool around the fluttering muscle between your lungs and squeeze it—tight. Hard. Hard, in absolute sorry fact, as your own dinosaur member, which—instead of wilting—just swells along with the flow, the sub-zero uprush, painfully full as a clogged artery, reaching for consummation. Blackout orgasm. Closed-heart surgery. Cooling it to a light sheen, to a frosty glow. Until it gives one last, convulsive clench, and cracks wide open.

Dark river, suck me down.

Now, if you ever read the paper for more than the Sports section, maybe you might understand *why* you're about to die. You might have seen the pictures of a woman's body, found naked and bloated in her apartment after a game that went too far. You might have heard the descriptions of her lover, garnered from friends and family. You might have remembered certain things Lisa used to tell you, before you stopped listening—those pseudo-Wiccan fatuities about how violent separation from the body sends what's left roaming aimlessly in pursuit of its most recent passion, of anyone who knows its name. How it confuses emotions: Pain for pleasure, rage for tenderness. How it forgets everything, except for the last person who touched it as though it was still a human being. You might, however briefly, even have time to pity the man she thought you were, for the horror he's going to feel once she finally finds him, and moves back in with him—moves *into* him, completely, never to vacate his heart again.

But you don't, so you don't. And so you die like she did, not knowing how or why things have gotten so far out of hand—in that most terrible of states, having expected only bliss.

* * *

Love, love. The worm in every heart. That little speck that keeps on burning after everything else is gone, right down to the bone, and the dust of bones.

Because you were right, after all—the world is full of thieves, baby. And so many of them have somehow gotten hold of your name, your walk, the same tactile net of warmth that used to hover between your hands, binding me to you.

But they all have the same face under their masks, once they're off: Slack, and white, and hollow.

I only want to be yours again: Only that. And with such a righteous goal to drive me, I think I can be forgiven for making a few errors in judgement.

They say the moment just before you die is the loneliest moment in the world. Well, I'm pretty lonely now. I'm full. I'm empty. I'm nothing but what I want, nothing but my own need. And when that's all gone, there won't be a part of me left to hurt.

So find me, baby, before I forget why I wanted you to, in the first place. Find me, and hold me.

Hold me—hard. Hold me . . . tight.

BLOOD MAKES NOISE

Depth drunkenness brings strange thoughts—stranger than usual, at least. Right at the moment, it's like I'm seeing my deaf paternal grandmother's hands hover in this darkening air, signing the scenes of my life away syllable by syllable: Old, new, in and out of order.

These slippery reminiscences, repetitive and elusive—squid-ink images written on oil, squirming from close examination. A memory flip-book, curling at the corners: Nanny Book's crepe-paper skin, laced with pale blue veins; the vestigial webs between her arthritic fingers, spread to catch the light.

My unit bracing to take their turn—pulses shallow, impatient with dismay, most of them more terrified to gauge the true limits of their shameful, mounting fear than consider the circumstances prompting it—as Captain Kiley lies propped up against his bunk, making rabbit-shadows on the holding cell wall.

The sky over Pittsburgh when I was five years old, dirty as a bed of nails.

A map I saw once of the twin moons of Mars.

Hit, flash: Popped bulb, clicked lens—image, then absence. Whispers in my skull, like the roar inside an empty shell: Blood echoes. Music to—in—my ears.

And just what the hell is that word for the fear of fear, anyway?

Fear: Phobos. Fear of: Phobia.

Phobophobia?

. . . must be it.

I press my eyes closed, momentarily forgetting to remember just how deep we must already be. HPNS regulations at least breached, for certain—sure, if not exceeded—more than deep enough to check my hands for tremors, and count off the rest of those prospective High Pressure Nervous Syndrome symptoms our mission literature listed:

Increased excitability, motor reflex decay; aphasia. Mental glitches.

. . . under the deep black sea, who loves to die with me . . .

—glitches. Psychosis. Cyanosis.

And eventually . . .

I slam my head back, skull on wall, hard enough to ring myself true—short, sharp shock, broken left incisor into lip, tweak of clarifying pain. Instant coherence. Kiley's rules, channeling themselves: Keep alert. Tell it through. No opinion without research. No solution without . . .

. . . with—out . . .

"Book," the Doctor whispers, beside me. I shift a bit towards him, deliberately trying to find the floor's sharpest angle, to bend my hip in such a way as to make the pain flare just so, girdling my pelvis. Making myself uncomfortable.

"Doctor," I answer.

"Book, Regis. American. No . . . registered rank."

"Specialist."

He coughs. "I . . . didn't know that."

"No reason you would."

The Doctor give a snuffling gasp, a liquid retch. Something catches in his throat, rattles there briefly—then flicks out again, splattering the floor between us with wet, red bile. I glance back at the wall I just used for a memory aid, which could frankly use a few shadow animals right about now. And as though he's read my mind—

—which may, I suspect, no longer be quite as hard to do as it once was—

"Black . . . Ops . . . operative. 'Wet . . . boy.' Yes? C . . . I . . . A—puppet."

I smile, thinly. "Whatever."

But at least you know my first name.

"You . . . are a—coward, Book," the Doctor tells me. Then lets all his breath out in one big rush, ragged with the effort, like he expects me to pause, to take note—to congratulate him on his sudden insight, his startling perspicacity.

As though this were really some big revelation.

* * *

Okay: Step back. Start over.

To call the situation bleak would be an understatement. Down to our last few hours of oxygen, high on our own fumes and drifting blind: Trapped inside a lost, crewless, experimental submarine—make and model strictly classified, even if it mattered—trolling rudderless, black and silent, along a smoking ridge of volcanic fissures at the bottom of the Subeja Trench. Engines blown, no fuel reserves, interior lights dimmed down to a thread or two of emergency luminance along the hallways. With nobody left to tell the whole tale but me and the Doctor, enemies in an undeclared Lukewarm War, huddled across from each other behind the blackout blinds, the two-way mirrored walls, of what we used to call the Waiting Room.

Me sitting quiet, chin on knees, cradled by a weak but quenchless glow that emanates from somewhere deep inside me—quivering, almost imperceptibly, against the back corner of my former prison. Watching him, on the floor, slumped in on himself—curled, fetal. Broken. Moving just enough, every once in a while, to give up the occasional cough—weak and wet, greased with pinkish phlegm; visible fallout from a buried haematoma, a crushed rib, a punctured lung.

Blood whispering in my inner ear, static between stations: Radio Tintinitus, the voice of the virus. Of that indefinite thing to whom I owe my freedom, my breath and life itself, but whose true nature remains as much a mystery to me now as when they finally threw me into this same room, head-first, to sweat and scream out my appointment with its presence behind a triple-mag-locked door.

The barely-there voice of my master, my soon-to-be savior.

It cajoles, flatters. It says: *My love*. It says: *You know I will honor my promises*. It says: *Time means nothing*. And in the same non-breath, self-contradictory, it says: *Soon*.

Soon, soon.

And I sit here, still, not answering. My whole body nothing but a thin skin suit, stretched tight over an endless scream.

* * *

When three of the Doctor's largest "orderlies" finally dragged me down to the Waiting Room, they had to break two fingers just to get me through the door. I lurched, tripped, came down face-down and felt my bottom lip split open on impact against the floor, left eyetooth cracking right in half like a piece of candy-corn.

Mouth full, head tolling, I spat, swallowed, screamed back at them—and him, for all I couldn't see him through the two-way's glare—every invective phrase I could form in their wonderfully poetic native language: "May goats rut on your grave! May nuns use your bones for dildos! May God fill your heart with shit and drown your grandchildren in blood!"

And then, reverting under the stress of the moment to pure all-American: "Fuck you! Motherfuckers! Fuck, fuck, FUCK *ALL* Y'ALL!"

Unlike the rest of my former unit, you see, I knew exactly what to expect—because I'd already been there behind the mirror myself, helping the Doctor record what happened to each and every one.

I felt like I'd broken the rest of my fingers on that fucking door, before the pain calmed me far enough down to get me thinking straight again.

So: Slowly, I turned. Made myself look back.

And there it was, in the Waiting Room's far corner—almost close enough to touch.

The thing.

They found it at the bottom of the sea somewhere, in relatively shallow water. Took it out real deep to test it, just in case—a fairly good idea, in my personal opinion. Given what I've seen it do.

White coil of unknown—metal? Bone?

Silence. Compressed dust.

What*ever*, Doctor.

A funneled, calcified glass shell, an empty tube-worm knot, utterly alien. Shedding icy light the way we shed blood, and looking somehow slick while doing it. Somehow . . . unclean.

But that might just have been the fear talking.

Blink-flash fast, I conjured a mental image of the Doctor comfortably ensconced behind that mirror, taking his notes, making his calculations, running his useless experiments; the same fucking data, over and over:

You go in. And it sits there. And you sit with it.

And then—the glow begins to change. To grow.

And then—

—you die.

Five times out of five. Granted, I'm a traitor, not a scientist—but to me, those odds do suggest a certain pattern.

I felt myself freeze, then, settling instinctively into much the same position I hold now, except with my back up against the door instead of the corner. Freeze and listen, straining for a hidden warning, some cold whisper beating up through the rush and gasp of my own hot blood—a hum *beneath* the hum.

Beneath the *human*.

The flutter of my pulse, quick and light with morbid anticipation. The—

(Phobo)

—inescapable fear—

(phobia)

—of my own fear.

. . . and why do I keep forgetting that *fucking* word?

Oh yeah, right; brain melting. Memory—drowning.

Terror-struck, I held my breath, tried to slow it down. Closed my eyes and prayed to simply disappear, before the sheer, dull, palpable horror of it all ate me alive.

But I didn't piss my actual pants until the first time I heard that noise in my blood begin to talk.

* * *

Two weeks, ten days and five other men ago . . . five men I knew well—my trusting comrades, my trusted co-operatives . . . five men plus dear, dead Captain Kiley, that old Cold War-horse, who once let slip (in strictest confidence) how he considered me his second son . . .

The call came straight from the top, wherever that is: A need-to-know mission with an unstated goal, just a set of coordinates and a schedule on a sheet of flammable fax-paper.

Search and destroy, no questions asked. So we smuggled ourselves into the area, clinging barnacle-fast to the hull of a rented ship—dropped blind, docked ourselves at the base of volcano 037, got equalized with the pressure, and spent the rest of the day marking off time. And when the sub's shadow fell over us, we swum to meet it in perfect formation, convinced—like the brave little hardbodied boy scouts our training had made us—that the computerized codes we'd been issued with would be enough to trick our way inside. Which they were, of course; when you're working for folks who routinely drop $50 million or so on new toilet paper dispensers, a string of numbers probably comes comparatively cheap.

No, it wasn't the codes that betrayed us, or got us captured within an insulting half-hour. The codes didn't give us up to the Doctor, to serve as cannon-fodder in his continuing quest to find out what that thing in the Waiting Room was—aside from almost-instant death for anybody he threw in with it.

'Cause codes, you see, don't really come equipped for treason—hold no political opinions, weigh no options, covet no raise in monetary reward. Risk nothing and nobody on the simple hope of gettin' pee-ay-ei-dee-paid.

So who?

Well . . .

* * *

Like participants in any arranged marriage, The Doctor and I agreed to consummate our vows only after an exhaustively negotiated ritual of long-distance courtship. Acting under Kiley's orders, I used my satellite access as the unit's translator and intelligence liaison to track the sub's location and eavesdrop on its internal mutterings—and when his back was turned, I used the same good ol' U.S. technology to slip inside the Doctor's laptop, read his notes. Send him e-mail. Tell him he could protect his precious project, and gain a core group of experimental subjects, for the one-time-only price of a hefty Swiss bank-account deposit, a trip back to the surface and an artfully-faked sole survivor scenario: Me cast momentarily adrift in the unit's life-pod, beacon on, with an enemy bullet lodged in some suitably fleshy body-part (exact location to be determined later on, at both our conveniences).

"You tellin' me all this's about money?" Kiley demanded. And I just shrugged, snapping back: "What *else*?"

Thinking, all the while: *Disappointed? Well, fuck you, dead man. You can yap all you want about honor, and duty, and the idiot joy of the holy patriotic Cause—but from where I stand, you're nothing but worm-food with an attitude. So go ahead, strike that pose. When you're being buried with full military honors, I'll be cutting myself a slice of apple pie and negotiating a thousand-dollar blow-job.*

"You know when the Old Ma'am and the rest of those REMFs back at HQ find out, they're gonna cancel your sorry ass."

I smirked. "Find out from who?"

"Ain't you got no pride at all, boy?"

"Well. I guess *not*."

Behind me, somebody spit on the floor. All of them glaring through me, turned back first: If looks could eviscerate. Even fey little Ed LoCaso, the training camp's token cocksucker, suddenly pumped full of indifferent hauteur and undying contempt—if the situation hadn't been just a little too butch to bear it, he looked like he might have given me the finger-snap, or maybe just the finger.

"You just better be ready to live with yourself, Book," Kiley told me, finally, right before they hauled his kneecapped ass onto that medical stretcher and took him down the hall to meet our mystery guest. Last words, and he knew it, so he thought he had to make them count—make his point before it was too late for me to repent, and come to an impressive eleventh-hour understanding of the error of my ways.

"Is that meant to be some kind of challenge?"

A frown—a wince, almost. Like: *Jesus*, Regis!

"History—"

"Yeah, right. Now, let's see: Who is it writes history, again, exactly?"

We both knew the answer, and so did everybody else—it'd been one of Kiley's favorite saws, back up top. So no one bothered to reply.

Not even him.

* * *

Distant echoes, as the dim lights fade further: Roils and rumblings, metal gamelan trills. The odd hollow clang, barely audible, as the Waiting Room floor's dip slowly steepens. Behind the two-way, I hear the Doctor's autopsy equipment start to skitter down the counter, catch and clatter on the fixtures—all those poor lonely clamps and scalpels, laid out in eager anticipation of my corpse.

And cheated instead: Cheated, cheated.

For now.

The voice seems to smile, seems to agree. And tells me:

Soon.

* * *

Oh, Book, Book—shape up, soldier. You think you really got all the time in the world? You believe everything some fossil full of prehistoric bacteria tells you?

... can't believe I even just *thought* that sentence ...

So talk it out straight, for once, you crooked motherfucker—before your brain turns irretrievably to mush.

Regis Aaron Book: Me. 28 years old. Specialist rank 4, Lang-Intel. Cheat and smart-ass. Traitor.

Coward.

Born in Louisiana, raised in Pittsburgh; deaf grandma, absent Mom—gone so long, all the photos burned, I barely remember if she had a face. But I suspect she was probably pretty; I sure am.

After she ran off, Dad re-enlisted, went to Germany. Got all ripped on LSD one night and drove his tank into the Rhine. The government sent us a letter. I got to it before Nanny Book could see, read it, and flushed it down the toilet.

No great conversationalist, my Nan, and that wasn't all because of her pronunciation problems. She did teach me ASL before I was five, though.

Ever see the sign for drowning? It's kind of cute.

I played football in high school, got a university scholarship. Fucked my left foot (deliberately, I must confess)—hairline fracture, long-healed now. Transferred streams. Did languages: French, German, Hungarian, Romanian, five different Slavic variants—the USSR grand tour, they used to call it. Which is how I caught certain people's eye.

When I went ROTC, I told people it was because the recruiting officers said they'd kick me $40,000 toward the rest of my fees. But that was a lie. I joined the army so I could kill people—after which I joined the CIA, so I could do it for no good reason and be virtually assured of getting away with it.

I'm an American, born and bred. I like money. I like power. I like sex, as long as it doesn't lead to anything too permanent. I—

. . . blood in my . . .

—what else? Anything relevant?

(*there*'s a concept)

Oh, fuck: Shut up. Will you just shut the hell up, already?

. . . noise. In my . . .

My name is Book, Regis—Regis Book—and yes, I am a coward. And you know why? Because the proper synonym for coward, in this messed-up post-Berlin Wall world of ours, is "smart person". Cowards always come out on top. We try harder, and when we screw up it hurts worse, so we make damn sure it never happens again. We're the ones who live to fight another day—or just to live.

. . . blood.

Stay alive: My sole, my only legitimate consideration. The only one that matters.

Five more minutes, five more hours. Five more days, more years. Fifty. Five hundred—I don't discriminate. But I *am* selfish: Oh, yes. You damn betcha.

Because I'm not going to die, not here—never here, never like this.

Watching image- and word-meaning shuffle off into disintegration as my mental deck of cards deals me a dead man's hand, and the air runs out. Watching the Doctor cough his life away. Watching the lights dim, and hearing this thing inside me hold its figurative breath, waiting for me to get so loopy I don't care whether or not I'm part of it, or it's part of me. Or if there's any me still left for it to be a part of.

No. I'm not going to die like this—or any other way, if I can help it. I'm coming out of this sub just the same way I came in, the same way the Doctor and company found me when they opened the Waiting Room's mag-locked door, after the manditory five hours had finally elapsed: Alive alive-oh, just like sweet Molly Malone . . .

. . . before the fever, that is. Before the last verse.

Yeah, well, what*ever*; folk music was never my strong suit.

Alive, spelled ay-ell-ei-vee-ee.

Anything else is gravy.

* * *

The Doctor has lapsed into some kind of half-sleep. In the two-way, I catch a glimpse of my fine new self, post-*thing*: My bone-blonde hair, my bleached-out skin. My eyes like bruises, cilia purple with broken blood-vessels. I sniff the air, and decide that my skin has begun to smell like hash packed in sulphur.

And this glow, this glow, around and inside me. This inmost light.

The whispers tell me: *You are a chrysalis*. And I counter by forcing myself to think hard about the shriveled husks I saw left behind in Nanny Book's back yard, after the butterflies had gone on their merry way. I imagine my mouth splitting slowly open, ripping. Bending like vinyl under the eruptive strain, as a hitherto-hidden larva sloughs me off like so much deluded dead skin.

I feel the fear rise up in me again like wine, like flame—the salt and spices of it distributing themselves through my body while I struggle in its slow-cooking flame, rendering me ever more tender, more juicy. More appetizing.

'Cause fear is what this thing goes for, see? It loves it. Eats it. Got it in little tiny jolts from Kiley and the boy scouts, one by one by one; suck 'em dry and move along, bub. Skin packets, lit and hollowed from within, irradiated with detritus radiance. One big bruise, left to rot: An empty, man-sized wrapper, stuffed full of crumbly bones.

And why was I the only one, apparently, to ever figure this particular connection out?

Just my luck, I guess.

Dribs and drabs, after the long drought on the sea-bottom—aside from stealing the occasional muffled howl from a passing, boneless thing or two, in between geological epochs. From me, though, a veritable stream of terror, so constant as to skirt actual saiety. Fear-engine Book, running on empty: C'mon in and make yourself at home.

The Doctor turns his head again, heavier. Barely able to open his eyes. And tries to ask:

"What . . . happened . . . to—the—?"

"The shell?" I shrug. "Dust in the wind, Doc." Adding, as though in explanation: "It was old."

"Pre-. . . Pleistocene."

"Yeah, that sounds about right."

A wheeze; a cough. "And—what was . . . inside . . . ?"

To which I smile, curling back my bruised lower lip. Showing the tips of all my remaining upper teeth—my ill-set front caps, my jagged, half-missing left incisor. And reply:

" . . . Went—inside *me*."

* * *

And hey, there's even evidence: The Doctor taped it all, obsessively anal to the last, with a camcorder installed (as per tradition) behind the two-way—images skipping and fading between intermittent washes of static. I wound it back, watched it, in those first dim eons after I knew for sure that no matter what, the sub would just keep right on drifting further down and faster. Talk about post-modern: My cruel apotheosis, shot by shot, in all its real-time glory.

Hour one: Me pounding, pleading. Slumping. Turning.

Hour two: Me and the shell.

Hour three: The glow, beginning. Spreading.

Hour four: My hypnotized attention. Our conversation, me and it—that *thing*; not something which really seems to register, actually, on the purely visual scale.

Cajoling, flattering. Saying: *My love.* Saying: *You know I will honor my promises.*

The glow increasing steadily throughout, meanwhile; a slimy glitter. A blazing smokeless cloud, pillar of salt-white fire. A certain sense of boiling. Of moving outward, then—inward. Saying: *Soon.*

Soon, soon.

And in hour five . . .

* * *

The Waiting Room door clicks open, admits four—Doctor and goons, the original three-pack, already braced for action. They see me on the floor, face-down; the declining line of my limp back, head clutched in hands, shadow-rapt. No more light, bright or otherwise. No more shell.

 . . . *this quintessence of dust* . . .

"Bastard ate the fucking thing, fuck your mother," I hear one blurt. And think:

You could say that.

The Doctor kneels, waves them closer. One kicks me over. They see my face, hesitate as one—

 . . . *this noise* . . .

—and I feel my hands knot, my insides furl. I feel them start to reel away from me, then stop dead—sway, dazed. Instantaneously lulled. All of them, Doctor included, plunged into a kind of half-intoxicated trance brought on by my—(its)—proximity. Like standing next to a generator, invisible energy pouring off me in waves. Drowsiness seeping in through the pores.

I feel their fear, like I feel my own. And I feel what was once inside the shell—what's now inside me—sniffing at it: My mental tastebuds, gearing for the feast. My mouth, watering. The glow rekindling, a slow flame under my skin. This radiance looking out through my eyes, bruising them from the inside with the pressure of its glare.

 . . . *in my blood* . . .

Disconnected, surfing the current: A battery. A contained conflagration, run on incipient panic. I lever myself up with both hands, mirroring the Doctor. Look around. See them return my look, all of them—helpless *not* to.

"Bet you wish we were back in El Salvador *now*, fellas," I remark. Conversationally.

And I feel it let go of me, the thing, exploding outward like a concussion bomb-blast: Blow out the bridge, bring the bulkheads down. Crush the goons back against the Waiting Room walls. Crumple the Doctor in on himself. A surge of pent-up energy, driving me upward—haloed, paralyzed, cocooned in power. Catapulted into some pupa stage, lapped in adrenaline and brain-opiates. I feel the shell's former inhabitant slip away from me, in search of fresher fields, and my terror surges, babbling. I match it, promise for promise—set myself up as its carrier, its willing Judas Goat.

Succor and repair me—love me for real, like you love yourself—and I will bring you prey and praise.

A modern Prometheus for the century's end: Eat my fear anew each day, that I may live forever. Trying my level best to make it understand, through instinct rather than intelligence, that I'm not just a host—not just some new flesh shell for it to hide and sleep in, hibernating until the next best thing comes along. Wordlessly eloquent, I vow to trade keeping myself in a constant state of fear and pain for a vaccination—however temporary—against the whole concept of death: Death by drowning, by slow suffocation, death here at the bottom of the deep black sea, in the pressure-drunken final fathoms.

Making sure to also point out—with strictest possible attention to detail—that if I lose my personal identity, then I won't know what I have to be scared of anymore.

And you'll starve.

I hover, wait for its reply. Until the words come, soft as necrosis. Cells collapsing. A lie for a lie:

Time means nothing . . .

Yeah, yeah: To you.

. . . to us.

* * *

Which brings us, I believe, right back to where we started.

* * *

"Book," the Doctor whispers, now—so soft I can barely hear him, over my own constant internal whisper.

"Doctor," I reply. The word not meaning quite what it used to: Two empty syllables, ringing hollow in my skull. Language no longer seeming *necessary,* even as a nervous tic.

He clears his throat, or tries to, blood rattling in his lungs. Spits, or tries to. And shapes the words, with a last feeble breath:

" . . . I'm . . . a—fraid."

I shift my gaze back to him, slowly. Take a moment to remember his title, his significance. Then nod. And think:

But not as much as me.

Thankfully.

* * *

Here on the Subeja Trench's second shelf, already too far down to hope for rescue—anytime soon, at least—we drift past holes belching black lava, coral mountains crusted five arms deep with vivid, fleshy anemones. Everything watches us go by, large or small. They give us sidelong glances, and bare their teeth. And we keep on slipping down, fathom by fathom, until the foliage thins and the light falls away. Until there's nothing to note our descent but a congregation of boneless, blazing things which regard us with a total lack of curiosity.

While I note the Doctor's broken corpse, sprawled and sloughed on the floor beside me. Feeling similarly little.

Wondering: *Did I really strike a bargain, just then? Or do I only THINK I did?*

But if I can still think coherently enough to even consider the question, I guess, it probably just doesn't matter all that much.

The sub buckles, twisting in on itself deck by deck. But I hold fast, footloose and evidence-free, to the improbable notion that I have been promised exemption—that even when the water seeps in under the Waiting Room door, this *thing*'s infernal patronage will render me impermeable, slicked with infection. No swelling, no softening, no gentle nibbles from passing teeth; just a long sleep, a long, long dream. One long nightmare, a phobophobic haze, during which I can jim in my own stew—

(you fucker, you promised)

—stew—*swim* in my own . . . juices. Awhile.

. . . *a while, a minute, a century* . . .

And when they (the CIA, the Doctor's bunch, a salvage crew, whoever) finally find us, and pry open this busted can, how very sweet I'll be. Well-marinaded, and ready to serve: To be my prehistoric savior's chosen liaison, its translator. Its face prepared to meet the faces it will eat.

Or maybe we'll just stay down here, forever, unfound and unmourned, until entropy eats us both.

I raise my hand, look at my fingers. See my vision narrow. My pressure-drunk brain, squeezing itself flat. Glitches, sparking and fading: Images fizzling. Kiley's shadow-animals. Nanny's hands.

The two moons of Mars, on that childhood chart. Deimos and—
(Phobo)
—Phobos. Meaning panic—
(phobia)
—and fear.

Fear, my motive, my spur. My dark and guiding star.

All my life, I think, *my fear has driven me to take the easiest way.* And where does the easiest way lead, usually?

Well, that would probably be—down.

Down here, at the bottom. Where there are a lot of things, and most of them glow . . .

Thinking: *When you get what you ask for, you really have no right to be surprised.*

. . . including me.

SKELETON BITCH

Rictus. That's the grin a corpse gets, when it knows you're just too chicken-shit to bury it yet, and I should know.

I looked it up.

* * *

So—Friday night at Jaime's, two months back. Somebody's earrings caught the light from over by the john, and I couldn't believe anybody could possibly wear that many rings at once without ripping their lobes wide open, so I leaned past Doug Whoever's shoulder for a closer look. she was up against the wall with a speaker at either hip, all black on black, thin as sidewalk chalk. White hair, white lips with an irregular flash of blue teeth laced between them in the kitchen light-spill. A chemical warfare jacket to mid-thigh over tights so old they were mostly runs, flag of South Vietnam dripping blood along one arm, the other nude and unexpectedly track-free. Element of surprise aside, it all seemed like the same old poser Goth shit to me—I mean, just about everybody there was trying to look dead.

But she was the only one doing it right.

"'Scuse me," I said, and pushed off to investigate. Some proto-grunge epic blasted so loud my fillings ached as I stepped up beside her, but she didn't even turn. Just said:

"Like this song?"

I took a second, got a smear of lash mixed with red-shot iris in return for my tact.

"Yeah, classic. You?"

"First time I heard this . . . it was 1987. Ozone summer. Kicked some kind of door open in my head, and I—"

"Don't tell me. You wanted to hunt him down and do him on the floor, right?"

She showed those teeth again—wet, this time. A little internal thrum of laughter. Then, in that prepubescent headcold purr of hers, entirely too detached to charm:

"No, Mr. Man. I wanted to *be* him. Just like you did."

I followed her down the hall awhile. Pretty soon, she pulled me through a door with a big splash of paint above it, and we fell against the wall. I felt her breasts move under the jacket, pointy little nipples piercing through like slate chips. Five cold fingers toying with my fly, diffident, like she could take it or leave it, depending on how slow the music got.

"You keep on doing that, I'm gonna have to take you into the john." Her hand moved a little lower. "Hey," I said, trying to keep it light—but it was drunk by then, and it came out wrong. "You think I'm joking?"

That made her look up, for the first time. And answer:

"No."

"Oh, so you're one stone bitch, I expect."

A narrow blue rim of smile, like frost.

"Yeah," she said, with absolutely no change of tone. "I am."

And I laughed.

* * *

But by the morning after—when I woke up, alone and hurting—I believed her.

* * *

A couple of days later, I met Jaime on the street. "That chick I went off with—" I began.

A wave of laughter. "Oh, yeah. Dawn of the Dead. How you make out there, anyways?"

I shrugged. "Okay, I guess." Then: "Listen, man—is that her name?"

This time, he had to hold onto the wall.

"Jesus, buddy," he said, finally. "Next time *ask*, okay? It seriously helps."

* * *

That was the same week we cut the demo. The same week I wrote it. We liked to leave things as close to the wire as we could, back then—before the money started coming in, and our lead guitarist started worrying about who our "real fans" still were.

The song was "Skeleton Bitch"—just the B-side, originally—and it broke us wide open, just like we always wanted. Just like nothing we did before ever could, and nothing we've done since ever has.

But I'm not here to talk about the *band*.

* * *

Next time I saw her was at the launch party, wedged between a cluster-fuck of drunken music critics and the kitchen counter, keeping herself amused by making anagrams from mine honorable host's (a.k.a. our agent's) Froot-Loop-bright fridge magnets. I slid in behind her, one arm under her breasts, and whispered in her ear:

"I do got a *phone*, you know."

"That's nice," she said, making S-H-E-S-V-A-I-N into V-A-N-I-S-H-E-S.

Something in her voice told me to gulp my drink, and when I shook the one I'd snagged for her in front of her face, she turned—to study me close, like we'd never even met before.

"That's nice too," she said, taking it. Then, sipping: "Do I know you?"

For a minute, I couldn't speak. Literally.

"Last I heard," I said, finally.

* * *

Because, Goddammit, it *was* her. Same white hair. Same white lips. Same cold limbs all aroll in their sockets, lithe as bones. And her pale, thread-veined eyes, beneath their fresh black diamonds of mascara—still shiny, still blank, like old blood under ice.

We ended up in the cloak-room, that time, doing it like dogs on a pile of coats worth more put together than I'd made in my entire life. She was all slick and tight under that jacket she wouldn't take off—wet but frozen, her inner ridges icy slipknots, pulling me down. She popped my zip and ripped her tights wide open with one long thumb-nail, sliding back onto me like some well-oiled, key-swallowing lock. And her nipple seemed to burn a hole right through my palm as we fell the full fathom five together, down deep to where the only fish are blazing ghosts and the pressure crushes you flat.

When I came, I heard "Skeleton Bitch" playing somewhere. "Wrote that for you," I gasped, in her ear.

She just smiled. And asked:

"Wrote what?"

* * *

Hours later, I woke to find Jaime gingerly trying to extricate his date's velvet cape from the mess underneath me.

"Chris," he said, "you're one exotic guy, and I mean this in the nicest possible way—but anyone ever tell you 'bout beds?"

I coughed, mouth full of cat hair and whiskey fumes. "Her name's Rictus," I told him.

"Yeah, great, man."

And he passed his date her shroud, just in time for me to stumble past them both, not quite making the washroom door before the rest of my brains all boiled up through my nose.

* * *

That was how it went, from then on. She was everywhere, like an itch—capillary-deep, unscratchable. If I'd had any trouble pissing, I would have thought she gave me something.

But I wasn't getting off *that* easy.

Things got dark, then darker. I'd snap my alarm off at eight, open my eyes what felt like a few minutes later, only to find it was two in the afternoon. The phone rang, intermittently: Relatives, old acquaintances, other band members—replaced, eventually, by their lawyers. They talked about stuff I'd signed. Contracts, whatever; that fabled three-album deal everybody'd dreamed about for so long, each side at least five songs long, with not one track of it written or recorded yet.

It didn't matter. Turns out, I'd only had the one song in me.

And now it was gone.

* * *

Anyways, enough said. I'll cut to the chase.

Three weeks of hell later, I was standing in front of Lovecraft, comparison-shopping for "marital aids"—dipsy-doodle half-inchers, bright pink rubber cartoon Japanese animals full of rotating plastic balls, two-foot ebony Pulverizers ("life-like in every way, complete with veins!").

And I saw her. A little black dot on the street behind me, tourists recoiling as she limped past them down the avenue with that sidewinder strut of hers well in play, swaying like kelp on a dark current. Blind, but purposeful.

Yeah, I called after her. What do you *think*? And no, she didn't turn.

So I followed her down.

Down past the Strip, down past Front Street, down through the underpass. Right on down to Harborfront. Down to the cold and slimy shore of Lake Ontario itself, where ducks float and fish-bellies flash, surfacing intermittently against the dark green waves. Down to the end of a long, long pier, its foundations slicked with chemical foam, where yuppies from the condos on either side stand arm in arm each night, to sip their take-out cappuccino and watch the Island ferry go by. Down where the land runs out, which is—naturally enough . . . where I stopped.

But she didn't.

* * *

Happened so fast, after our hour-plus meander, it took a breath just to register. One minute she was there, the next—

I heard myself scream, and plunged in after her.

* * *

When I made the pier again—which was a lot harder than it seemed like it would be, from dry land—I just lay there, panting. Soaked through. Jesus, that water was cold.

The sun moved higher, drying my clothes. Dogs came and sniffed at me. Shadows flickering across the mirrored windows and distant highrises. Clouds. I shut my eyes, retreated into a dim, red roar, and lay there playing dead man—which, at that point, I very seriously felt like I might as well be.

I just couldn't get my head around it.

When my back hurt too much to lie on anymore, I shuffled away; I don't know where to. Vague images of hats and sports equipment hanging in space, mannequins contorted in pointless displays, my own eyes staring back at me from a series of department store windows. I picked yesterday's newspaper out of the garbage and dissected it, unread. I hung around the pay-phones, hypnotized by their calling-card readouts.

By six, the sun was setting, and I found myself back at the shore, stumbling along a seemingly endless stretch of what passes for beach in Toronto. My shoes were full of sand, so I stopped to knock them out. Right one first.

A few drops of what I thought was rain kissed the back of my neck.

Then a shadow fell across my bare foot.

I looked up.

Rictus stood there.

* * *

Her clothes hung slack on her, shiny and deflated, like popped seaweed pods. Water in her hair. Water in her kohl-smeared eyes. She gave a great, jaw-cracking yawn, through moist black lips, and I heard it rattle in her lungs.

She cocked her head at me, inquisitive. But only mildly so.

"We met before," she said. "A while back."

My heart was a fistful of broken glass.

"Oh, Jesus Christ," I said. "You're dead." A beat. "Aren't you?"

She made that thrum again. Just as low. But more—liquid.

"Well, you tell *me* . . . Mr. Man."

I know what real contempt is, now. Not what we think hurts us. Not words, not deeds. Not even physical pain. Real contempt is a waterlogged corpse you've cried over for a day, wordless and amazed at the depth of your own loss, who stands in front of you at sunset with her hair like a bloody halo—and doesn't even have the decency to pretend she remembers your name.

"You bitch," I said, dry-mouthed. "I'd do anything for you. Don't you even *care*?"

She smiled, then. And I saw her mouth was ripped at one corner—not much, just enough.

A freshwater leech pulsed, black and fat, at the base of her pale tongue.

"Care," she repeated, as though tasting it. "There's a word for you. Impressive. Like it should mean . . . something."

Smiling wider. Showing more.

"Problem is, I don't know what."

She sank down in front of me, there on the dirty sand. Lay right on back amongst the fast food debris and the frost-bitten weeds, easing her chemical warfare jacket's front flaps slowly apart.

Clip by painstaking clip.

"We *did* meet before, though," she said. "Once or twice. Your name—is—"

"Chris."

"Oh, *riiight.*"

She pulled it open, then. For the first time. Saying, not unkindly:

"You're all the same to me, man. Nothing personal. I just am what I am. And being what I am, I take—what I—can get."

And when I finally saw what was under it, I heard myself mewl like a crushed cat.

She just looked up at me, from under her wet white lashes. A level gaze, flat-eyed. Not *secretive*, so much—as patient. Like dust.

Because I wanted her. Still.

"So," she said. "You coming?"

Still. And always.

"Or what?"

* * *

And I let her draw me down. Like she always knew I would, whether I'd ever found out or not—what she was. I mean, is. Rachel, Ruth, Rebecca, maybe even Rita-turned-Rictus, mouth open wide, some milky kind of liquid spilling up from deep inside her like an undertow. *Oh, Christ, suffering Christ.* A real man-sized portion poking up from me into the dark beneath her coat, sausage stuffed fit to fry and pop, right on up where it's tight, and slick, and ragged, and cold. *Christ.* I knew exactly what I was doing this time, and it didn't even matter. Up through the snapped wishbone of her pelvis, nudging aside a few soft coils of intestine, up through the muscle wall, up as far as I could go into that clotted seam full of black blood, the autopsy scar I'd thought all along was her vagina. Deep into the black, sweet, caustic heart of the matter. The core. Where it all gets broken down to the lowest common denominator, meaning eff-all. Nothing to the infinite power. A dead girl's stinking stomach flapping open in the wind, cold enough to burn.

Then a rasp of unstrung suture caught me on the back-stroke, and I screamed as I came, clutching her close—'til her corpse's grin finally got too much for me, and I jack-knifed my face hard into the top of her spine.

This time, when I bit her shoulder in the grip of my passion, a bit of it tore away.

And I swallowed it.

* * *

"Skeleton Bitch" went top ten in a week. I don't care if I never sing again.

Because somewhere out on the Strip, she's there. I know it. My white doll muse, washed unrecognizable. Got stitches from her throat to her twat, black on bruisy white, left nipple gone limp as any supernumerary mole. Back of her right ear, under the dark roots, there's a triangular gash—the place where somebody's steel-toed boot went in. And part by part, she's ugly. Part by part, she's poison. But if you ever catch her eye, even for a second—those wide, ivory eyes, like bone, like stone, so level and calm and dead under their maps of burst blood-vessels—she'll wipe you raw, she'll drag you down, down deep into the trash at the bottom fo the Lake, where the big fish breed. H-shot to the spine, lighter-fluid spurt, imploded orgasm cold as nitrogen, freezing your brain 'til it shatters at a touch. And you won't mind at all, man.

You'll even get to like it.

* * *

This is what she said, that last time—a breathless breath against my ear-lobe:
"Bite down, baby. Bite right down. 'Cause this is all of me you get."

Skeleton bitch, see her grin
As the knife goes in and in and in and—

End of story.

FOLLY

Pentheus: You say you saw the God clearly. What was he like?
Dionysus: Whatever he wanted. I had no control over it.
—Euripedes' *Bacchae*, Cambridge University Press translation.

Good evening, ladies and gentlemen—very sorry for alarming you, if I did. Yes, the lights have been out for some time up here; it happens rather frequently, I'm afraid. Localized brown-outs; that's what happens when you have an entire town practically running off the same generator. Yet we manage, nevertheless.

At any rate: Again, welcome! Please step through into the front portico-hallway, where our tour will begin as soon as everyone on the list is assembled and accounted for. I've sent my assistant Stephen for candles, but it may well take him some time to return. Until then, I guess we'll just have to rely on my trusty flashlight.

Very well. And . . . here we go, then.

Though the foundations of the Peazant house—or, as its re . . . *inventor* liked to refer to it, Nova Mephitium—were first laid in late 1887, most of what you see here is far more recent. These alterations and additions date from 1947, when Dr Denys Peazant took control of his grandparents' estate. Using old money from the family business (importation, curiosities), which he augmented with a series of governmental grants that may or may not have been under-the-counter "rewards" for his extensive but secretive service in the field of post-mortem communications research during World War II, Dr Peazant made extensive modifications to the house. So extensive, in fact, that many family retainers quit in horror during the process, accusing him of "defiling" and "gutting alive" the very home where he and his siblings had been born and raised.

A bit strong, perhaps. But it's certainly true that absolutely nothing now remains of the house Dr Peazant's grandfather built except its exterior facade, this hallway we stand in and a wing of personal apartments to which Dr Peazant used to laughingly refer as "the Sacristy", which lie through those doors to your left. These are potentially of great interest, but I am restrained by court order from exhibiting them to you—a codicil of Dr Peazant's will, you understand.

Interestingly, as a sidebar, you may have noticed that the locals—from whom the insulted retainers were recruited, and to whose ranks they later returned—still never use Dr Peazant's own nomenclature when referring to the house. They call it variants on the original, instead . . . Peazant's Hulk, for one. Peazant's Ruin. Or my personal favorite, for reasons I'll revisit in good time . . .

. . . Peazant's Folly.

* * *

Outside, nothing too spectacular. A typical red-brick monstrosity squatting at the top of the hill like some overfed gentleman's angioplasty-courting heart, cloaked by firs and lapped in gloom, apparently content to grow mainly by osmosis: Extrude a fresh lobe of windows, turrets and buttresses for each new decade and spread wide, sinking ever deeper inside itself, 'till its original shape disappears from view completely.

As you approach from below, the silhouette of the house seems to reach out in all directions at once; its proximity comes with a subtle aftertaste attached, pungent as the smell of burning rubber along some otherwise charming but inexplicably accident-prone road.

It makes little attempt at concealment. Any passerby has only to look at it once to know: This house, this house. THIS house, beyond the shadow of a shadow of a doubt—

—is haunted.

* * *

If you would please keep to our original path, however—yes, that's the door to the interior up ahead. And what a very good observation: The hallway *is* indeed designed to seem considerably shorter, and less narrow, than it actually is. The source of this illusion lies in Dr Peazant's use of multiple archways whose columns are just wide enough to mask the next archway lying beyond; it's an architectural trick called "forced perspective", usually used to make things seem *larger*. And another interesting turn of phrase, too, considering its application.

You will also note that the walls are hung with deliberately foggy mirrors made from hammered bronze. This serves to fracture the reflections of approaching... Dr Peazant, I am relatively sure, would call them pilgrims, or even supplicants... in such a way that, very occasionally, one might almost—

—ah, yes. But it would probably be far more effective simply to show you.

Look into the mirrors, and keep walking. As you do, you may begin to see something take shape behind your own reflection, a vague shimmer at the edge of your vision. As it does, watch the way that this doubling effect seems to spread across your own reflected face, obscuring it like some sort of metallic caul; like the tough white facial membrane some children are born with, seventh sons of seventh sons and such, which must be first cut away in order to free the breathing passages and then dried, saved, worn around the neck in a small leather sack. A presentiment of prophecy made flesh, signifying some inborn ability to see your own future—or that of others—coming, ahead of time.

Some of you may also glimpse something more, however. An actual *figure* rather than simply the implication of one—back bent, hands and face obscured, draped in what looks like a length of lightish colored cloth. Its frame will be unmistakably human, yet dsiturbingly thin; it enters the mirror sidelong, from an unwatched corner, to hover by your own image in an obscurely threatening pose. Turning, shoulder outthrust as though its arm were about to rise, its shrouded hand about to *reach*, to *touch*—to lay itself, suddenly, upon the unwary supplicant's all-unwitting shoulder—

Or not. The effect doesn't manifest itself for everybody.

Yes, those sconces near the ceiling *are* for gas, and provided the bulk of the house's emergency lighting until only a few years ago. No, I will not be lighting them tonight.

Yes, there will be an explanation.

I must ask you to enter into the house's interior single-file, now—one by one, with a minimum of straggling. You may well wish to muffle the lower part of your faces while you step across the threshold; this part of the house is not very efficiently ventilated, frankly, and visitors often find the smell somewhat disturbing until they have a chance to get used to it.

Now just keep close, if you please, while I shut... and lock... this door behind us.

* * *

One of the most enduring tales told about Peazant's Folly long pre-dates Dr Peazant's subsequent remodeling. It implies that Edmund Peazant, the house's original builder, buried the first of his five children alive in its foundations so that the baby's death-agonies would help keep the structure strong and erect. This rumor has never been substantiated, though it may explain why Mrs Peazant later—after so many births, plus a few more "miscarriages"—chose to commit suicide by first thrusting her head through the stained-glass window of her husband's study, then slitting her throat from ear to ear on what shards of glass still adhered to the frame.

The true reputation of Peazant's Folly, however, only began to grow after Dr Peazant reduced his grandfather's home to a shell behind which he could arrange things to his own very particular, semi-arcane specifications. Periodically, its status as Canada's least-habitable residence has since been challenged by reporters, historians, parapsychologists, exorcists, businessmen, the unwary of all stamps and stripes. Few have emerged from the experience unaltered... but such a place will attract tourists, even so. Even now.

Outside, then, all as expected. Inside, however—

—the flashlight's beam choking to a dim glow, its lens a windowpane clogged by insects' wings—

—a sudden snap of wrist-deep dust, filling your throat to bursting—

—panic narrowing your chest as you cross the doorsill, and that smell, that SMELL—

* * *

So here it is, at last: Peazant's "Folly" itself, in the truest sense of the term. A plaster and limestone reproduction, built to scale, of that Mephitic Temple Dr Peazant himself discovered in a series of caves near

Delphi—"Mephitic", meaning "up from underground", underside of the Apollonian, most mysterious of all Mystery religions. Like their more legitimate neighbors, the Mephitium had its oracle too. But while the Delphic oracle merely squatted over a crack in the earth and breathed in the sulphurous, volcanic fumes which produced her prophetic trances only when she was directly requested to, her Mephitic sister-seers lived their lives out in the same cavern from which those gases were produced.

The fumes in *here*, however, are somewhat less than natural, let alone sacred. As my employers eventually discovered, not so very long ago—after they opened the Folly to visitors in order to defray rising property taxes on the one hand, while cutting local incidences of vandalism and trespassing on the other—the smell you're reacting to comes from the gas-sconces Dr Peazant's grandfather once installed, way back when. Dr Peazant had them soldered permanently open, so that they would admit a steady stream of near-fatally pure methane mixed with hydrogen sulfide from the (only partially drained) swamp old Mr Peazant built his house on top of. I could take you down to the basement right now and show you what's left, but I wouldn't advise it . . . it's really *not* a pretty sight.

Here, then, is why I've been instructed not to turn the sconces back on, let alone light them. *This* is the invisible contagion Dr Peazant infected his family's home with, hoping its influence might convert whoever was unwise enough to live here into a modern-day Mephitic priest or priestess whose constant oracular trance would doom them to live—and die—in the same eternally-receptive state as their predecessors: Perpetually open, perpetually God-possessed.

But by what God, you ask? Another good question. Not Apollo, certainly; Apollo had no truck with the underworld, even in his less—appealing—aspects . . .

Ah, but if we *knew*, it wouldn't be a Mystery. Would it?

* * *

After thirty years of incident, recorded and otherwise, some patterns do tend to emerge. The 1983 Jay Expedition case is particularly typical of what would become known as the Peazant's Folly "experience": Two parapsychologists (Drs Jay and Jay, husband and wife) plus a mental medium (the late Guilden Fisk) vs. two scientific skeptics—an archaeologist (Dr Meulendyk) and a forensic psychologist specializing in suggestion-induced psychoses (Dr Lean). Each team had publicly vowed to expel, or expose, the house's secrets before the other could finish its initial diagnosis. They entered Peazant's Folly en masse, but left it one by one . . . in body-bags, straightjackets, or simple police restraints.

Whether their tenure ended by murder, self-mutilation, suicide or insanity, however, each survivor told a strikingly similar story. Approaching the Folly in accordance to Dr Peazant's instructions, they had reduced themselves to playing the part of worshipers at the Mephitium's figurative altar; they had passed through the hallway and over the inner threshold single-file, making a ritual pilgrimage from the above-ground world of the living to some all-purpose underground Land of the Dead: Hades, Styx, Acheron, Elysium, Heaven and Hell all rolled into one.

So: Imagine, if you will, this disparate group wending its collective way down that long bronze hallway like a trip through the birth canal in reverse, watching their reflections split and blur and peel away before their very eyes—cracking their civilized shells open, just as instructed, in order to render themselves more properly amenable to the Mephitium's inherent range of—suggestions.

They all say they saw that faceless figure hovering behind them, eventually; saw it reflected in each other's eyes, if nothing else. Even the ones who, like Meulendyk and Lean, had taken as great a care as possible NOT to research the house and its various phantoms beforehand, for fear of tainting their on-site findings.

Maybe a God. Maybe a ghost. Maybe something else, something specific to the house itself. Self-created, maintained by a steady stream of fresh minds to infiltrate, fresh dreams to occupy . . .

Given enough of a head-start, a house like this probably becomes its own haunting. Don't you think? I mean—

* * *

—don't you?

Please excuse me, ladies and gentlemen. I appear to have let my thoughts run away with me.

What? Oh, no, no—believe me, if there's one thing we've learned over the years, it takes a considerably longer period of exposure to the Folly and its fumes for oracular madness on a Jay Expedition scale to finally manifest itself than this tour is likely to consume. No matter *how* long it eventually takes Stephen to get back here with those candles.

Actually, since we seem to have the time . . . and yes, those carvings really are lovely, aren't there? There's more 'round the back, which we can examine further once the lights are on—

At any rate: Like most tour guides, not to mention most frustrated academics—I certainly didn't take this job for the pay, after all—I have my own theories about what Dr Peazant's little experiment in enforced prophecy may have succeeded in invoking. Not so much an ancient God reborn, to my mind, as a completely new construct: The Folly itself, made phantom rather than flesh. That cloth-draped vision, expressing itself through an endless series of unwilling human visionaries.

Dr Peazant wanted his Folly's supplicants to become oracles themselves, answering their own unspoken questions about the past, the future, what lies beyond. Instead, he made his *house* into the oracle. We come and go, but it remains—and as long as we come and go quickly enough, it has no choice but to keep its own counsel.

I wonder, though. What does a prophet prevented from prophesying feel, exactly? Does it feel relief, freedom, a welcome escape from using and being used in return? Or does it feel loneliness, depression . . . the terrible pain of being left perpetually alienated from its deepest, most integral calling?

Nova Mephitium. It reminds me of the question posed to yet another ancient oracle, the Sybil at Cumae, who grew so old and shriveled that her worshipers were forced to keep her in a huge glass bottle, like a genie. And like some clever Arab giving away his last wish to the genie itself, one supplicant once used his—or her—turn to ask, on the oracle herself's behalf: 'Sybil, what do you want?' To which she replied, wearily:

'I want to die.'

Thirty years, fifty years, a hundred years: You show no one anything they really want to see, tell them nothing they really want to know—nothing they can profit from, nothing *good*. And then, at the end of it, the ungrateful bastards leave you all alone here in the dark, in the middle of this awful smell, with nobody to even try and understand you but the man who leads gawking groups of tourists back and forth through your hollow guts a minimum of three times a day, seven times a week, fifty-two weeks a year with almost no time off for sickness, vacation or good behavior . . .

Which makes it rather one hell of a lot of time I've spent in here already, really. And I can't believe, what with all the thousands of hours I've spent thinking about this house, Peazant's Folly, its Mystery, one way or another—

—that I've never, but *never*, thought about that before.

Um . . .

. . . just one moment, all right? You—just stay right there, together. *Close* together. And I'll be—right back.

Oh, God.

No, no, I'm fine. Just . . . over there, by the door? The door I *locked* behind us, and I think you all definitely saw me do it—

No, *don't* turn to check—really, *don't. Really.*

Well, if you feel you have to . . .

No, you're right. You're right. It's gone now.

Hah.

Well, that was a nice little scare to end the tour on, wasn't it? Things you'll convince yourself you see in the dark . . . might be more fumes left in here than my employers have been letting on, I guess.

And where the hell *is* Stephen, anyway? With those—

—candles.

Fumes.

Look does anybody smell anything, aside from me? I mean—

—something worse?

Uh . . .

. . . maybe that wasn't the best idea, all told. Maybe—I'm just going to unlock the door, and maybe we should all just—leave. Quietly, single-file, like the guidebook says. But, uh . . . quickly, too. Before Stephen decides it's just the right time to finally show up and, um—

—Steve, is that you? You look—*bigger*, somehow . . .

* * *

That same figure you saw inside the Folly's door, back bent, hands and face obscured. Turning with its draped shoulder outthrust, its shrouded hand about rising to reach, to TOUCH . . .

* * *

Oh Christ, it's—it's right *behind* you, right fucking now. You know, the—*Christ*, Steve, *you* know what the fuck I'm fucking talking about—

* * *

'Sybil, what do you want?', you ask. To which I reply . . .

* * *

—fuck, don't *look*, moron, just *don't*—

* * *

I want to DIE!

* * *

—STEPHEN, FOR FUCK'S SAKE, DO *NOT* LIGHT THAT FUCKING CA—

MOUTHFUL OF PINS

Sometimes I dream that my father, who's been dead for eight years now, appears at my door in the middle of the night and tells me he's actually been living in another country with a whole new family—but he won't tell me where or who, no matter how I plead and cry. Sometimes I dream of rain. But mostly I dream of Yle'en, the Drowned Land. I dream of the Twins and the Green Lady, of the Monocle, the Hammerheads, and the Unseen King. And that frightens me.

* * *

There were five of us in the game of Yle'en—Mary, and Eunice, and Ray, and Trevor, and me. We were all quite young when it began, friends mainly by virtue of our shared pain. We met at school. Hurried conversations in the yard at recess soon revealed our remarkable similarities. Mary and Eunice received midnight visits from their live-in uncle, as I recall, while Ray's highly religious relatives' ideas about child-rearing had left him with an awful stutter. Trevor's father ignored him. Mine beat me. We would all have gladly traded places with each other. That not being possible, we escaped—as far as we could—into Yle'en.

We were model children, all told—quiet, neat, polite. Our bruises kept well-hidden under slightly unseasonable clothes, we faced the world each day with the calm aplomb of prisoners of war. We never talked back, or broke things, and didn't seem actively unhappy. We simply hadn't the strength to be.

So we created Yle'en, which slowly gained strength enough for all of us.

Eventually, we grew apart. Our time in hell done, we exploded out into the world, and haven't stopped moving in completely different directions since. Ray lives with his lover in Vancouver, making sculptures from "found objects". Eunice has three kids of her own. Trevor is a homicide detective in Winnipeg. I'm still in Toronto, working for an ad agency. You may have seen a few of my commercials for beer, cars, or the Canadian National Exhibition. I put in too much overtime, drink more than I should, and—once every two years or so—precipitate a brief but painful affair by picking up a similarly ambitious young woman in a downtown gay bar. Late at night, I often go into the bathroom and press a lit cigarette into the crook of my elbow. Just to prove that I'm really alive.

But Mary is dead.

* * *

Yle'en is a cold place with a very rigid hierarchy. Being more than a little intimate with the power of fear, we populated it with the things we each feared most. I contributed my twin brother Ian, who fell from a second-story window when we were five. His memory took fresh significance as the glass-armored Twins, one of whom lies forever coiled inside the other like a twisted reel of tapeworm. Ray, who had a morbid dislike of flowers, which possibly stemmed from his love/hate relationship with female genitalia, remade himself as the Green Lady—her arms and her legs articulated like a praying mantis's, her face a ravenous lily. The Monocle was Trevor's father's geometry set—Yle'en's executioner, cutting variables viciously down to size with his razor-edge calipers. Eunice's repressed rage finally found form as the Hammerheads, a whole shoal of sleek, stupid ghost-sharks bent on mutilation.

And Mary was the Unseen King.

She brought a book on Antarctica to school one day and spread it out excitedly beneath the jungle-gym. "The most inhospitable place on earth," she called it. Faced with the facts, we had to agree.

Turning and turning at the world's utter end, breaking apart only to reform again with a slowness which makes fossils seem hasty, Antarctica is an abstraction made real upon which nothing was ever meant to live for long. It *is* nothing, an inexhaustible waste stretching as far as the eye can see—numb, blind, and devouring.

It was the way we felt. We loved it for that, and made it our own.

In Yle'en, no clocks run. In Yle'en, the ice is made of glass. It freezes the breath solid in your lungs everywhere you touch, choking you, cutting you to the bone. Blood is its art, cruelty its highest form of compliment. Our horrid avatars move with ritual politesse across its blank, lidless eye. Their hunger is an incurable virus running rampant and unafraid across the crevasses, inexorable.

We exiled our parents to Yle'en daily, and tortured them without pity. We murdered countless generations there, and reanimated them to face the knives again, at a whim. We exterminated a slew of civilizations, just for fun. And, along the way, we instilled Yle'en's citizens with our own values—the wit and wisdom of abused children, laid down as unbreakable law.

We took comfort in it, outgrew it, and forgot it.

But it never forgot us.

* * *

A week before she died, Mary called me up. I had just broken with Babs for once and for all, and was drowning my sorrows with creme de menthe in the kitchen. I let the phone ring ten times before I picked it up, more out of respect for the caller's tenacity than curiosity.

"Hello, House of Pain."

"Zara?"

I sat straight up when I heard the voice. Not just because it had been six or seven years since the last time, but because she sounded so desperate—as if her telephone box were underwater, and slowly springing a leak.

"Mary, where are you? Christ, it's been—"

"Zara, it's coming," she said.

I absorbed that. "What is?" I asked, finally.

"Yle'en."

There was a pause. She spoke across it, the words tumbling out without waiting for a response. Like a cry for help, or a confession.

"Trevor's father is dead. They found him at home, all over the place—upstairs, downstairs, in my lady's chamber. Blood everywhere—but it wasn't liquid or dry. It was frozen."

A bird tapped lightly at my window, making love to its own reflection. Probably deranged, as most city animals soon become.

"And Ray's aunt, too. She suffocated in bed—her lungs were full of pollen.

The cops said the whole house smelled like lilies. When they broke the door down, it was so cold they could all see their own breath. Zara, this was in August."

I studied my right hand. My cuticles were speckled with what my father used to call gift spots, but which I later discovered to be the residue of slow-healing bruises on the flesh beneath. Apt.

Mary was still ticking off her mental list. "And then Bob Shand—you remember our uncle? It got the bastard in September. Dogs, the cops told Eunice. But she knows better, and so do I. *Dogs* don't leave triangular bite-marks."

"I would've thought you'd be glad to see him go," I said. "All things considered."

"I was, that's not the point." She paused. "I've been in therapy for a while. It helped a lot. I managed to forgive some people—my mother, for one. But they found *her* last night, in her car, in the river. Floating in a block of ice."

The sun stood still and white in a pale grey sky. Beyond my garden, people were laughing.

"Have you called the others yet?"

"Of course."

"And what did they say?"

She sighed. "Eunice didn't want to be bothered. Ray told me to get professional help. Trevor's line's been disconnected. Zara, they've changed so much."

"And I haven't?" I felt like giggling, but my mouth wouldn't move in the right direction.

Silence and hissing, across the miles. Then:

"I've been thinking about it. There's one chance—slim, but I've got to take it."

"Which is?"

"I was the one who started it all. I showed you guys the books, I sowed the seeds. I'm the Unseen King, right?" Her voice quavered. "If anyone can stop Yle'en—reason with it somehow—it should be me."

"And if you can't?"

No answer.

I absently wondered how she planned to whistle them all up. Long-dormant images sprang immediately to mind, but I held onto my stomach, and pushed them firmly back down.

"But it's changed too, Zara," she whispered at last. "I can feel it. It hates us now."

"No, Mary," I said softly. "It hasn't changed. We have. And that's why."

For a moment, I almost thought that I could hear her heartbeat.

"Good luck," I said.

"I'll call back in two days," she replied.

We both hung up at once.

Three days later, the police rang my bell.

* * *

It wasn't much of a surprise, though. Because the same night, about 11:15 p.m., I was looking for a scar-tissueless patch of inner arm on which to test my theory that writing advertising copy makes you a zombie when the bathroom door opened. It was Babs, her face wrinkling in disgust.

"Shit, not this again," she said.

"Apparently so," I said. "Forget something?"

She'd used her key to get in, which I—in the heat of the moment—had forgotten all about. I leaned against the bedroom wall as she rifled through our drawers, stuffing odd articles of lingerie into a big plastic bag.

"There's a name for that problem of yours, you know," she told me. "It's called Borderline Personality Syndrome, and all it takes to get rid of it is a little effort. I read about it in *Cosmopolitan*."

"A little effort," I repeated. "Boy, I never would have thought of that. Thanks, Babs."

And the argument began afresh. I didn't get to talk a lot after that, as she went over the usual complaints with new vigor—my lack of commitment, my lack of imagination, my lack of passion.

"You blame everything about how you've fucked up your life on this thing with your Dad! If *I'd* been abused, I'd at least be sad, be angry, be *something*! But you're just cold, Zara! There's nothing inside you, and that's why you do that to yourself—because you know that if you couldn't feel pain, you wouldn't feel *anything*!"

The gospel according to Babs, drawn from a bevy of self-help gurus, each one devoured, considered, and discarded within a week to make room for the next.

"No one could love you, Zara! You don't even love yourself!"

Cold.

I could see my own breath.

And an overpowering smell of lilies filled the room.

Babs' hand was on the knob when I suddenly yelled: "Wait, don't!"

She turned back. Just for a second. And her lips curled back, showing even teeth.

"You sad bitch," she said, quietly. And pulled.

The door fell open. Beyond it were the Twins.

And they ate her alive.

I suppose I could have done something to stop them, done anything other than just watch. But I'm not *sure*. Because, as they left, they looked into my eyes. And I saw them smile. Their teeth were made of glass.

Why should they love us? I thought. *We're their parents, after all.*

I might have been able to help her. But probably not. And, at least in that respect, she was right. I just didn't love her enough to die with her.

* * *

I've told you that Mary's dead, but I can't actually say for sure. After all, the police never found her body. Just her skin.

And I've remembered since then that, in Yle'en, the most loving tortures of all are reserved for those guilty of treason.

I really hope she's dead.

I watch the news whenever I can these days. They say that large clumps of ice have formed overnight in the Kansas cornfields. They say that Antarctic explorers were recently surprised to find lilies growing along the southernmost ice-ridges. They say that snow fell in Bombay this year. Only for a day, but even so.

But, as Babs used to tell the office gossips, they say a lot of things.

* * *

Sometimes I dream that I hear great machines grinding away slowly, deep under the ground. Sometimes I dream that my mouth is full of pins. Sometimes I dream of sheep. But mostly I dream of Yle'en, the Drowned Land, whose borders are growing wild as crabgrass and eating whatever they touch. Almost every night now, in fact. And that frightens me more than I can ever say.

PRETEND THAT WE'RE DEAD

The first time I cut myself, on the lid of a tin I'd been opening, it was inadvertent. I stumbled as I lifted it free, and the sharp, round edge slid deep into the fleshy underside of my arm, freeing a flap that swung wide with every movement. Blood broke from the wound in a full, black pulse; I had to hug it closed, the knuckles of my other hand white with effort.

But when my mother saw it, her eyes went wide as stars. She cooed encouragement to me all the way to the hospital.

It was the first time she had spoken directly to me in over two months.

Afterward, when her interest dimmed again—directly proportionate to my rate of healing—I realized that I had been once more consigned to the roster of the invisible: All those inconvenient living shadows who walk, and speak, and have the unmitigated gall to get between her and the endless current of the passing dead, whose faces she spends her days scanning for any sign of recognition. For the familiar features of my brother Ethan, born ten years before me, who joined the Parade when I was only five.

Because we are none of us so real to her as he has always been, haloed like we are in mundane and unwelcome skins of light. We're chores, tying up her time, diverting her attention from the *real* task at hand.

Weekends, I walk the streets with my Ghoster friends, all white-face and caked mascara—cheekbones and noses colored out skull-style, conspicuous by their absence. We go coccooned in velvet and chiffon, in white and black and grey, shod in claw-toed boots with heels too high for comfort, our veils and trains left trailing. Strutting silent, our walkmen left ostentatiously blasting—a steady stream of noise-whisper from one-name bands, recognizable only in closest proximity: Curve, Coil, Hole, Tool, Lard.

And in and about and around us, always, the real ghosts glide—vivid phantoms that eddy like smoke, glitter like scales. A mist and a haze of constant motion, flashing by like spokes in some profane prayer-wheel: Brights slices of darkness, strobe-quick, trimmed in self-doused light.

A girl with jewels for teeth, eels for hands. An old man inching himself up the street, slithering belly-down, pulled along on an anchorless rope of shining hair. Shark-toothed grins. Silent, watch-face eyes.

The facts, then: It all started the year I was born; we post-Ghosties call it the Infestation. And what it means is Toronto remade, slipped through some cosmic crack and out again onto an "other side" that soon turned out to be *the* Other Side. Phenomena aplenty, both actively malign and strangely beneficial, measurably physical and apparently spiritual: Cold spots, words written on walls, knockings, mutterings, whisperings, ghost lights, radiant boys, warning shrieks; apports, transports, automatic writing, ectoplasm, mediumistic possession. Anything and everything "weird", with only a sort of consistent inconsistency as the sole established rule.

Faith doesn't seem to help, or hinder, for all the varieties of faith we have to spare—the multiculti mosaic at work, church to mosque to temple to bank to whatthefuckever. And sure, people naturally want to think there are rules to discover and follow—that if Torontonians only found out what it was that they "did" to "deserve" this happening to them, the'd be somehow able to defuse the situation; repent, atone, stop digging up the old Indian burial ground—no rules, or reasons, seem to apply.

Or, to put it another way: Clean, neat and boring as we've always been, we still might've done enough dirt to attract this, if it's even the kind of thing *needs* "attracting". But there's not one damn thing from before or since to proves that anything *we* did is the reason it began . . . or the reason it continues.

So: Spirits, phantoms, specters, dopplegangers and harbingers erring always on the side of the surreal rather than the traditional; dog-headed men in tuxedos rather than werewolves, palely loitering *belles dames sans merci* rather than vampires. Monsters and witches and freaks floating 'round on every corner, dead men—and women—dancing down every street.

But Cherry Street in particular, of course . . . home, weekly, to the Parade. Which Ethan watched, and followed, and—finally—

—joined.

Because much as Mom would never want to admit it, Ethan spent most of—my—life aping Toronto's ghosts too, almost the exact same way my friends and I do now . . . aside from going farther with the imitation, of course, and for substantially different reasons. If the papers I found hidden behind a grate in his bedroom wall are any indication, Ethan was seeking some kind of shortcut away from mortality—a crack of his own to slip through, sideways. To fall and lodge forever between those sharp, sharp teeth that hide unseen beneath the "normal" world's tight-shut lips.

And oh, it must've taken such amazing concentration, such amazing *effort*, to seek out his own demise at the Infestation's—hand? To engineer, single-handedly, his own transition from flesh to phantom.

But let's face it: Effort like that never goes unrewarded for long . . . as Ethan, along with all his fellow Parade Day attendees, soon found out.

They went out in the morning, to the top of Cherry Street, and they waited for the Parade to begin. And then, when it did . . . they followed it, all the way down to that bleak brick wall at the bottom that the Parade walks *through* each and every Saturday afternoon. Followed it out of this world—

—and into another.

Twelve years on, meanwhile, my mother still drifts alone in the wake of Ethan's disappearance. The fallout from his last gesture draws her like a tide, even now—especially what with him being no longer around to repeat it.

So I Ghost up, and go out, and stalk around the shadowy streets of my half-dead home-town, imperiously brushing elbows with the same *things* that took Ethan in: Ate him whole, washed him away, leaving nothing behind but the dry, picked bones of my mother's love . . . nothing left for me to hold onto, aside from a dull pretense to the same spectral status.

Sun editorials aside, though, I don't Ghost up because I want to die. I do it because I want my mother to see me—or *want* to see me, at the very, very least, at least as much . . .

. . . as I already know she wants to see *him*.

* * *

Which is why the second time I cut myself, it was intentional—and the third, and the fourth, each time a little deeper: A nail from my pinkie, shed to win a wan maternal smile; the top joint of my index finger, to extort one more sympathetic word. Each a sacrifice spent on the altar of Mom's absent attention. Each gaining me just a hint of response, before she slips right back into the fog.

Lost and groping, over and over. And over.

But hey, I can wait. I still have both my eyes left to give, after all. My breath. My name.

"Ethan—"

"I'm Monica, Mom."

"Yes, Ethan. I know."

Well, she does *talk* to me, now; that's got to count for something.

Or so I struggle, mountingly, to reassure myself.

* * *

Because: In a city full of *real* dead children, it's me, my friends, the whole pathetic Ghoster subculture who've ceased to register—born on, around or after Parade Day, shoved aside under the shadow of a generation lost. Doomed, always, to make room for our parents' grief, to step aside for one more gulp of a far more precious sibling's enduring but elusive scent. To catch the waft of their hair—a passing, spectral caress—as they slip by.

We're memory's exiles, mere brief flesh. How can we possibly hope to compete?

Days like these, between dressing up and posing all weekend and working like a neutered dog all week (nose to the keyboard, bent almost double to peer blankly at the readout of my cubicle computer's screen), I swear I start to feel as though I already *am* what I only try so hard to seem: An unlaid ghost, eternally left behind—

—and not even *my* ghost, either.

It's on days like these that I feel the urge to cut myself rise up, and bite it back down so hard blood salts my mouth. Remember how good it once felt to be loved—*me*, for me alone—and then wonder, in turn, if what I think I remember is anything more than plain old wishful thinking.

At which point I cast my mind back even further, to my precocious high school days, reminding myself how—in Old English—the word "ghost" is the same as the word for "anger".

I plan out my own final gesture, on days like these—something far too grand to ignore, far too big to overlook. Dream absently of how I'm going to make my mother watch as I act it through, and practice the speech I'll make for the occasion—the one that goes, and I quote:

"Look, Mom, look. So—how you like me now? Better . . . "

. . . or . . . worse?

Because—when I pretend that I'm dead, like the rest of my Ghoster friends, *that's* when she likes me best; when I cut myself, scar myself, slash over my half-healed scars and let them form again, keloiding the wounds 'til they puff like pastry. When I pepper my skin with fresh flesh flowers on her uninterested behalf, blood-blister-bruised and purple with relevance—always just one more, freely given, payment in pain for pain. One more for each of my mother's ceaseless, careless tears . . . the current of her mourning, washing me away piece by piece by piece: Tide to my rock, wave to my sand . . .

Yeah, she likes me "dead", because it makes me more like Ethan. And the more I'm like Ethan, well—the more I'm like him, the more I *count*. Just a little.

And one day, maybe—one of these Infested Toronto days, when there's nothing left of me to cut away—I'll find the strength, at long, long last . . .

—to finally stop pretending.

NO DARKNESS BUT OURS

*We will pull down the mountains
And devour the stars
And there will be no darkness but ours.*

Rhodajean Sokoluk walks with steady steps up the dark highway, toward a blurred mass of thoughts the signs on her path name Toronto. It's 3:35 on a Thursday morning, late November—though since Arjay's watch broke eighty miles back, she wouldn't know. Mickey Mouse's tiny hands hang loose beneath cracked glass, describing spastic arcs with the jolt of each new stride.

The night presses down on her with palpable weight, unbroken by headlights, unscarred by neon. A fine mist rises to cover her tracks.

Somewhere above, a 747 screams.

Look at her now. Thirteen years old, five feet seven inches. She wears a baggy grey sweatshirt over a brown-and-yellow plaid kilt whose hem barely brushes her knees. Across her flat chest, in pale mauve letters, the legend SACRED HEART OF JESUS BLEEDS FOR YOU may be dimly made out. Her arms swing limp at her sides; slender fingers, meant for a piano's keys or a guitar's strings, now tipped by splintered nails and caked with mud. She walks quickly, her eyes never leaving the unseen horizon. It's cold, but Arjay doesn't mind.

Her bare feet leave small, bloody prints in the gravel by the side of the road.

Arjay's thin mouth shapes a faint, triangular smile. No need to hurry.

What she is coming for has waited this long—a few more hours changes nothing.

And the air around her takes on a quality suggestive of storm clouds massing to the north, black and heavy with snow.

Passing her, uncalled images spring to mind—reflections of a cold life in a distant land. Birds hanging frozen from telephone wires; milkweed caught by frost in mid-launch. Shallow bedrock graves.

* * *

Take me down baby
Take me where I wanna go
Take me down down down
Baby take me where I wanna go . . .

"Forget it, booger. 'S mine, anyway."
"Daddy said it was my turn! You don't play fair!"
"Says who? Besides, you'll just break it."

Take me down baby now
Baby take me down

"Will not!"
"Will so, booger."
"Won't! And don't you call me booger!"
"Why not? Broke it quick enough last time—snot-nose."
"Don't you call me snot-nose, you—*rat-turd*!"

All the way down down down
Baby take me where I wanna goooo . . . .

"Snot-*nose*, *snot*-nose. Booger, booger, *booger*!"
Harold Monkson Junior, call him Hank, braces himself for a screech from the back seat. He isn't disappointed.
"Dah-*dee*! Jeannie called me—"
A booger, and she wasn't too far off, you little shit.
"Ronald, If I hear one more peep out of either of you about that Goddam Transformer, it's straight back to Buffalo and I'm not kidding."

Vicious whispers greet this announcement. Under the parental guidebook, they qualify as silence. Hank inhales and coughs, spitting Marlboro smoke. The car reeks of three parts enforced proximity and one part greasy Chinese food. His vision started blurring at the border, and that throbbing just behind his left eye is surely an incipient migraine. And he can't find one station on this entire radio that isn't playing fucking disco.

Take me down baby now
Take me where I wanna go
All the way down down down
Take me where I wanna goooo . . . .

Christ, yes, Hank pleads, inwardly. *Take her. Don't wait on my account.*

Hank's a real estate agent. He lives in Toronto, his ex-wife—as of gaining custody—in Buffalo. So far, this simple strategy has kept his visits down to a minimum. But last Sunday, fortified by five beers and the promise of three weeks vacation time, Hank drove down and demanded his fatherly privileges. A decision he has since come to regret.

Heavily.

In fact, further discussion on the Transformer notwithstanding, he's beginning to seriously consider just turning the car around and—

— driving straight up the white line until he hits a truck.

What?

The disco singer croons on, her backup vocalists lapsing into a seemingly endless series of deep, orgasmic grunts. Behind him, Jeannie and Ronald have struck up a blessed truce, Transformer discarded in favor of comics and green Day-Glo Slime. Before him, the road falls away without a moment's pause, smooth as a lidded eye. Around him, silence.

But Hank feels a sudden prickling of sweat. He grips the wheel, cold. His palms are wet.

And he couldn't tell you why if he tried.

* * *

A quarter-moon sweats over Barrie.

Seven miles gone, police have just entered the last gas station Hank drove by while Jeannie and Ronald set up a steady whine, imploring him for ice cream, phone calls and trips to the little boys' room. Officer Sam Woo throws the adjacent diner's kitchen door wide, gun up. The owner lies slumped in one corner, holding a shotgun and wearing a big grin. Nearby, his wife Marie sprawls face down in a tepid pool of rotisserie grease, a stencil of Goofy staring from her discarded apron.

In the TV lounge of Toronto's Gorman Manor, a halfway home for newly-released mental patients, a lanky man with grey hair works on a picture of Princess Leia in his Star Wars coloring book. Being very careful to stay within the lines, he gives her red eyes and navy-blue skin. His name is Myron Sokoluk, and he is Arjay's father.

Forty miles away and closing, Arjay runs her tongue across her teeth.

There are no stars left visible to watch.

* * *

Jeannie Monkson shifts irritably. She has a whopping crick in her neck.

Glancing over her shoulder, she sees her brother Booger—a.k.a. Ronald Jerome Monkson—gearing up for yet another whine about how he's so cold, or he really needs to pee, or can't we stop for a burger? Like nobody else in the whole wide world was every chilly, or hungry, or waiting for a try at the next available john.

How'd you like a "mixed-fruit cocktail" instead, Boog? Jeannie thinks, taking mental sight on the back of his head. Kpow, kpow, kpow-pow-pow.

Nothing happens. She turns away, sighing disgustedly.

Fact is, there's shit all to do on these trips with Dad except pick on Booger—no pun intended—and dream about Christopher Walken.

An utter hunk. Turns MY crank.

And *The Dogs of War*—what a bitchin' flick! Good plot, great locations, and beaucoup de good-lookin' babes dripping with sweat, up to their necks in mud. What else could you possibly ask for?

Real life pales by comparison.

Especially when the most immediate slice of that life involves being trapped in a rented Honda that stinks of stale cigarettes and egg rolls, out in the middle of fuckin' nowhere with a man she hasn't seen (or missed seeing) for the last five years, and a little brother she sees constantly every single day of her miserable existence.

Jeannie scratches idly at her cheek, testing the latest spot where she knows a pimple will sprout before morning.

Suddenly, she can draw the next three weeks like a map. A stream of lackluster events and petty annoyances, oozing inevitably toward the last big blow-up. Then a ticket home and a stiff good-bye at the station. With no parting gifts. With Booger weeping and drooling all over the seat near the window. With even the faintest possibility of a bus accident just stranding them in some roadside dive until Mom's newest flame can drive them back home, where they'll be grounded for three more weeks for causing her the trouble.

Booger stares intently at his left shoe, freckles swollen big as mumps in the dashboard's light. In the rear-view mirror, Hank's eyes seem the same red-shot shade of grey as moldy bologna.

Who are these people? Jeannie thinks. *I don't know. And I don't care.*

And she sees a hail of bullets peel their faces back to free the blood inside, their brains painting the wilderness.

Her hand tightens on an imaginary trigger.

Yes. ANYtime.

For a split second, she's all alone in somebody else's skull. Crushed silent by the view. Walking into the night, every pore gorged on its darkness.

Just breathing in and out, in and out, in and out.

* * *

Under the cornfields which bracket the highway, animals stir restlessly in their long sleep, hearing the beat of a measured tread which chills their cold blood even further. A raccoon curls tight, cracking open the end of a rabbit bone as his teeth grind together; sharp white splinters pierce his gums. Mice put their tiny paws over their ears, and burrow deeper. A knot of garter snakes strangles itself.

An ant-hill's entire winter supply of eggs withers, as the sole of Arjay's left foot blocks out the sky.

Suddenly, she pauses in mid-stride. She sniffs the air.

A car is coming.

* * *

Never, in his dreams, is he Booger. They call him by much sweeter names in the world behind his eyes, which he visits as often as the bark and babble of more mundane reality will let him. That candy-colored world where no one ever yells, whose inhabitants comprise the entire toy section of his mother's consumer catalogues. Like Chuck E. Cheese, but better. Where it's his birthday every day.

Where he is absolute ruler.

Where Jeannie and Hank lie, screaming, stretched taut on the rack of his fertile imagination.

In Booger's world, he is King Ronald, the First and Only. And they call him Master.

* * *

Ah.

Booger's thoughts graze Arjay, clumsily. They seethe, full of a bile she drinks like wine. Only a sip, though; he's young.

She turns her attention to the others.

Hank. And—Jeannie.

Scratch them. They bleed as deeply, if all unknowing. Very close. And getting closer.

Yesss.

And the hunger grips her, keen as love. Somewhere, someone whispers:

Feed and be strong, my love. Strong enough to kill them. Or anyone else.

Strong enough—

—to eat the world.

(Time enough for that, though. Later.)

With one foot on either side of the white line, Arjay turns, and pauses. Folding her arms, she readies herself. She holds up a fallow mirror to those shallow minds rushing toward her, paining her with their petty hopes and dreams. She holds it high, and a reflection grows, a more accurate one than any of them can stand to look at for long.

When they come, they will find her waiting.

* * *

"Are we there yet?"

For a moment, Hank stares. Jeannie meets his eyes, her own full of a contempt level enough to goad him beyond surprise. He snaps:

"What do you think?"

Jeannie leans forward. A smile tugs at her lips; almost, but not quite, a smirk.

"I think you're lost—Dad."

Click.

Stepped in it there, didn't you? someone says conversationally. *Traps work both ways, Hank-o. That's why they come with instructions.*

"Shut *up*," he hisses.

Jeannie recoils.

Booger's wide awake now, watching the two of them in rapt fascination. The green Slime drips, forgotten, down the side of his leg.

Almost as good as TV, Hank thinks. Then: *It's starting.*

What's starting?

Christ, I'm getting hysterical.

Jeannie's smile has hardened, near enough to grim to call it cousin.

"Stop the car."

"Don't be stupid," Hank says, automatically.

Quietly: "So now I'm stupid?"

Click.

All right. All. Right.

"Yeah," Hank begins. The words are a cut vein, too fast to catch and too wounded to plug. "Yeah, that's right. You're a stupid little girl who wears too much makeup, and listens to too much crap on that stupid walkman, and thinks the world owes her something, which it doesn't. Any more than I do." Pause. "And what do you think of *that*?"

Jeannie's eyes hold Hank's. Beneath them, something familiar stirs. Something akin to the same sticky stew of rage currently aboil behind his own.

"I think you can go fuck yourself," she says.

Booger shrieks, clapping his hands next to Hank's ear with all the subtlety of a mortar shell explosion. "Jeannie said the F-word!" he sings happily.

"Fuck you too, Booger," Jeannie shoots back.

Booger drums his heels on the back of Hank's seat, transported. "Jeannie said the F-word *again*!" he howls.

The road swims before Hank's eyes. "*Shut UP*, Booger," he hears himself say.

"*Dah-dee!*"

Jeannie knocks Booger aside and leans forward. "Gimme the keys."

Hank glances back at the road, and finds it whipping by so fast it's starting to blur.

We weren't going this—

The odometer, spitting miles.

And Hank realizes that the ache he feels in his leg comes from the fact that he's been pressing steadily down on the accelerator ever since this conversation began.

"Jeannie—" he starts. She squeezes—five sharp, pink-and-blue varnished points, stretching his jacket thin enough to rip.

"*Gimme.*"

"The *fuck* I will!"

Booger is in seventh heaven. "*You* said the F-word, Daddy!" he screams, slinging his full prepubescent weight against Hank's other shoulder.

Hank cries out in pain.

It is at exactly this moment that they see Arjay.

* * *

At first, a smear of black at the horizon—darkness on darkness. Then a stick-figure, draped in grey. The grey deepens, cross-hatches. She is an old woman now, whose hair hangs like frosted lead. Her shoulders scrape the sky.

They are twenty feet away. Nineteen.

With every foot, she is more inevitable. Her face smooths from faint stippling to moon-pale, and equally disinterested, features. She raises her head to greet them, brushing her bangs aside.

She smiles.

And their headlights catch her glasses.

God—

(No.)

Abruptly, the world is two white circles. White on white. The dark is gone, and Nothing takes its place.

Hank, Jeannie and Booger freeze, caught in their glare.

They see themselves reflected in her eyes.

* * *

Far away, Myron Sokoluk's crayon snaps in two.

* * *

Hank swerves, too late. His kick snaps the brakes. They tumble past Arjay in a clumsy arc, and come down hard. Three tires blow simultaneously, hubcaps drawing sparks across the gravel. They strike a handy fence-post and up-end, wavering a moment, before flipping over backward.

The gas tank goes a second later.

It's all a bit too quick for any last thoughts.

* * *

Back at the gas station, an officer exiting the rest room exclaims as an orange flower blooms against the sky.

* * *

Arjay walks on.

She passes the shell of Hank's car, cracked wide and bleeding blazing lines of oil across the asphalt—steps over one and onto part of another, leaving a sizzling black smear. She doesn't feel the flames; the damage she has done here is nothing to her. She isn't sad, or particularly elated. Just full.

For a while, at least.

She turns her back, and leaves it all behind.

North, always north. This is her country. Its frozen soil holds her up, as winter creeps a little closer with every step she takes. It knows her hunger. It knows her need.

Toronto. And Myron.

And—then?

Arjay was born at five in the morning. The Hour of the Ox. When the dead bell rings. Her father lived in a house full of carefully preserved lovers who never answered back, never grew old—just a bit dustier, and less elastic. From this house her mother ran, naked to the Winnipeg night, into the street to flag down the first truck she met. Arjay came a half-year later, suited in blood—her mouth full of half-eaten placenta.

Her mother took one look at her, and let go.

Now she moves, a canker on the world's dreams, past the houses of the unwary. A circle of darkness follows, constant and pure, impinging briefly on all she touches. Leaving scars. A rising flood, leaking through the ill-kept seams of neat yards and tidy gardens. A draining slough of numbness. Sleep.

And visions which vanish, on waking. Yet remain.

Arjay knows her path well. An inner compass keeps her steady, marking off the miles.

She has an appointment to keep.

JOB 37

Speak to me for Gods sake.
There are worse things than death,
though you and I are not likely
to experience any of them.
—Pat Lowther.

—... two, three. Okay: Looks like we're go.

This is session seventeen, research project 4.7, Freihoeven ParaPsych Department; we're interviewing subjects whose professions are associated, prospectively, with the accumulation of psychic fragments, and this particular tape will be filed under the heading of Job 37.

Anyway, uh—how's that mike sitting? You comfortable with that?

—Yeah, it's okay, thanks. (*Pause*) So ... what do you want to know?

—First off? Well, first off ... why this? Pretty—odd—career to specialize in, by most people's standards.

—I guess. (*Pause*) You mean *gross*, though. Right?

—Okay, I'll be a little more specific: You own your own business—a cleaning business. And you clean up ...

—Blood, mostly. Blood, brain-matter, decomposed flesh; sick, shit, kinda bugs feed on sick, shit, dead people. All that.

—How'd you decide to get into it?

—Um. (*Pause*) I've always cleaned, always been a cleaner. I never really went through any other jobs, when I was a kid—always did like janitorial work, maid service, hotel cleaning staff jobs, whatever. Because that was what I grew up around, right? My Mom, her Mom. They used to take me around when they were cleaning up office buildings, 'cause they couldn't pay for anybody to watch me at nights. One time when I was almost one year old I even drank some solvent 'cause I was crawling around in the supply closet while they bagged shredder waste two floors up, and my Grandma wanted to call 911, but my Mom was like: Hell *no*, they'll take her away from me for sure.

—Jesus. What'd she do?

—Just made me drink milk 'till I puked, made me puke again, made me keep drinking milk. She thought that'd get rid of the burning inside my mouth, and I guess she was right; I remember I was all swollen up for a week after, though. I mean, I could breathe, but I couldn't eat for shit. (*Pause*) And I *still* hate fucking milk.

—So you're working as a cleaner . . .

—Yeah. And I started my own service, right, 'cause I thought why not? I'm bonded, got a good record, so getting the licenses was easy enough. So, my third or fourth appointment, when I'm just settling into it—this guy was a lawyer, and he used to drink 24/7. Never a hair out of place, but you could *smell* it on him the minute you walked in, like he slept in a bathtub full'a vodka. Now, his regular day was Thursday, but when I come in, first thing I find out is he'd shot himself sometime the previous Friday.

So I call the cops, call the family; the M.E. comes and fixes time of death, means and method. It's not a *crime* scene, 'cause no crime's been committed; guy just checked out with this big-ass hunting rifle he kept in the closet, and the force of the thing was so heavy his whole skull sort of exploded, shot like ninety percent of his brain out the top of his head onto the carpet he was lying on and the wall behind. And he stinks. And the family are freaking out, A) 'cause they loved the guy and oh my God how could he *do* a thing like this, we never knew and blah blah blah, but B) 'cause they own the building, and they think they're *never* gonna rent the place out after this.

So I said: "I could do it." And they let me. And I did.

—How?

—Dumb fuckin' luck, mainly, 'cause I did *not* know what I was getting into. First off, you got brain dried hard on everything, and when brain dries it's just like epoxy or shit. Didn't have time to find someplace to buy the kind of disposable haz-mat suits we wear now, with a breather and everything, so I did the whole thing in about three layers of clothes—some sweats, a pair of overalls, a big jogging suit over that, plus rubber boots and dishwashing gloves and a big scarf wrapped around my head. Thought I was gonna melt away in the heat, and I had to burn it all afterwards, anyway.

So I went at the brain with a snow scraper I had out in the truck, and I got most of it that way; used a bristle-brush on the rest, and about ten bottles of industrial bleach. I had to sand the floor and varnish it over, but the fact he did it on the rug made it a little better than if he'd done it, say, in bed, or what have you. Bed's a motherfucker to clean if you even can, which most times you just can't.

When I was done, though, it was the craziest thing, 'cause it basically looked exactly like it'd always been supposed to look that way. Like he was never there at all.

—Was that why you kept doing it?

—A hundred to five hundred an hour is why I keep *doing* it. You get me?

—Absolutely. (*Pause*) Pretty high equipment costs, I guess, though.

—Eh. Not when you buy in bulk, so much: Suits, chemicals, what have you. Or the brain machine.

—The "brain machine"?

—Oh yeah, it's cool: This big truck-mounted steam-injector thingie. Whenever we have a job that looks like it's gonna take all day, we bring the brain machine in and it just melts all the crap up and sucks it into a tank, like gettin' dirt out of a rug. And that's a *real* fuckin' life-saver.

No, the all-star pain in the ass is paying for time on the medical waste incinerator, because the guys running that thing make you pay a big extra fee unless you've got at least a hundred pounds of shit to burn, minimum. So these days, we have to keep the waste on ice out at the warehouse 'till we've got enough for a trip—and that can get seriously disgusting. (*Pause*) You're not using my name, right?

—No, just like we discussed. Total anonymity.

—Then I'll tell you this much: First year or so, I used to take it down the dump, torch it myself. To keep us in the black 'till we built up a regular client-base. I remember one time, this *serious* de-comp job—chick was so slimy, she was practically jelly. So I spent about two hours out there throwing plastic bags full of maggots on the fire, and those things, when they go up? They sound just like . . . popcorn.

—Uh-huh. (*Pause*) You started out using bleach—what kind of chemicals do you use now? Special stuff?

—Ancient Chinese Secret, buddy ruff. No, look, seriously—we're selling that information over the website now, in Start Your Own Business FAQ-packs that go fifty bucks a pop. So what do you think: Am I gonna give it away to you for free? Please. We're doin' fine; I don't need the PR *that* much.

—Granted.

—It's a going concern, crime-scene cleanup. You know? And there's two reasons for that—well, three. Number one: Firepower. Number two: Drugs, 'cause drugs'll make you think and do some crazy fuckin' things. And number three . . . people are just a lot more *alone* than they used to be. No family, no friends. Nobody to give a shit. Even in the same building, the people you see every day—you think they're gonna give a shit if you go missing? Most they'll be doing is sitting around going: Jeez, haven't seen Mrs So-and-so for a while. 'Till the bugs start comin' down through their ceiling. (*Pause*) And then they'll call me.

So. That it?

—Um, no ... (*Pause*) What—what would be the weirdest job you ever did, in your opinion?

—You mean messiest?

—I mean weirdest.

—It's *all* weird. (*Pause*) But you're talkin', like ... "psychic fragments"-type weird. Right?

(*Pause*)

— ... well, yes.

(*Pause*)

— ... okay.
So. This guy killed himself while squatting; hung himself from the doorknob. And the house he did it in, it wasn't exactly abandoned, but it hadn't been checked for a pretty long time. Anyway, real estate agent found him. And he didn't want to tell the property-holder, 'cause then the holder calls the cops ...

—Like with the apartment, with that first guy.

—Yeah, just like that. 'Cause it's always the same story with these pricks.
So the agent calls us. 'S obvious what happened, and there is *not* a lot of the guy left, anyway. It was summer, it was hot; he was probably in there, like ... basically, he melted. Okay? Cranial fluid came out through his face, spinal fluid through his back. Fluid, generally. All this—crud.

—Brain machine time.

—Serious. Except we didn't *have* the machine yet. (*Pause*) But that was why we were gonna do it, right? 'Cause we know if buddy pays us to dispose of a body for him, we're gonna be the people he calls in to do his dirty work for the rest of his life. And I won't lie, man—we *wanted* to be those people, why the fuck not?

—And now . . . you are.

—Yeah.

So . . . back then, the whole company was just me and the S.O., basically—my "significant other". So this was pretty big of a coup for us. And 'cause we're bankin' on this little windfall, him and me decide we're gonna do what we were never able, up 'till now: We hire a third person. This girl, let's call her—Rosa.

I was the one knew Rosa, from my maid days. Sat her down, told her about the company, what the job was gonna be about. But we didn't have the puke book back then, either, and—

—Sorry. "Puke book"?

—Yeah. It's this book at the office we got now, full of photos from real bad blood scenes, and we run it past everybody who comes in, 'cause if they heave right there then this probably ain't the career they wanna get into.

So I don't know. I don't think she really *got* what she was sayin' "yes" to, even after we got her all fitted up in the suit, the breather, showed her how to do everything . . . not even then. Not 'till she went in there, and saw it.

But anyway. We get to the house, and just the night before, we'd suddenly figured out how if we bring Rosa along then we're gonna have to fake like it's all been approved already. So the S.O. sets up a video camera, like we're taping it for the cops, which they like us to do—they want to know what went where, after all the shit's been squared away. In point of fact, it's just in case buddy wants to screw us over, but how's she supposed to know?

I'm humping in the disinfectants, and he's pissin' around with the camera, and Rosa's out there parking the truck, so she comes in last. And because this guy did it from the doorknob on the front door . . . well, I guess it just didn't occur to me. How when you walked in, you were basically walking right over all the—stuff—that used to be *him*.

And that smell. More like a taste than a smell, really. 'Cause you get it worst in your mouth, all the way at the back, even with the breather. Like it's comin' up from inside *you*.

You do get used to that too, believe it or not. Eventually.

But Rosa—

She steps in, hears that sticky sound, looks down. Sees what she's steppin' in. And when I see her face I think for sure she's gonna run right back out the door, but instead, she runs *in*—into the house, away from the camera. Through the doors into what used to be the kitchen.

Well, we gave her about an hour, 'cause it took that long to get the absolute worst of this guy up. And then I go in, like: Okay Rosa, c'mon, man.

But.

No Rosa, for one thing. All right. So she's gone upstairs, obviously, or out the back. Or something.

Try to open the door to the backyard, but that sucker's locked—more like nailed shut, maybe ten, maybe twenty years ago. So I yell to the S.O., and he goes to check upstairs, and I go down in the basement. And there's . . .

(*Pause*)

. . . at the bottom of the stairs, there's this—I walk into this patch, this sort of—spot. And it's really cold. Really, really . . .

I thought I could sort of hear her, too, just for a second there. Like she was far away. Like she was—yelling.

(*Long Pause*)

Well, we get the rest of the guy all cleaned up—fast as we fuckin' can—and then we take the camera, and we get the fuck out of there. And we don't tell the agent, and we don't know who the hell else to call about it—her relatives? I don't even know who they are. Cops? Please.

A couple days later, we do an anonymous 911 call to say she was missing. But nothing ever came of that, I know of.

And a week after that, we finally put in the tape and looked at it.

(*Pause*)

Well?

— . . . well, what?

—You wanna know what was on it. Right?

(*No Answer*)

Okay.

First, it's just static. Not even the house, or the guy, or any of us. And then it kind of gives a jump, or a blip, or the light changes or something, and—

—Rosa, right there. But she isn't *there*. I mean . . . she's somewhere, right? But not the house. Not the way we saw it, anyway.

It's like a—construction site, or whatever. Support beams, sky; it's all kind of wet, like it's been raining. Like the place is only half-built, except for the fact that's just fuckin' crazy.

And Rosa wanders around in there, in her haz-mat suit. Takes her breather off, puts it down someplace. And she looks all seriously freaked, which is . . . understandable.

And then she goes off-screen, and she comes back on, and there's that static again. And then—

—she's in a vacant lot, in the middle of nowhere. No house at all. And it's winter. And she's still wearing the suit, but it's all ripped and dirty. And she's—thinner.

More static.

And then it's summer. And . . . she's in a swamp. And most of the suit's gone, 'cause those things—they ain't exactly built to last, 'specially when you get 'em wet.

And . . . she's getting older.

Static, and static, and everything's moving faster. Shit's goin' by like—I don't even know. And Rosa's all dirty and almost naked and her hair is all long, like down to her shoulders. And she looks kinda crazy, now. And she's so *thin*.

Treeline in the background comin' closer and closer, 'till it's really dark 'cause the trees block off the sun. And she's screaming and crying and goin' back and forth, side to side, in those shadows right by the front of the trees. And then—

—*something*—

—reaches out from the trees, and it pulls her in. By her *head*.

And she's gone.

(*Long Pause*)

Tape went on a while after that, like it kept goin' 'till we finished up in the house, shut it down and took it home. But there's no more static, and there's no more Rosa.

Thing is, though . . .

Later, we figured out—when I was down in the basement? Standin' in that—whatever the hell? When I was doin' that, it must've been like was standin' exactly where she would have been, at the same time. Right in the same damn spot.

Like I was inside her, or something.

(*Pause*)

There's a "psychic fragment" for ya.

(*Very Long Pause*)

— . . . what was it like?

—Bein' inside her?

—No, Christ. The, uh—that, uh, the . . . thing. You saw grab her.

—Fuck, *that*. Uh—

(*Pause*)

It was like . . .

(*Pause*)

Kinda like, um—one of those big bugs you see on the *Discovery Channel*, on those freaky "freaks of nature" shows. You know? But . . . with skin.

—Skin?

—Shit, I don't know. Like, like a . . . iguana, or something.

—Big enough to pick a grown woman up by her *head* "iguana". Are you—
—are we talking dinosaur, here?

—Look, fuck you, buddy. (*Pause*) I'd know it if I saw it, tell you that much.

—And you still have this tape.

—Sure.

—You didn't accidentally erase it, maybe, or—

—Sure. I mean, what'm I gonna do—tape *Wheel Of Fortune* over it?

—And—who'd you show it to, exactly?

—Nobody. I saw it, the S.O. saw it, but aside from him who'm I gonna show it to? Her parents, assuming I ever found out who they were? Tell 'em hey, your daughter slipped sideways in time, got herself eaten by Jurassic fuckin' . . .

(*Pause*)

Shit, right.

—But you still *have* it.

—Like I said two times already, *sure*. Why?

(*Very Long Pause*)

— . . . how much would you want for it?

BEAR-SHIRT

Wednesdays—Odin's day—I give my last talk at five. Afterward, as I walk out, I find the blond kid already waiting: A somber Aryan clone, barely out of his teens, puppy-fat still sleek and pink over his football-ready mass of cultivated muscle. I can tell he's one of Karl Speller's just by looking at him, though his face isn't exactly familiar. Far too young to be one the disciples I knew, way back when; a late convert, maybe? Fresh lower-middle-class meat, scooped straight out of school, fallen through the deepening crack between liberal cant and so-called "Equal Opportunity" in action? Somebody's—

(*Karl's?*)

—second-generation Separatist son, even?

(Ick.)

Another damn zealot out of the same half-cracked mold, anyway—pure white, not too bright, up all night every night stockpiling weapons and updating websites in the service of the holy Cause. Same philosophy I was supposed to share just because an accident of genetics left me looking like the RaHoWa's unofficial gay pin-up; same not-so-underground "culture" I now spend my days lecturing against, at colleges and universities from Vancouver to Florida.

The University of Toronto's more than a bit off my beaten track, going by these established standards—a bit too close to my former home for comfort, all told. But it had been a long time, and I was invited, and so I came: Back to Toronto. Back to where Karl and I first rubbed up against each other.

And now . . .

... now, I don't get much time to consider whether or not this may have been a mistake before the kid brings his fist up towards me, held at an awkward angle—and I feel my lips peel back, automatic front-or-flight reflex kicking in hard; get a sudden, giddy rush/flash of (*gun*), (no *time*), (screw it, screw *him*, just stand there and take it like a *man*, you dumb fucking faggot ...)

Because: You always knew this day would come, now, didn't you? In your heart of hearts. Or somewhere considerably—

(lower down)

As it turns out, however, all the kid has to offer is his palm, salmon-belly soft and city-bred callus-less—his palm, plus a dull brass key, half caught in the crease of his life-line.

"Brother Speller ... " He begins. And I think:

(Oh, be fucking serious.)

Flushing bright, temper flaring—snapping back at the very sound of that long-lost title, sharper than I need to, fear sliding fast into half-embarrassed anger:

"My name is *Hengist*, little boy. Okay? And I am *not* your 'brother'."

Because, sure, Karl might have pushed me into that fucked-up ritual acknowledgment of his—hand-fasting 'round the fire, calling me his "shield-brother" in front of the whole camp and daring anybody else to say different. And sure, I might have gone along, like I went along with most of Karl's suggestions—

(—to a point, anyway.)

But: Doesn't mean we were ever married, him and me. Doesn't mean I *took his name* like some housewife from the fucking 'burbs, or anything ...

The kid's eyes stay steady, under those blond brows—eyes pale as Karl's, brows almost-white as Karl's. Karl's chosen spawn, staring calm at Karl's chosen ... what?

Mate? *Friend?*

(fuck—)

—Buddy?

"Brother Speller," the kid repeats, calm enough to lull and freeze—a cheap postpube imitation of Karl's manly Fuhrer rasp, Novocaine-sting over sandpaper-rub— " ... left us this. And he told us it was for you. *Mister* Hengist."

* * *

When I turn my forearm over and look down, exposing the smooth inner flesh, I can still see Berkana—the bear-rune—imprinted just where the skin is thinnest: The slightly raised, black outline of two sidelong triangles on a stick, a Nazi letter "B". Comes complete with a sense-memory of it going on, faint buzz and hot metal stink as Karl held my arm out to the tattoo artist's gun, fisting my reluctant hand hard. Like he was helping a fellow soldier face down some battlefield surgeon—to stay brave while his bullet-wounds were packed with gunpowder and set alight, in tiny explosions of righteously-earned pain.

And speaking of pain, I remember *that*, too. Like getting stung by a bee, only worse. Longer. More intense.

But then, that was Karl for you: Pure intensity, constantly moving back and forth between himself and everything he touched. Including—

(me)

It's a complex rune, Berkana—one of twenty-four, hallucinated from fallen willow-twigs by the great over-God Odin while he hung nine days and nights on the World-Tree Yggdrasil, a sacrifice, himself to himself. The *Futhark* alphabet, Viking wisdom reduced to sketchy little bite-sized chunks, each one a mess of contradictory implications. So scratch 'em into stones, throw 'em down on a scraped-out hide, read the results and draw your own conclusions . . . and if you don't like the way your future seems to be turning out, so what? You can always cut yourself a handy mouthful of foxglove variant—belladonna, lady's mantle, laurel leaves, whatever—chew on it awhile, and make up something better.

Berkana's direction is the east: Spadina, Mimico, cottage country. Its bird is the swan, its color blue (like Karl's icy eyes, or my own), its tree the beech. It's the rune of birth, of creativity—children, or new ideas. A marriage—

(or *re*marriage)

—in the offing.

And even now, after I've had every other trace of that crazy man I once thought I loved lasered from my body . . . a demure swastika on either hip, palm-sized, like handles; an elaborate iron cross above my heart; Karl's name like a half-collar across the back of my neck, where the first big visible knob of the vertebrae nests, so he could read it aloud while he plowed into me from behind . . . I still force myself to look at Berkana every day. The bear-rune. The sign of Karl's chosen totem. The ancient, meaningless symbol that bound us together, then tore us apart.

I do it to remind myself why I left him, in the first place—why I ran away, and hid, and haven't seen him since, even assuming he was still anywhere he *could* be seen. And I do it to remind myself just how much, how oh so very much indeed, I once wanted—

—to stay.

* * *

So—stones on hide, falling, shifting; rune-magic, poetry and probability conjured together from the empty air. Berkana *in* air, first reading out of a possible four. Exciting family news quite probable. A birth or a new venture a distinct possibility.

I recognized the kid's key, of course. Last seen—Christ, ten—years earlier, on a chain around Karl's neck, swinging hypnotically between his pecs as he labored back and forth above me. Grunting low, right in my ear; saying, over and over:

Oh, baby. Oh, Lee, baby . . . you're it. You're . . . the one.

The bulky weight of him, all over me, making me ache and strain with secret heat: Big hands, big muscles, big, rough head. Mica-fine blond stubble of cheek, chin, scalp abrading my inner thighs as he rooted and lapped at me impatiently—forcing me open, willing me wet and slack enough to take all of him in one slick thrust. Karl never had any of the hangups my other nominally-straight tricks clung to; never thought twice about enjoying every part of me he could reach, as long as it made us both moan and snarl and sweat together. From the minute we met, he treated me less like some uppity academic fag he was way too cool to kiss than a long-lost brother, rediscovered at last in the very heart of the enemy's camp—some fellow warrior who'd fallen amongst thieves and picked up bad habits, not that he didn't like the result.

"Key to your heart?" I suggested, flicking idly at it, as we lay together after our first encounter. He snorted.

"Ma's folks left her a cabin, up Gravenhurst way. I go there, sometimes."

"To get away from it all."

"Yup." A pause. "That, and find my bear."

Uh—

(—'scuse me?)

My key, then, to Karl's cabin. Where I'm heading, by car, even as we speak—even as I cast my mind back further still, remembering how we first met: At a faculty do, earlier that same evening. I was there alone, bored and horny and single, just one more Media Studies T.A. backing up the Prof of the moment in return for some help with my never-ending thesis; my duties included Pop Culture and Literary Antecedents MMS301, which mainly involved showing up and grading papers.

Karl, meanwhile, was ostensibly "there" with Nini Machen—Barbie's thinner and far less smiley twin turned program student rep, the female equivalent of those straight guys you hear about all the time who think lesbians only exist because none of these poor, deluded girls has met *them* yet. She'd already tried that tack on me, only to be rebuffed. And now that I'd been officially erased from her personal radar screen, it just made it all the easier for me to sidle over and cast Karl the narrowed, flirty eye—which he noticed, eventually. And, eventually . . .

. . . returned.

Big and blond and peach-fuzz pink-and-white all over—he looked like me times two, the cartoon super-hero version, cut and solid, utterly unrufflable. Every fetish made flesh, every neo-fascist dream come true. Son of a bitch made my knees knock, and I'm not a knees-knocking kind of guy.

When Nini turned her attention on the Prof, we drifted to the door, swapping names as we went: Karl Speller, Lee Hengist; Lee, Karl. He smiled when he heard my last name— good Swedish stock, fair-skinned and fuckable, with no fear of contagion.

(Not racially, at least.)

"You're a fag, though," he said, a minute later, shattering my initial assumptions. "Right?"

No particular revulsion in his voice, just a seemingly genuine interest—a relief, coming from somebody who looked like they could crack my skull and eat my brains for breakfast.

I nodded. "And you're . . . not?"

A shrug. "I do what—"

(*who*)

"—I want." A pause. "You clean?"

I swallowed, mouth suddenly dry. "I've been, uh . . . tested . . . "

"Negative." At my nod: "'S good. Ma always says condoms are a Jew plot to keep us from breedin', but I just hate the way the damn things feel. That, and I like bein' able to—*taste*—"

(—what I'm . . . eating.)

Hunger boiling off him in a wave, too pure to even seem intrusive. He was up against me, looming, so close all I could breathe was his hot musk. I'd never felt so small, so slight, so patently unable to defend myself. Or so—weirdly—

—desirable.

I fisted my hands and gulped, through growing dizziness. Stammered, annoyed by my own inarticulateness:

"Uh, I don't, I don't go bareback, that's just *dumb*. I mean, you do two friends, and I do two friends, and HIV takes five years plus to even show up on the chart, so—"

Karl just looked at me, knitting those no-brows, like I was the cutest, dumbest little thing he'd ever seen. Making me . . . blush.

"But—you're not gonna *be* with anybody else, Lee," he said, finally. Simple as that: No one. Never.

(Ever again.)

I reddened. "Say what?"

Dick going: *Yes!* Brain going: *Nut.* And everything in between slapped suddenly awake, tentatively *up*, from the rising hairs on the back of my neck to the crawling skin of my balls, my widening nostrils, my fluttering pulse.

An hour later, we were back at my place, with him already in me deep enough to hurt. And me, already—

—pulling him deeper.

* * *

There are a lot of bears to choose from, but the one Karl had in mind was—naturally enough—the biggest aside from long-extinct *Arctodus simus*, the prehistoric short-faced monster bear, which ranged from six feet at the shoulder on all fours to fourteen standing up. Under the skin, Karl believed he was a Grizzly: *Ursus horribilis*, "The King Of The Brutes", able to weigh two thousand pounds, run thirty miles an hour, and survive four bullets in the heart just long enough suck the marrow from your bones.

He reeled off statistics like they were love-talk, or family anecdotes: Told me how bears eat each other, adult and child. How fights between bears lead to broken jaws, shattered teeth, lost eyes. How the female bear is called a sow, the male bear a boar. How female bears won't have sex while raising their young, which can take two to four years.

"Thought you were a cat, y'know, first time I looked at you," he murmured that night, into the sweaty side of my neck. "But now I think maybe . . . maybe *you're* a bear, too."

(Uh *huh*.)

Nini aside, you see, Karl wasn't faculty—but he *did* teach: White Power cant, liberally admixed with a highly personal form of Viking Shamanism. The first he'd inhaled, almost literally, with his mother's milk; "Ma" was Verena Speller, called Vee, currently serving twenty-five to life on a particularly grotesque beat-down that turned into a full-scale race riot—payback for Karl's father, Grand Wizard of Klan North, who died of a heart attack after getting into a fist-fight with the Holocaust survivors' group protesting his initial public appearance. Karl, a toddler at the time, could no longer remember seeing her outside of a contact visits room.

"She knew what she was doin'," was his only comment, the one time I asked about it. "Ma's a soldier. She knew the risks."

We went to visit once a month, after Karl and I had become an item. But I usually stayed out in the car, because Ma had "issues" with "my kind"; she was old-school to the bone, and didn't want to be anywhere near the narrow faggot ass of any white guy who wasn't doing his level best to replace the race. Karl was safe enough, though—he'd already done *his* bit, and then some, sowing his seed with nine good Aryan wenches he'd met through ads in the backs of Heritage Front hand-outs. He got baby, toddler, preteenage pictures through the mail and took them in for Vee to coo over, destroying them ritually at each visit's end to keep the guards from confiscating them.

And every time, he left saddened in a way that made me sad just to witness it: Revolted, horrified, shaken to his unshakable core by the spectacle of his mother stuck behind bars, penned and prowling restlessly as a lioness confined to a stall built for dogs.

"They're never gonna put me in a cage," he told me, with equal emphasis on all parts: Not them, not me, not a *cage*. Not *ever*.

Oh, no.

I kept my opinions on the subject to myself, for then. Things had already gotten complicated enough once news got around, and my friends started telling me I was screwing Hitler. I'd scoff: *Rommel*, maybe. After all, he'd never said anything too repulsive to bear without response about non-white people around *me* . . .

And was that rationalization? Bet your ass. And did I need it, just to make my own behavior endurable, and still dream myself moral?

Not—

—as much—

—as I *should* have.

I told myself what Karl told me—that he didn't really give a damn about "the Cause", about paramilitarism, neo-Nazism, racial Separatism, any kind of ism. That all he really cared about was the grail he pursued to the exclusion of virtually everything else: The maddeningly elusive goal of evolution—or *de*evolution—into his own "natural" animal form.

It was the second part of Karl's creed, the one he'd been left to come up with all on his ownsome . . . a Frankenstein faith patched together from romance and ritual, mythology and madness, snips and snails and old wives' tales. Put simply, he aspired to remake himself into a *berserkgangr*, or berserker—a bestial warrior-poet, Odin's champion, intoxicated with blood-mad ecstasy, who could wade into battle naked except for his totem animal's flayed hide, the ritual bear-shirt.

Pretty nutty, huh? So much so that even other Aryans considered Karl cracked. To the Far Right Christian coalition he was a renegade, an unrepentant Pagan, maybe even a devil-worshiper. Straight-up paramilitarists, meanwhile, thought his time would be better spent fighting the good fight on a battlefield the rest of them could share—down here on earth, where the usual weapon of choice is rocket-launchers, not shape-shifting.

But Karl didn't care what they thought. He truly believed this state of holy fury was the true nature of every white man—*his* true nature. What he wanted to be. *Could* be, with just a little more . . .

. . . application.

Go out into the woods, find your bear, kill it and wear its skin—into battle. And then—

"Battle?"

"Find a fight, get in it; shit, baby, what'd you think I meant?"

(I mean, this ain't *rocket* science, here.)

"Okay: Skin, battle. Because . . . ?" I prompted.

"'Cause that's how you change." A pause, while I took this in. Adding: "Won't work if it's not *your* bear, though."

"And you know this—how?" I asked. He just shrugged. And replied, simply—

"'Cause it hasn't worked yet."

(. . . *yet*.)

* * *

Skirting the lake, Karl's key already pulse-warm beneath my shirt; haven't driven this route for two presidencies, but it's not like I have to check the map. So I here I sit, letting the engine's drone pull me past an endless panorama of long-forgotten sense-memory material: Grey walls of rocks, green-brown blur of trees—reflected light lapping back and forth, setting sun gone liquid all along the shore. Berkana in water, my tattooed rune's next logical reading made flesh. Synchronic or coincidental, sports fans?

(*You* decide.)

The books agree, mainly: A time for self-assessment, for inward thinking. A time to relax, and count your blessings.

And: *Ten years*, I think, as I take the next hill. *Three with Karl, seven without.*

Ten . . . whole . . . years.

(Christ.)

Because sure, I know you must all be saying to yourselves, right about now: The sex sounds good, but there has to have been *something* else to keep Lee with this nutcase after the lovin' was done, smart guy that he obviously are. Right? I mean, let's not fool ourselves—freak sex, good or not, is kind of like pure Scotch: You can only drink it every day for just so long, before your insides spring a leak.

So what was I doing, exactly, while those initial years flew by—besides letting Karl have his wicked way with me anytime he wanted, that is? Well—

—not . . . a lot.

But lest you think I just lay there and took it the whole damn time, I might as well mention the other primary component of the whole Lee/Karl melange—the not-so-hidden character flaw Karl sniffed out in me that very first night, and lovingly nurtured every subsequent second we shared: My aforementioned temper, which tends to range—on a daily basis—from simple finger-snap snarkiness to outright barfight-picking piss-artistry. I've struggled with it all my life, and turning out gay has neither helped nor hindered, especially since the men I sleep with usually seem just as uncomfortable with my sudden flare-ups as those few women I forced myself to get jiggy with ever were. More so, in fact—because most guys don't really know *how* to deal with rage, except by producing some of their own.

Not Karl, though. He didn't want to be placated, or reassured, or soothed. Culturally, conflict was his medium; he expected it, required it.

Hell, he reveled in it.

"'Anger management problems,'" he repeated, after I—reluctantly—let slip the reason I still saw a psychiatrist twice each week. "You."

I felt heat boil across my face, jaw- to hairline. "Yeah, *me*. So?"

"Like when you get riled you go all psycho, that it?" I stayed silent, as he continued, teasingly: "C'mon, seriously—like you can't think? And you see red? And when some guy keeps comin' after you, you start wantin' to rip his guts out with your bare hands?"

Teeth gritted: "Something like that, yes."

He chuckled, deep in his throat—came in close, doing that looming thing again. But this time, my blood was up. I showed him my teeth, all white and sharp . . . and he just laughed again, even harder, at the sight of them.

"Naw, don't think so" he said. "Little pretty kitty fag-boy you? Be serious." Leaning closer, showing me his: Bigger, whiter, sharper. "Believe *that* when I—"

—see it?

(Well . . . okay.)

And then, with a growl, I was on him—had him on his back, struggling, before he even had time to count his losses. We went at it hand to hand, no holds barred. I kneed him hard in the groin; he roared but sucked it up, cracking me across the jaw so hard I bit my own lip. Finally, as I hissed blood, he got his knees between mine and spread them hard, pinning me. I raked his face, so he flipped me, bit into my nape, and gave a flesh-smothered crow of surprise and delight. Rumbling, while I thrashed beneath him—

"Ah, now—that's better."

I bucked up like a hard-rode horse, made it to my knees—then froze as he slipped into position, humping me higher, drawing a helpless moan. So quick, for all his bulk. And the touch of him, raising hairs where I barely knew I had them—so raw, so rank, so right. So utterly, unnaturally Goddamn . . . natural.

"This," he told me, firmly, "this's how it should be. Way you're feelin', that ain't something you *manage*—that's an ancestor-gift, Lee, pure and simple. The very best part of your heritage."

Trying to unseat him, and failing miserably. I gave one last half-hearted flail, one last hoarse groan, then managed:

"This's me getting pissed, that's all. Nothing more, nothing—"

A snort. "That's your *bear*, Lee, lookin' out through those baby blues. Sayin' 'hi' to mine . . . "

(. . . the way bears do.)

All hot breath and hunger, carrion-rank, honey-sweet. Grappling and snuffling. All claws and jaws and *blood* in every part of me, pumping me hard enough to pop on contact. Making me feel alive in a way I've never felt since:

Not then, not now. Not before. And sure as hell not—

(after)

"Oh, shit," I hissed, finally. "Just . . . shut the fuck up and fuck me, you fucking freak."

Another grin, into my spine. "Whatever you say—"

(shield-)

"—brother."

Karl didn't just accept my unsociably low tolerance for annoyance, he encouraged it; we'd fist-fight as foreplay, go straight from making bruises to licking them. While all around him had been trained to try and *keep* their tempers—keep them on a leash, keep them in check—if Karl felt it, you knew it. It was like breathing to him, like sex. Like prayer. For Karl, rage was a means to its own end, its own energy and its own purpose: A negative rush, infinitely destructive and potent. It was meditation, masturbation, sex and drugs and rock and roll, all rolled up into one. An in-body out-of-body experience. Losing yourself.

Or, maybe—

—finding yourself.

"These guys I run with," he said, "they're weekend warriors, mostly. Talk big, sure, but ain't nothin' under their skin worth the lettin' out. *You*, though . . . " He paused. "You could go all the way, you wanted to."

"All the way where?"

Well . . .

. . . that'd be the question.

(Wouldn't it?)

Wherever Karl went, I suppose, all those years ago. Wherever he left me for, after I—finally—

—left *him*.

I try not to think much about that last night we spent together, if I can help it. That time we went up alone, just the two of us, with no disciples invited—when we built a fire so big it felt like we were cooking in our own sweat and fucked in every splintery corner of the house Karl's Grampaw built, 'till we were both so hot and tender we could barely move. And then, when everything was at its peak . . . when Karl, who never drank, had already downed what seemed like a potentially fatal load of fermented honey-mead he'd bought from some fellow Viking-obsessed freak in the Society for Creative Anachronisms, and made me match him slug for slug from a couple of dirty steins . . .

... then, if I force myself, I can just about barely remember what it felt like to find him pulling me outside by my hair, holding me upright against the wind and pointing me towards the trees. Crooning so low I could hear it move through his chest and into mine, like some subsonic earthquake-warning; pressing a knife—a Goddamn *knife*, serrated blade long as my femur—into my limp right hand, and telling me:

C'mon, Lee—tonight's the night. Can't you feel it comin'? My—

(*our*)

—bear.

Naked, sweating, barely upright. His fist on my hip, over that left-side swastika—fingers spanning my thigh, nudging my half-hard cock. Steering me by it, practically, like it was a magic wand that'd make me do whatever he wanted me to . . .

(. . . whatever . . . I wanted to.)

Because here's the truth, all right? It was never what Karl wanted that scared me. It was the part of me that desperately *wanted* to be what he wanted—to do whatever it took to keep him with me, on me, *in* me. The insatiable part. The angry part. The—

(*bear* part)

That voice, murmuring—was it even coming from him, anymore? Or from somewhere deep inside me?

So c'mon, baby: Into the woods, knife out. And I'll get mine, and you'll get yours, and we'll be together, always—

Hunt together. Kill together. Eat . . . together—

(—forever.)

And at the last second, the very last second possible . . . I turned, and I dropped the knife, and I punched him in the face, so hard I broke a knuckle. And then I took off, running. And I have never looked back, never. Not *ever*.

* * *

. . . 'till now.

* * *

Say it with me, once again: Right *now*. Which is when I find myself turning sharp off this last, gravel-paved trace of road—eyes burning, neck stiff, limbs fatigue-cramped, with memory still lodged bone-deep and burning sharp in every part of me, like too much lactic acid after a long, hard race. When I pull over into the trees at the bottom of Karl's hill, turning the engine off, getting out, kicking my joints awake again . . .

Then look up, squinting into the sun. And easily spot, even through seven years' worth of encroaching overgrowth, the door of what that blond kid says Karl's *will* says is (from this moment on) "my" cabin.

The key still works, albeit with a rusty click. Inside I find a homespun panorama of decay—wood-rot and silence, dust rising like ghosts, screen-doors black with caterpillar corpses, cobwebs laden deep with mummified flies. That oil-lamp we used to see by, its wick only half-burnt, waiting for a match's kiss; that unvarnished pine table-and-chairs set Karl once bent me across, splintery as ever. That same fireplace, full of cold ashes.

And everything I touch, everything I don't—just, plain, everything—still smells . . . exactly . . .

. . . like Karl.

Musty, musky. Earthy as a cave. Like somewhere you can sleep all winter, hibernate 'till spring—live off your own fat and dream, *willing* yourself into another shape by the time you finally wake.

(And how the fuck can that be, anyway? After seven *years*?)

I feel a shiver go up my spine at the very thought of trying to answer that particular question, quick and cold as the phantom lick of long, grooved tongue.

Because: It's been quite the ride for me, one way or another. And now that it's finally over, I find I have almost no idea—

(good *or* bad)

—why I ever actually bothered to come back up here again, in the first damn place.

Dust on the floor, dirt smeared black on the dimming windows. That earthy scent. Berkana *in* earth, third reading of four: Unsafe footing, shifting ground.

The rune-books' advice? Hold back a little. Take stock. Try "not to be so pushy", because—

(*things*)

—could rebound on you.

Jump-cut, moment to moment; lost time, skittering sidelong between action and re-. And suddenly, it's later—maybe *very* late—with the oil-lamp's shine joining a shifty play of firelight across the dusty floor . . . a huge, blood-warm, spark-leaking blaze I must have worked at least a whole half-hour to build, being the woodcraft-unfriendly little city mouse that I am.

(Late.)

The fire, the lamp. And me, looking down at something laid out across my lap, all big and stiff and . . . *furry*.

Something with a hood-like, floppy, shaggy head.

Something that smells, worse than the cabin around it. Worse even than my own stink of cold-sweat incredulity.

Something with empty eyes, and sleeves—their seams sutured fast with dried gut—that end in claws.

Something I know—must be—

(Oh, go on ahead and say it, Lee, baby. You *know* you want to.)

The bear-shirt, itself.

(Karl's . . . bear)

—or what little's left of it, at least. After he finally got through with it.

(Ah, *shit*.)

I feel my eyes sting, my head buzz; feel my inner arm hum with sympathetic pain, my Berkana tattoo puff rug-burn raw, just like it did the day Karl let them draw it on me. Make it to my feet, swaying slightly, and watch this terrible artifact I hold unfurl to brush the floor beneath me; Jesus Christ Almighty, but the fucking thing's fucking huge. Big enough—

(—for two.)

Questions reeling through my head, answered practically in their moment of asking: So where'd I *find* this particular haphazard masterpiece of outsider art, anyway? Must've been in that closet gaping open by the bed—the one that looks so very familiar, 'specially when I squint. And why am I having so much trouble forming these questions, in the first place? Well, the empty bottle by my boot might hold a key, rolling to clack against a few of its similarly empty buddies as I stagger back towards said closet, trailing Karl's precious shirt in the dust—but barely make it to the bed before this subtle numbness in my face and hands spreads southward, felling me onto its rumpled sheets.

And yes, that *is* me crying openly now, all salt and snot. Me knotting tight into a wet-faced human ball, kicking off my offending Docs, shucking the rest of my trendy clothes to crawl inside this dead animal husk; me, slicking this unsanitary parody of a fur coat over my own naked skin and hugging it to me, sobbing.

I think about Karl, and wonder: Was it just too much for him, in the end? My desertion? This latest—last—failure? Or a self-image-destroying combination of the two, that awful morning after . . . cold light of day, the hard death of a lifetime's dreaming, cut with blood-stink and mead-hangover?

Bear-grease on my cheeks, mixing with my tears. Bear-head pulled down over my nose like a mask, toothy jaw flapping to knock against my chin. And Karl's spoor shedding everywhere it touches, marking me with his scent—its sheer bulk so like his, warm and heavy on all my most intimate parts. As I think, hysterically:

Got me under your skin, Karl, baby—down deep in the heart of you. So deep, I'm really . . .

. . . *a part of you.*

Just like you always said I was.

I still don't know where he went, and maybe I never will. But—wherever he is, *this* isn't with him. Which means it sure as hell can't be where—

(or *what*)

—he wanted so desperately to be.

And the sad fact is, I think know Karl well enough to know that if he couldn't be what he wanted, then—in the end—he'd probably rather be . . .

. . . nothing at all.

* * *

So I cry myself to sleep, and dream my own dead dream—face-down, tapped out, crushed flat under ten years' worth of retroactive anger and bitter regret. I dream of one more reading, the final one available: Berkana in fire, hot and close as this cabin, sliding swift towards incineration like one of those volcanic islands off Iceland's coast, the kind that rise and fall in a flood of lava and a matter of days. Danger, Will Robinson; you don't know as much as you think you do, not by fuckin' half. So pay attention to detail, or pay—

—the price.

Rune-knowledge, hard-learned, flickering in and out like light through the Yggdrasil's narrow leaves. But paying attention's not exactly top of my list, right at this very moment. Instead, I find myself slipping down fast into a morass of memory crossed with fantasy—"feel" the bear-shirt part beneath Karl's phantom hands as his stubbly profile glides quick across the sweaty small of my back, leaving a trail like the scratch of an open matchbook-cover all the way up my spine. Submerged, swamped, moaning and drooling in my drunken daze, I "hear" him snort and snuffle between my shoulderblades as he pulls me up by the tail, rooting and spreading and puppeting me around in that way he's always liked best. "Feel" my mouth come open as he thrusts inside, coring me, and think:

Oh Christ, Karl, CHRIST . . .

Christ but I've missed this, you could-be-dead-for-all-I-know Nazi nutbar of mine—missed *doing* this, *with* you—

But: It's not true, and I know it, even as the charge begins to build. It's just my fume-filled mind tricking me, my body looping back into those painfully pleasurable patterns of hurt and hunger it knows so well. And the idea that I could be such easy prey, even for my long-lost lover's ghost . . . the mere idea of me overtaken by dumb ecstasy, rucking the sheets and howling, then sagging forward like I've just been disemboweled: A corpse myself, skinned and gutted and left to soften like the splayed remains of some—

(bear's)

—last meal—

Jesus, it all just makes me so damn . . . *mad*.

And I come awake, mid-spurt, amid smoke and mess and oh *fuck*, are those *flames*? Fucking cabin's on fucking fire, how the fuck did *that* happen—like I kicked the oil-lamp over in my sleep and it hit the rug, spread and sparked across those bare pine boards where my boots fell and shit, can't believe I'm gonna have to run *barefoot* through this crap—slamming hard into the wall where I think the door should be and bouncing, spinning into that filthy screen, my Berkana-arm punching through in a spray of wounds, broken metal threads already hot enough to cauterize on contact—

Stumbling out into the cold night air, with pine-needles stabbing the soles of my feet; turning back, squinting and gasping, to see the whole damn thing engulfed beyond saving. Shivering in the bear-shirt, clutching myself. Thinking—

Hey, look, boys 'n' girls . . . a real live Viking funeral, just like on TV. Everything Karl ever had, gone up in flames—

—all except me.

More questions, though, as the ash flutters upwards: Where're my glasses? Inside, of course—unsalvageable by now, mere melted slag. But . . .

. . . I can still see.

And that smell, mounting, that back-of-the-throat strong stink—that must be me too, right? Burnt hair, burnt flesh, burnt bear-hide. Looking down to confirm it and seeing the charred palms of my hands poking from the bear-shirt's paws, my shins already swollen with water-blisters . . . but why can't I *feel* it? And—what—is that—

(*other*)

—smell?

At which point I turn again, further, towards the first shadowy rim of trees, and see the bear come out of the woods.

Five feet at the shoulder. Twelve standing up, clawed hands tentatively drooping inward, childish as a Tyrannosaur's vestigial clutch. Its fur is sandy, touched with dull hints of gold; its muzzle matted with blood and honey, underbelly-fur shaggy with burrs. I can smell its breath from here, even over myself, over the fire: Old bees, fresh carrion. Honey-sweet blood-reek.

The bear is huge. The bear seems hungry. And its tiny eyes, so dull and atavistic, which widen almost beyond the limits of their narrow orbits as they turn my way—as it catches my (familiar?) scent, and moans with goony ursine lust—

—are blue.

(Karl.)

Karl, in *his* shirt, in "his" bear. In his *natural animal form*.

(That bastard.)

Because if this is Karl's shirt I'm wearing . . . and that's *Karl*, then . . .

. . . I have been seriously screwed.

Find your bear, kill it. Wear its skin—

Yeah, okay, got it. But once you put it on, once you change—

(as is becoming *more* than obvious)

—you can't ever take it off again.

Which makes this not Karl's shirt, then, at all. Made *by* Karl, for certain-sure, back when he still had hands—imprinted with his musk, his enticing flavor, before he traded his tender human skin for the far less permeable coat he now wears. But not on his own behalf. No.

Because just like he said that night I ran away and left him—holding his knife, alone in the darkness—this bear whose hide I wear now, *this* bear was meant—

(—for me.)

The final puzzle-piece, gut-feeling intuition made explicit. Bears are predators, omnivores, opportunists, pure and simple; they don't tend to think strategically, if they think at all. And in the wild, just like everywhere else, the only animals who lay traps for other animals . . . are humans.

Giving that kid the key, making him wait. Making *me* wait, and brood, and convince myself I wasn't thinking about Karl at all—even though I rarely thought of anything but—for seven long years. Then sending it to me, and sending me up here, where the trail was strongest—where my memories would finally rise up, break their floodgates forever, knock me down and drag me under like a dark, sweet, dreadful tide—

(Bastard, you *bastard*, you)

—but that's no good. Gotta stop that, right fucking now, before the final phase of Karl's plan kicks into gear. Before he provokes me into battle.

(Fuckin' "battle".)

Yeah, that'd be about his style, that racist son of a racist *bitch*. I mean, what's the definition of Valhalla—Viking heaven—if it isn't getting to fight the same worthy opponent . . .

(and that'd be me)

. . . over and over, world without end, amen?

Which is why, to be frank, I'd be a hell of a lot more worried about these burns of mine if I couldn't already feel them healing.

So I stand here trying to rip the shirt off, before my own inner Grizzly has a chance to really sink its hooks in me—but Goddamn it all, I just can't. Feel it sealing fast, the claws clicking in and binding to my fingers. Feel my broken knuckle ache and blaze, a white-hot arthritis-flower just about to bloom, like it's going to rain and never stop. Feel my mind getting bear-slow, bear-petty. Bear-

(angry)

Yeah. 'Cause my blood's up, and I'm panting, and that bear—

(*My* bear?)

—if I didn't suspect it was physically impossible, I'd say that bear was fuckin' well *smirking* at me.

And: Ah, but Lee, that treacherous little inner voice whispers teasingly, soft as rot—if you really didn't *want* to wear it, then you never should've put it *on*. You know what I'm sayin'?

I mean, if the shirt fits . . .

(Oh, fuck *you*, you fucker.)

Lowering my head, lips peeling back over teeth, all sharp and white—sharp*er*, whit*er*. Feeling blood in my head, my face, my heart. Feeling my cock jump, bone-harden, and my pulse pound like a war-drum. And wondering, with what might be my very last—intelligible—thought: Is this how they felt, the *berserkgangrs*? When they chewed the edges of their shields flat and bloody, then tore off their mail to reveal the fur beneath? When they threw their swords aside and ran into the fray, like they were finally going home after a long, long journey in the upright, lying, divided world of men—biting, clawing, changing, gratefully—as they went?

History in motion, good Swedish stock. "A part of my heritage."

(The very *best* part, to be exact.)

I feel my jaw seize up, shallowing—my words deform, as a groove carves itself down the center of my tongue. And snarl, with my last human breath:

"Well, fine. You want me back this bad, huh? C'mon on ahead, motherfucker. C'mon and—"

(—*take* me.)

HIDEBOUND

. . . he howled fearfully:
Said he was a wolf: Only the difference
Was, a wolf's skin was hairy on the outside,
His on the inside: Bade them take their swords,
Rip up his flesh, and try . . . .
—-John Webster, *The Duchess of Malfi*

Contrary to popular belief, no security guard is automatically issued a gun. You have to pass a special six-month training course for that, which hardly anyone ever does, because they make you pay for the privilege, as with so many other things—-your P.I. license, your uniform shirt, your on-site shoes (black, thick-soled, equally presentable for PR or plain old patrol duty), your First Aid expertise, even your clip-on tie, with its risible little cloisonné company insignia. And since the unspoken rule of security is do exactly as much as your bi-weekly direct deposit check dictates—-no more, often less—-I'm sometimes surprised anyone ever ends up packing heat at all.

Besides, as everybody who's seen an action movie knows, the security guard is always the first to go if anything actually does happen. So the best you can do is just ride each shift out, calm but cool, taking your mortality as a given: Become a Zen master in 365 easy steps, for only seven bucks an hour.

So no, I don't carry a gun, just like I don't drive. I'm a Toronto girl, after all, downtown born and bred; quite frankly, I've never had to go anywhere that required me to learn how to do either.

I got my security job for exactly two reasons: Because I could speak and write fluently in English, and because having a certain quote of female guards was necessary in order for Saracen Security Limited to retain its licence under the new Ontario government (of the time), which supported the idea of job equity. This is how I ended up drawing my current site, subsequent to spending a week at 1088 Dupot, the events of which tenure comprise much of the following story.

And since I was originally referred to Saracen by a friend of my ex-fiancé Colin, who had worked her way through Theater at Ryerson, by taking night shifts at some deserted office building in Scarborough, I guess that's yet another thing I have to thank him for.

Like so many others.

* * *

Much later, sitting on the couch with Colin, watching him trying to be calm—fingers knit, and shaking—as the music wove gilt swooping arcs around us, effortless trailing ribbons of sound, I thought: So this is the end of everything. And then, no doubt misquoting Shakespeare's *King Lear*:

What, will my poor fool ne'er come again?
O never, never, never.

My teeth dancing. My cut heart twitching at our feet, pumping painful gushes of dust. The whole room shimmering with a kind of heatwave, a pricked-bubble haze, seconds after the pin. No explosion, simply absence.

Except, of course, that everything was still there, untouched. And so was I.

"I don't get it," he said, over and over. "I mean, I . . . just . . . don't get it."

Eventually adding, in a slightly more aggrieved tone: "I mean, I *said* I was sorry."

Like he was annoyed, was disappointed, with me for being so obtuse as to actually believe him when he told me our love was just a little more trouble than he felt like going to, anymore.

I twisted the (dis)engagement ring on my right hand and bit my tongue, hard, ready to bleed before I'd let myself agree again to this impossible fucking dream, this useless fucking ostensible marriage of ours, to salve his aggrieved and swelling eyes.

* * *

When I first applied to work as a security guard, the boys down at Saracen made me take a detailed—-but apparently routine—-psychiatric test, much of which involved checking "yes" or "no" boxes next to a series of statements, like these:

I enjoy life. (Yes.)
I would enjoy working with dogs. (No.)

Next came a multiple-choice, aimed at identifying the best type of site to assign me to. It contained my single favorite question, which ran thusly:

Would you be more likely to prefer a site where:
A) You had a lot of personal power, but were required to deal with people all the time:
Or one where:
B) You sat in a room by yourself, doing a repetitive task, seeing and dealing with no one.

Being misanthropic by nature (when it comes to my choice of straight-up, purely-for-the-pleasure-of-rent-payin', uniform-wearin' asshole jobs, at least), I checked the latter. I told Colin about it, laughed, and forgot.

But it wasn't until two years later, when I turned up at 1088 Dupont, that I ever considered it possible someone had actually taken this response into account.

There were a lot of firsts for me on that site—-my first night shift, from 2345 to 0800 hours. My first site outside. My first site with no partner, and no one coming to take over after I booked off, either, since the only reason they needed anyone on site in the first place was to make sure nobody ran off with the construction company's expensive equipment before morning. Up until then, I'd mainly guarded college campuses, a couple of office buildings.

But 1088 was none of these things . . . yet. 1088 was a work in progress.

Lit mostly by the giant neon crucifix on top of the church across the street—an extra implication of moonlight occasionally smearing down through the clouds, touching its incomplete lines with snail-track grey—1088 looked like a serial killer's dream house: Stately Dahmer Manor, replete with shallow trenches and stacks of dry cement bags, a bleak theme park of prospective murder and burial scenes. Below, nude walls held up the faceless, backless concrete doll's house: Above, girders barely made a roof, let alone an upper floor.

"So," I delicately asked my trainer for the night, former site S.O. Sonny Rehan, "are those holes up there just left ... open ... all the time?"

He laughed. "Oh, yeah, man. I wouldn't even bother going up there. Seriously, I mean. Saracen got no medical plan—you break your neck on patrol, nobody's gonna care but you."

Sonny, a gangly young Sikh from Kenya, had spent much of his career with Saracen so far assigned to 1088. And since both his parents also worked for the company (mother staring down potential shoplifters at the Eaton Center, father wrangling illegal immigrants up at the airport), he knew every angle there was, not the mention how they could best be taken advantage of. Now, after two years' weekend training and a written recommendation from his site supervisor, he was off to fresher fields—the far more lucrative double shifts of Dispatch, where he could spend his time tagging lucky winners for the same shitwork he'd finally escaped. But he wasn't gone yet, and a surfeit of solitude had obviously made him talkative.

"You know that part in *Indiana Jones and the Temple of Doom* where they eat the chilled monkey brains, man?" he demanded, at one point. "We used to do that—my uncles, my Dad and me. Little grey bush monkeys. Hold 'em still, saw off the top of the skull, then just go at it with a spoon while they're still kicking. Nothing like it, man."

Sonny gave me the grand tour. He read me the site standing orders, which required me to make a complete patrol every forty-five minutes—checking specifically for squatters, vandals or thieves—before returning to the portable office where I was to sit between said patrols, filling out my Daily Occurrence Report and reading day-old tabloids. He pointed out the "cop button", conveniently hidden just under the lip of my desk. which had to be pulled out and pushed back in with a special key that looked like a taken-apart can opener.

"How long does it take them to get here?" I asked. "I mean, usually?"

"Five minutes. Probably."

I looked at him. "Probably?"

Sonny shrugged. "Oh, man, depends." Adding, cheerfully: "But I never had to push it more than twice, anyways."

These, then, were the major drawbacks of 1088, according to its most regular custodian:

1. No lights on the upper floors of the building.

2. Permanently open holes in said floors, so big even a novice such as myself would notice them.

3. No interior toilets.

4. No flashlight on site.

This last item frankly amazed me.

"First two months on the site, man, I put in a request at end of every D.O.R.," Sonny said. "They had to call and tell me personally there were no extra flashlights anywhere."

"It's like some bad fucking horror movie."

Sonny grinned. "Can be."

* * *

When I look back on how I was with Colin—what I did, what I said, what I allowed to be done . . . it all seems so . . . improbable. Like a fever dream. The shed cocoon of my own sweat, facing from bed sheets hung up to dry: Invisible ink run backwards, wilting from the flame of clear-headed examination.

I tell myself I loved him then, which I know to be true. I tell myself I had no control.

I tell myself it was love, as though that mere fact explains anything.

* * *

I called Colin that first night, before I performed was was to become my normal "patrol"—stepping outside the portable, walking around the building (keeping a careful space between me and it), peering inside and scanning for any moving shadows, before retiring to falsify the D.O.R. My fingers sped through the flat little song of his phone number. He picked up on the third ring.

"House o' Colin."

"Hiya."

What did we talk about? I couldn't tell you if I tried. Probably the dog we'd bought together. Probably the movie we'd seen last night. I know we didn't talk about how we were supposed to get married in three months, our agreed-upon deadline, to commit to each other and stay together the rest of our lives—even though my mother couldn't stand him, and his mother wouldn't even acknowledge I existed. Except for that one time she'd taken him aside, during our sole joint visit to homey old Brantford, and told him, "You know, Colin—you sleep with trash, you become trash."

I know we didn't, because we never talked about any of that. Not even when we broke up.

* * *

Ever since I was a child, I've had a running debate with my mother over whether or not there's something "wrong" with my bladder capacity—a nagging fear reinforced by a nightmarish visit to my grandmother that ended with her counting every time I went to the bathroom during the night, giving us a full report in the morning, and telling me (very seriously, in her Scots-Canadian burr), "You really shude think aboot consoolting a doctur, Lee. It's jist nut nermal."

But I'm a big girl now, supposedly. So after I'd held it in for about three hours, I decided I'd rather take my chances with one of the portasans than risk getting fitted with a colostomy bag.

Inside this unlit, upright plastic coffin with a septic tank, however, I found not only no toilet paper, but an overwhelming stink to boot—a nose-and-mouthful of warm European cheese, the kind so bad you can barely stand to taste it, let alone smell it. Not to mention I was desperate, but couldn't let go . . . which actually had less to do with the situation as I've painted it above than with an overpowering feeling of being watched.

You know how it is sometimes, when you're caught unaware—that impassable glitch between reflex and realization? You're seconds from sleep, dreaming a busy daytime street, until you feel yourself step in the gutter and jerk awake again, bruising your foot on the bedboard. The plate's left your hand, and you know you'll never catch it. But you can't stop yourself from jumping, even as it slowly arcs down to break apart on the floor.

A flash of movement, right at the edge of my vision. Next thing I knew, I was up—standing so quickly that the whole portasan gave one big jerk—and out. I strode behind the nearest truck and squatted, scanning the bushes: There was nothing to wipe myself with but leaves, naturally, which seemed more than a little sixth-grade, so I pulled the tail of my shirt free, planning to use it and tuck it back in before I could think about what I'd just done. And I sat there on my hands, listening to my heart hammer in the hollow of my throat—my breath ragged, like I'd run a mile through some seashell.

My throat was sore. My lungs felt full of blood-warm mucus. But all I could think of was the figure I thought I'd seen loping past in the crack of dark between door and jamb, its face the barest Pierrot mask, two smudged eyes in a white oval, with an uneven red thumbprint for a mouth.

I sat there on my heels, knees pulsing with fatigue, and felt the warmth drain out of me, spurt by uneven spurt.

Under the truck, a shadow in its shadow, some pile of half-crushed stuff nested by the back tire. Having nothing else to focus on, I stared at it until it resolved into a calcified cache of turds—animal, presumably, given their location. Except that I could see a glinting twist of metal protruding from one cracked fecal egg. A bright, bent hook topped with a ragged glass sliver.

It looked like a chewed-up earring.

Then the church across the street's neon Passion Tree winked out, and I decided to call it a night on external patrols.

* * *

Night shift is different from anything you've ever worked, though it doesn't usually feel that way: After the first day, your clock turns with an audible click. But it's not a simple thing. You lie awake in what now passes for darkness, with the most opaque towel you can find triple-folded and draped over your eyes. Breathing slow. When it finally comes on you, you sleep like a dog —mouth open, tongue like old flypaper by the time the alarm goes off. A noose around every limb, pulling you downward.

When the phone rang, I was still dressing.

"Late dinner sound good about now?"

"Sure. Muggs okay?"

"Sure."

I peeled sleep from one eye, struggling to keep my thoughts stacking up in a straight line.

"I think," I said—and it was at exactly this point, as I heard myself say it, that I knew for certain it must be true—"that they have people living on that site. Not . . . legally."

"Mmm." I heard Dewey the dog in the background, making that asthmatic little pug whine of hers. "Yeah, wouldn't surprise me. Ontario's Common Sense Revolution in action."

We set the time. We called each other pet names, told each other how much we were looking forward to our upcoming meal. But as I hung up, I finally remembered my dream—the same dream I'd had for months, on and off. The dream about the woman with hooks for hands, holding Colin's mouth open in a too-wide smile, pulling so tight the corners were already starting to crack.

Turning him to me and grinning (just a touch) herself, like it was some new kind of party trick she'd just mastered, and she needed my reaction to know whether or not it'd go over well in public.

So smile if you like it, baby mine. Smile.

* * *

The second night, I hit a nearby 7-11 to stock up on fast food and napkins, planning to pee in a wadded up paper bag and bury it at the bottom of a wastepaper basket. As I approached the counter, a man and a woman were already investing in their own little haul—or rather, he was buying, she watching. Sometimes he'd smirk and whisper something to her, adjusting his toque. She was one of those bendy girls, double-jointed and voluptuous, but with lips so thin they barely masked the points of her small, sharp teeth. It was late September, colder at night—sky a black vault, like an open door into vacuum—and he was dressed accordingly, his Maple Leafs jacket bulbous with down. But she wore a slip-on smock dress and a shapeless grey sweater, her sockless feet stuffed into a pair of too-small, open-toed summer sandals. Whenever she moved, I thought I could hear her exposed toenails rasp on the floor beneath her, like the stealthy claws of some passing animal.

The man finished his business and drew her away into a big, tonsil-polishing kiss: She twined one leg around his, leaning back. There were almost no other customers in the store, and the clerk kept his eyes firmly on the free show by the door. I briefly considered just grabbing what I wanted and telling him I'd already paid for it.

A minute later, they were gone, and I was telling the clerk to add on the big bottle of cranapple juice I'd spotted on display near his elbow.

So: Back on the site, still with no flashlight. (I guess I might have put myself far enough out to actually bring my own, had I cared enough to do Saracen's job for them. But the way I saw it, if a flashlight had ever suddenly appeared in that desk drawer, I would have lost my sole excuse not to do a real patrol.) Since Colin wasn't in, not even by 0200, I polished off the last of the cranapple juice, and almost threw the bottle away before I realized its other possible uses.

Three hours and a half-full bottle later, justifiably paranoid about an unannounced visit from my site supervisor—they usually come on the first night, just to see whether you're sleeping, smoking or entertaining guests on the job—I capped it, zipped up my parka, and stepped out to dump this impromptu toiletry aid on the nearest waste-pile.

I saw them on my way back, through one of 1088's wall-high "windows": Toque-man and the girl from the 7-11, knit and heaving against one of the support girders. She had her skirt hiked up and her underwear bunched around one ankle; he had apparently decided it was too cold to risk opening more than his fly. Both of them were a little too busy to notice me, frozen in the glare of my own embarrassed annoyance (because this was the first situation I'd ever come across on a site that I felt I might be required to actually do something about)—until the girl's nostrils flared, suddenly, and she looked up over his shoulder, meeting my eyes just as the headlights of a passing car caught her pupils, bleaching them blank as the silver coins on a corpse's eyelids.

The guy would have kept on grunting even then, if she hadn't nudged him. He squinted at me, unafraid, demanding: "Shit you want?"

"You're trespassing," I said.

He snorted. Behind him, the girl gave a laugh—high, husky, curled back in on itself: The brief bark of something not entirely tamed. It made me shiver and the guy smile, like it sent some hot needle of fresh desire tugging up through his buried dick.

So: "Fuck you, bitch," he replied, and went right on back to what he was doing.

The cops got there at 0525 (ten minutes late, according to Sonny's predictions), and one of them had a flashlight. But all we found where she and Mr. Toque had been was a stain at the base of the girder, a dark spot that could be anything—blood, oil, sperm.

"Nothin' we can do," the older, bigger one told me. "It gets cold out, people end up wherever's open."

"Not to mention you wouldn't believe some of the places we've found 'em goin' at it," the other one added.

I nodded. I said I understood.

As they got into their car, the older one offered: "You should tell your boss he wouldn't even have this kinda trouble, if they'd let you guys carry guns."

* * *

Over breakfast, I got into an argument with my mother, who was on her way out to an audition—the first in a long time, so she was irritable to begin with, but I didn't think that excused her then, and I don't now. She said that somebody had said that Colin had jokingly said that he was going to hire a hit-man to get her off his back, and I said that I didn't understand why she felt she had to tell me what somebody had said Colin had said about her. And so it went, escalating in volume, until her cab came and I stomped away upstairs, put a facecloth over my eyes and lay down in the half-dark to dream.

I dreamed I was standing in front of the bathroom mirror, flossing my teeth so hard that one of them fell right out in a gush of blood, clattering in the sink. Causing my mother to lean over my shoulder, exclaiming: "You know how much fixing that is going to cost?"

And I dreamed I turned, slapping her hard across the face—but that the movement broke my hand open at the wrist, peeling it back like an empty husk to reveal the glint of a sharp, blood-stained hook.

* * *

You're wondering, about now, why I never told anyone about what was going on—why I never said: "Hey, Colin? Those harmless homeless people I was complaining about, down at 1088? One of them laughed at me like a wolf last night, and I also think she might have eaten this guy I saw her doing the nasty with. Now I watch the building all the time, I see people come and go, and more of them than I like to admit look familiar to me—bums on the street I pass every day, guys hanging around outside the liquor store, women I've seen on the subway and thought they were just coming back from work, so bone-tired they were holding their romance novels the wrong way up. Some come back out. Some don't. And I hear the ones who do come out talking to each other, but the words they make are all sound and no sense, like those cats people train to sing Christmas carols, or those dogs that bark like they're saying 'herrow' or 'goorbai'. I sit there and listen to them all night, and pee in my cranapple juice bottle, and never go outside after the big neon cross turns off. I keep the door locked until 0800, and everything I've written in my D.O.R. for the last three days has been a lie."

Or maybe: "Hey, Mom? You know how you're always saying I'm so distracted, how I'm no fun to talk to or be with anymore, how we can't say two words sometimes without our necks going up, how we're verbally pissing on each other's shoes all the time to prove whose opinions are more worthy of respect?

"Well, part of that is natural: I'm getting older, we're growing apart. And part of that is because I'm just beginning to see that Colin has handed me a line of bullshit from day one, and you were right about him all along, though I will never admit it.

"And yet another part of that is because every night I spend eight hours in vague fear for my life, not even knowing really what the hell it is that I'm afraid of, and it's all so improbable that I forget about it as I'm coming home, only remembering it when I'm back on site and I can't do a Goddamn thing but wait it out 'til morning."

But I told neither of them any of this. I told no one anything. I had my own wound to deal with, and it took up all my free time. I drifted in a growing batch of silence, uprooted. And though I seemed to move further down with each new kick, I can't ever remember touching anything like a bottom.

I left Mom's place, went to Colin's, cried on his plaid foldout couch. I told him I'd had all I could stand of being their Goddamn emotional go-between, and begged him to settle things with her himself—before the wedding. Before it was too late. He made soothing noises, kissed my breasts, ignored every word I said. And all the while, Dewey whimpered in the corner of his bedroom, staring up at us with her poached-egg eyes.

Oh, Jesus: Whatever. Fill in the rest of these blanks yourselves, why don't you.

Because how can I ever expect to explain to you how preoccupying the pain of knowing I was losing Colin's love was—so vast it drowned everything, even my own fear? Even then it was ludicrous. Laughable.

Which sure as hell leaves with no excuses now—when I don't really recall myself how it felt to love him, in the first place.

* * *

Nights, I sat in the protable and filled out personality tests in the backs of old teen magazines like *Sassy* and *Y.M.*, aka *Young Moron*; days, I lay in Colin's bed, staring up at the ceiling and wondering who the uncalled-for denizens of 1088 Dupont could finally be. Until, finally, a certain woozy dream logic looped what facts I already knew together, stringing them like beads on a thread of unprovable intuition. What if, what if.

A nomad family who weren't even a family, not criminals or cannibals, but predators who hid themselves by taking on the protective coloring of their chosen prey. Cultureless, rootless, migratory, instinctual. Not people who acted like animals, but animals who had learned to act like humans. The girl, staring at me. Her numb cat's eyes, shining.

And the funny part is, I thought, *it probably wasn't all that hard.*

Intermittently, I slept and dreamed—mainly of the woman with hooks for hands, of course. Only one of them remains particularly clear: Getting up to go to the bathroom (that weird sensation of "relief" that's actually the anxious ache of automatic retention), bending over the sink to rinse and spit and then feeling a touch on the back of my neck. Looking up, seeing the woman with hooks for hands standing behind me in the mirror, her points laid lovingly under either ear, poised to dig deep, to rip me open.

To unfurl my innards like a flag for everyone to read, a red warning shout, with 1088 Dupont as its theme and title.

* * *

And then it was Thursday, the night my site supervisor finally turned up—a man I knew, as they say, of old.

"Hooper," he said. "Heard this was where they put ya."

"Sir."

His name was Czolgoscz (first initial L., so you just knew we were fated to be friends), and unlike me—unlike most security guards, to be frank—he considered himself "career", which apparently required growing a brush-cut little pseudo-cop moustache, with a gut to match. To normal people, this job was a step on the way to something better. But since Czolgoscz had no better thing to go to, he spent his time trying to make everyone as clinically depressed and constantly paranoid about their lack of employment options as he was.

He gestured for me to let him in, which I did. As usual, his first stop was my D.O.R.: A quick flip-through later, he went rooting for the site standing orders, eager to compare and contrast.

"No patrol since 0200," he noted. I nodded. Always so impressive to find a site supervisor who can count.

"I was just going," I said.

Czolgoscz smirked. "Yeah, well, you better put on your parka."

I nodded again. He kept flipping.

"You cover the whole site when you patrol?" he asked.

"Yes."

"Even upstairs?"

"Yes."

"Everywhere upstairs?"

I fixed me with what he'd probably call his "got 'em on the grill" look—a Dennis Franz-like glare absolutely made for admiring in bedroom mirrors. I wondered whether he was seriously still nursing a grudge from that time he'd tried to get me fired for supposedly deliberately leaving a janitor stuck in a George Brown campus staff elevator, and merely succeeded in having me moved to another site. (Though not this one.) I also wondered, idly, whether anyone had ever thought to put Sonny Rehan through this kind of bullshit.

"There's ... holes in the floors upstairs," I said. "As you may have noticed from my previous reports."

He wasn't about to suggest I'd lied in the D.O.R.—but then, I wasn't exactly about to volunteer that information either. So instead, he got up, shrugged his own parka back on, and opened the door again. Saying: "Think I'll tag along tonight. If you don't mind."

"I don't suppose you have a flashlight," I replied, without much hope.

He chuckled, and gave me an abortive kind of slap in the general direction of my back—nothing he could find himself facing possible harassment charges for, if I happened to take it the "wrong way".

"C'mon, Hooper," he said. "We're both old enough to vote, right? Think we can find our way around a *hole* or two."

It was raining when we left the portable—sleety, half-frozen rain that seemed to fall in gushes rather than drops, street lamps mere hazy smudges of light through the gathering fog, and with no neon cross to see by, just the phosphorescent glimmer of the water-heavy air itself. We clumped along like top-heavy navy-blue astronauts, wreathed in the milky nimbus of our own breath.

Czolgoscz and I went around first one side of the building, then another. We checked behind the parked trucks. Nothing.

We went around the piles of earth and the stacks of gravel-bags, through the main body of the first floor, picking our way between the open dirt trenches and an intermittent sprinkling of dismayingly sharp-looking beds of metal rods set in concrete.

Again, nothing.

And now we were at the bottom of the stairs leading to the second and third floor, right beneath the largest of the holes, on the threshold of a part of 1088 Dupont that I had never seen before.

Not finding any of 1088's usual residents around so far hadn't really made me feel any better about being in the building after my chosen cut-off point, even with Czolgoscz's big, beer-swilling ass at my side. Inside my pockets, I felt my hands curl in on themselves, as though tunneling for invisible weapons.

Czolgoscz put his booth on the last step. He looked at me. I looked back at him.

Then we went upstairs, together.

* * *

Romantic love. "Real" love. The kind of love where you're so far into the other person they seem like a part of you, like they are you. Until it falls apart, that is—and the other person comes to you and tells you everything that's gone wrong, how it can't be fixed, how it's all your fault.

And you think: *But if I'm you and you're me, honey-bug, then why the fuck didn't I already know that?*

I mean, I can live alone. It won't kill me. I've done it most of my life. I'm doing it now.

But the thing is, I don't *want* to.

* * *

Czolgoscz had just cleared the top step when an arm reached out and caught him around the throat, hauling him upward, two more sets of arms worming around either bicep as the first hand turned, dug, freed a wet, red starburst so suddenly I barely avoided being splattered, recoiling, catching the back of my parka on the ragged edge of the nearest hole and jolting myself so badly my feet slipped, losing the stairs altogether. Falling down, parka ripping as I hit the nearest girder, falling down hard on one knee and skidding, skinning it to the meat on 1088's unfinished ground floor. Falling to sprawl (pretty damn near) right at the bare, clawed feet of the girl from the 7-11—my nubile cannibal rover, still wearing the same dress, the same blank eyes. The same stained smile.

(Her relatives making short work of Czolgoscz, meanwhile, up above both our heads: Up in the rafters, where they'd been sleeping like extras from *Aliens* or something, apparently, ever since I'd called the cops that one time. And me too distracted, one way or another, to even credit them with enough sense of self-preservation to hide.)

Thinking: Now I'll never get to read those extra hundred pages of "Amazingly Accurate Information about My Secret Self" in *Young Moron*, or find out if *Sassy* thinks I'm a "Bad Girl Bud or A Substitute Sister".

The girl just kept on smiling, enjoying the luxury of taking her time. I guess she thought I was too stunned to move. I guess maybe I thought so too.

But we were both wrong.

* * *

Next thing I know, I'm back in the portable, holding the door closed behind me with all of my body as the girl crashes against it again and again. I dump out the key cabinet, scrabble through, grab the can opener, hook the cop button, back away. Looking for anything I can use for anything that'll keep me alive until they get here.

Under the desk, the cranapple bottle, full and capped. By the door, a fire extinguisher: Type 3—Industrial Fires. Hefting the one. Unhooking the other, as the door heaves one more time, comes off its hinges. The girl's arm coming through. Her face, her smiling mouth.

"Faa hew, bisssh," she says.

And then I break the bottle across her face, and start spraying.

* * *

I learned two things that night (among others).

First—a little liquid nitrogen goes a long way: And second—on occasion, the cops actually arrive within five minutes.

I ended up at the hospital, which pleased the whole hell out of the guys at Saracen: With something this public, even they had to start thinking about compensation. Which was just as well, since it turned out I'd burned my hand pretty badly on the fire extinguisher's spray, and had to wear one of those weird plastic gloves for the next month or so, just to keep it rigid. When they finally pulled it off, my hand shed its skin like a snake, leaving a fine vellum glove on the examination room counter.

Two weeks later, Colin and I broke up.

* * *

One night, weeks later, when I was booking on, the usual Dispatch deadpan gave way to Sonny Rehan's cheerful voice, brimming with gossip. He told me how my former supervisor's jawbone had been pried out from under the seat of that famous lightless Portasan, half his dyed brown moustache still attached, along with a full bottom lip.

"Pretty freaky, huh, man?" he asked.

"Guess Saracen lost that contract."

Sonny guffawed. "Oh, no shit. Seriously though, man, you got out just in time."

My new site is up in Scarborough, somewhere—a mere apparent bus stop away from the ass-end of beyond. Mushroom cloud country, with way too much skyline and not enough pedestrians for my liking. Another night shift, roaming from dusk till dawn around a square of Ontario Lottery Corporation offices, checking to see the computers don't overheat, counting the fire extinguishers as I card-key each successive door. Looking out the windows as I pass.

Scanning the parking lot for shadows.

Last week, on the street, Colin came up behind me, seemingly not realizing I had my walkman on. He got within an inch of the back of my head, shouted, "Hello, Lee!" and stalked off. As though I'd insulted him with my lack of notice. As though either of us really gave a good God damn anymore.

But this is the truth: I tried. When he came begging back to me—when he told me he hadn't known what he was saying, that night in the restaurant, when he told me it was no use going through with the wedding, and could I please pay back that $150 I owed him from our vacation in Ireland—I made excuses, made allowances. Because hey, it was probably my fault, anyway. As so many things are.

So I went out with him again. I sat with him, talked with him. I kissed him. I let him kiss me. And I felt—nothing. Except that I wanted less and less to sleep with him, to touch him, to be in the same room with him. And the real joke of it was, I didn't even know what was wrong. It didn't even occur to me.

'Cause when you get right down to it, I guess I'm just stupid. When people tell me they don't love me anymore, I tend to believe them. (And what was it you did mean to say, then, Colin? Exactly?)

I should have known a long time ago that I will never marry anyone, except maybe myself.

I hear noises at night, now. One the bus, riding up, my two-hour trip is dogged with the steady pad of bare feet on asphalt, with the scratch of clawed toes. On my rounds, I carry a plastic bag full of unpopped soda cans, swinging it like a weighted sling. I memorize the exits, and check the walls for fire extinguishers. I listen carefully to each new person I meet, trying to decide what they're hiding, what they really are.

Because the pain is draining away now: Taking my well-worn detachment with it, leaving nothing but the fear I never felt—glinting sharp.

The knife in my unhealed wound.

And whenever I stop long enough to consider it, it occurs to me that breaking a bottle of my own urine across the face of something with an animal's sense of smell may not have been the best idea I ever had.

I think of my dream, of the woman with hooks for hands, Our Lady of Self-Protection, who can only wound, never touch.

Never touch. Not even herself.

SKIN CITY

The street lamp's glare leaks in over her windowsill, unchecked by blinds, to touch what little furniture remains with a bleak light. Before her, a table—actually, three upturned boxes topped with a plank stolen from the construction site just north of the railway tracks. On the table, a tape recorder. Next to it, an empty cassette case.

Her suit waits, thrown over the end of the bed, for her to make up her mind.

Adage swallows.

The bright eye of her cigarette blinks, as ash dots the rug beneath her feet.

Useless even to try and tell you what she looks like: She's naked now, though not as we know the term. Naked and red and wet. And it's so comfortable to be hidden away here in the dark, she almost wishes her cigarette would last forever.

But that's impossible.

Soon the clock will strike, and she'll get up. She'll dress herself, as carefully as she can. And then, when she's presentable, she'll go out.

To meet somebody.

Anybody.

Adage takes a last drag. She drops the butt on the rug and lets it lie, smoldering.

She leans forward into the dark, feeling for the "record" button.

* * *

A month later.

Mike Grell sits by the window nearest the front door, looking out. In one hand he holds a postcard, in the other his walkman.

Outside the bus, Chinatown blurs by, trailing pennants of red lacquer and neon.

The postcard is custom made. One side's a holiday snapshot: 13-year-old Adage tilts her head back, laughing, as the sun bleaches away her face.

Mike touches his wallet, where the original lies folded between bank card and expired driver's license.

The other side is a scribble. Deciphered, it reads:

It's happening again. In Toronto. At the Meat Market, there's a girl named Sherri. Ask her where I am. Find me.

Please.

Adage.

Below that:

P.S.: If you got the tape, listen to it.

Ahead, a couple with matching Mohawks argues with the driver over what currently constitutes exact change. An elderly woman squeezes past, cradling an overweight pug on one hip and a bag of groceries on the other. Somebody drops a dime. Dust motes tremble, caught in mid-flight, as the doors slam shut.

Mike sighs.

He flips the cassette case open, and lets the tape fall into place.

* * *

A low hiss.

"Testing, one, two, three. Testing. Hello?"

Click.

Rewind, and press play.

"Testing, one, two—"

Click.

Softly: "All right, then."

* * *

"July twenty-third, nineteen-ninety. About . . . quarter to twelve."

Silence. In the background, a distant sitcom's laugh track seeps up through the floor like a forming blister.

"Okay. I'm gonna tell you a story.

"It's a red one, through and through. The words I'll use are stained so deep nothing could wash them clean. They reek and shine. Red the same way the moon would be red tonight, if you could see it. Red the same way the river is red. A red moon, a red rising tide, a red river breaking its banks, and a deep red tale somebody beside me has to hear before the world ends or I do, whichever comes first. And Larry's dead, so it might as well be you.

"Here's how it goes."

* * *

Mike hops the curb and stumbles, nearly sprawling waist deep in a puddle.

Uck.

He scans for the Meat Market sign—a steak on a phallic neon stick—as his mind races backwards.

Larry.

Last name—Gurley? Garvey? A skinny kid, bigger even than Adage, who'd spurted to full height that year, the way girls tend to. They spent their summers at the cottage—Mike with his parents. Adage her grandparents—and played in the woods, down by the lake. Always together, but always alone. And not minding.

Right up until Larry's Winnebago pulled into the vacant lot across the road.

Mike shuts his eyes. Beneath his coat, against his side, he feels the cold iron weight of his father's gun.

* * *

"Late July, nineteen eighty. You, and me, and Larry. Out in your Dad's truck, in the woods, before it got light. You wanted to go spot birds, and I wanted to go home. But Larry said no, let's do something different. And he took out the cards. So okay, you said, you want to play gin rummy? And Larry laughed. It's not like that, he said. Now draw.

"So we all took one card. And then Larry made us stop the truck, right near the shore. Just before the sun comes up, when all the stars are dead. And the lake was still. Now look at your card, Larry said, and I looked down. And my card was a picture of four sticks, lashed together and hung with some kind of fur, standing in front of a river. Like a door.

"And underneath it was written the word: SKIN."

* * *

Inside the Meat Market, girls jiggle and sway like parade balloons—white, swollen, shiny as plastic wrap. Strobe lights pulse. Squinting, Mike spots the bartender: A tall skinhead, deep in conversation with an even taller transvestite wearing a lime-green minidress.

Up and down the bar, tattoos bloom, bright as mold.

Mike elbows his way in. "'Scuse me—"

Next stool over, a yuppie with his shirt open to his waist howls with laughter. Bottles click together.

"I said, 'scuse me?"

The bartender turns, slipping his customary scowl back into place. "Can I help you, buddy?"

Oh, Christ.

"Well, yes," Mike replies brightly. "Actually, you can. I'm looking for a girl—"

Deadpan: "What a shock."

"—named Sherri."

No immediate reaction. The light turns orange. Cheers greet the next number.

"Sherri?" Mike repeats.

The transvestite blows a smoke ring. The bartender jerks his scalp toward the front. "Back there. In pink."

Mike turns. One door's propped open, spilling noise. Beyond, shadows move and posture. A faint gleam of rose-colored plastic shimmers, becomes an arm clutching a battered leather bag whose long white fringes seem chewed. Now a profile, once pretty, but equally worn. Between them, couples thrash.

"Thanks," Mike says, pushing off.

* * *

"There's nothing on my card, you said. And Larry smiled, like he expected it or something.

"Nothing on mine either, he said.

"Then he looked at me.

"Later, you told me Larry said I should stare at the card and try to make the door open. To want it to. So I did. And you started feeling like there was somebody watching us. Let's go, you said. And Larry said no, something's gonna happen. Like he knew it would. And when he said that, I started to make this noise deep in my throat.

"So then you got mad, and you said you were going to start the truck, and Larry could go to hell if he wanted but we were going back. But as you reached past me, I grabbed your arm. Hard. And it was like my nails were longer or something, because I was hurting you. And you said hey, Adage, let go, hey, what's wrong with you?

"And then I looked up, I grinned. And you screamed.

"You told me my mouth was full of blood."

* * *

"Sherri?"

The girl—15? 30?—jumps, catching Mike's sleeve with her cigarette. A tiny circle of pain stamps itself inside his wrist.

"Oh, man. Man, I'm sorry. I—you okay?"

"Fine," he lies. She beats ineffectually at the damage, making it worse. Through gritted teeth: "Please. No problem."

A shrug. "If you say so." Sherri drops the cigarette, face falling into more familiar lines. "Looking for me, huh?" she says. "What for?"

Instinctively Mike reaches inside his coat—whether for his gun or his wallet, he couldn't say. "I—I'm a friend of a friend."

Sherri smirks. "Got a lot of friends, baby. Refresh my memory."

Mike swallows, hard. Something seems to be caught in his throat. It knocks against his tongue when he tries to speak, deforming the words. "A—dagebeck."

"Come again?"

Much slower, this time: "Adage Beck."

Sherri recoils, slipping on some stray garbage. When he tries to help her, she avoids his touch. "Get *off* me," she snarls.

"You knew her, right?"

"Damn straight I knew her. That chick was stone crazy. Nuts. And you're her *friend*?"

"Look, it's important. You know where she is?"

Sherri wrenches away, flattening herself against the inside of the door.

"One time," she says, suddenly clear and calm. "Only one time, and then I don't ever wanna see your face again. Me and Susan, we had a room down in Chinatown. And one night she brings back another chick she found on the street. Your friend."

Adage, Mike breathes.

"So we're doing pretty well here, right? Except our johns start disappearing. And they turn up dead, all over the Strip. It's in the papers. Cops're finding them in pieces. And none of them got any skin, right? Like somebody tore it off."

And Mike sees early morning. 1980, peering through the windshield of his Dad's truck at something. Something small, and nude, and black with flies. Something without a face.

As the smell rises and settles, rises and settles, like a tide.

"So I start noticing stuff. Like how she smells weird, like meat that's gone off. And she sleeps all day, and she's always wearing the same clothes. Whatever. And then Susan's gone. And they find another body, out back of Ryerson. And that night I come home early, and your girlfriend's standing there—"

Sherri chokes.

And: *I don't want to hear this*, Mike thinks. *I really don't.*

"She was wearing Susan's—Susan's—"

A nearby street lamp goes out.

"Sherri?"

Sherri looks up, mascara dripping.

"I'm going now," she says, and does.

* * *

"I was three months in the hospital, but I don't remember any of it. Just a long, red blank.

"And the silence.

"When I resurfaced, they told me Larry was dead. They said it was suicide.

" . . . likely.

"So I got better, and moved away. You wrote for awhile, and I appreciated it. Then, eventually, you stopped.

"I wasn't too surprised.

"I went to Toronto, and I was fine for a long, long time. I lived in the waking world, and brushed my teeth twice a day. I thought bright little thoughts which flashed once and were gone, just like everybody else. I went to school. I even had friends.

"Years slipped by.

"Until—it happened.

"Again."

* * *

Across the street from the Meat Market, Adage leans against a lamppost, waiting for her evening's prey to reveal itself. It's finally stopped raining. The gutters overflow with light.

At 12:22, a girl in a tight pink plastic slicker breaks rank—struggling, briefly, with some unseen partner—and jumps the last two steps, falling into her customary strut as she clicks away.

Sherri, Adage thinks with a little stab.

She didn't expect it to be her tonight.

Other—worthier—candidates still linger outside the Market's doors: That older woman, whose smile seems penciled on over a lipless slash of a mouth. The boy in the leather jacket, whose ears are fringed with tiny silver rings. The girl with a freshly-bloodied nose, whose pendant proclaims her to be a HOT CHICK.

But take what you can get, babe, and count yourself lucky.

Adage lets Sherri's footsteps die away before rising to follow.

The moon sees her coming, and narrows appraisingly.

* * *

"Graduation night, I let a boy I barely knew drive me up the hill to that spot we'd all heard so much about. And we sat there, side by side in the car, staring at the city below. He shuffled his feet, and coughed, and finally put his arms around me. And there in the dark, between the bars of a Depeche Mode song, I felt something change. A key in a lock. A red river rising, a hot red tide finally coming in, high enough to drown us both.

"And when he turned to kiss me, he sniffed the air and gagged.

"And I just smiled."

Then, in a whisper:

"And it was so sweet, Mike. Like sex. Only so much better.

"Like Larry.

"And I remember it all."

* * *

Pushing her way past the Totally Concerned With Sex Shop, Sherri hangs a right in front of Girls! Live! Girls! Nude! and disappears. Her scent remains, though fading fast.

Adage swallows, tasting dust.

It'll be over soon enough, she thinks.

And walks even faster.

* * *

Mike rounds the corner and sees her up ahead: A slight woman in a long, cloth coat, fashionably cut. A toque pulled down over her ears. Shabby. Anonymous. Totally unseasonal.

Adage?

She pauses at the crosswalk. Her face is very pale against the dark. White and flat, and oddly limp. Motionless, except for a pair of searching eyes.

As she bends to press the signal change button, a lock of hair spills from her hat—

Ad—

Blonde.

Mike feels his heart deflate.

You stupid sucker, he thinks. *She's dead in a ditch somewhere. You blew your education to get here, and she's dead. Probably died while you were still on the bus.*

The woman reaches up to scratch behind her ear. Maybe to tuck back the lock.

Stupid, stupid, stupid.

Instead, she—

what?

— digs her nails into the side of her neck, and rips.

The skin flaps slightly as she shifts weight.

Oh, God.

Delicately, Adage reaches further in, to scratch the raw flesh underneath.

* * *

The signal changes. Adage spots Sherri on the opposite side—twenty feet ahead, and gaining speed.

Behind her, a movement.

Sherri pauses, nose wrinkling.

The wind has changed.

And the smell boils up from Adage now—an invisible glove of uncured hide, reaching in every direction at once. Prodded by the stench, Sherri turns—

— to meet Adage's eyes.

"Uh," she says, then, "Susan?"

Hardly.

And Mike freezes, as Sherri starts to run.

* * *

"So why am I telling you all this?"

"Larry was dumb. He wanted power, but he was too lazy to take his own risks. So he tricked me into opening the door, because he thought he could control me. Afterward. When what was always inside me finally came ripping up to meet the waking world, all raw and naked and hungry.

"And he was so wrong it's kind of funny.

"I live my life the way I was meant to now. I get up, and I get dressed, and I go out and meet someone new. And then we dance. And then I take what's left of them home and sew it back together, and the whole thing starts over again.

"Winter's better. They can't smell you coming, at least not as well. But summer's okay too, because by the time the cops find them there's very little to even identify, and I'm gone long before they can.

"I keep my nose clean. I don't get caught.

"But I'm lonely.

"And I don't know how long I want to go on like this. But I don't know how to stop, either. Or even if I can.

"So—

"—find me, Mike.

"And do whatever suits you, when you do."

* * *

The parking lot behind King Fook's. *This is it,* Adage thinks, through her haze.

At last.

She takes a last step, mainly for effect.

Sherri moans, runs straight into the back gate, scrabbles at it for a moment, then bounces back. It holds, locked tight for the night.

"God!" she screams.

Adage pauses to remove her coat, which is far, far too expensive to dry clean.

Sherri falls to her knees, sobbing, as much with anger as with fear.

And Adage starts to shake.

Sherri looks up, her cupped hands full of snot.

Adage throws her head back. The naked moon, visible at last, ripples in time to her shivering. A red joy cracks her ribs.

And Sherri just watches—

— as Adage rears up, full size, the corners of her mouth breaking open. Rips inch towards either ear. Impatient, she thrusts her hands inside, and pulls.

"Adage!"

To her right. From the elevators.

Sherri stumbles vertical, using the fence for support.

Adage turns, drooling blood.

In surprise: *Mike?*

He came.

The fence's lock explodes.

Sherri shrieks. Adage matches her, high and harsh, like a carrion bird sighting a hearse.

She lunges.

"Adage—no!"

And as she turns again, Sherri slips under her arms, disappearing around the corner.

Mike and Adage are left, face to face, with only a gun and ten feet left between them.

Hesitant: "Adage?"

Slouched like a praying mantis, the thing wearing Susan's skin gives a dust-dry laugh.

"See—for—your—self," she says.

And steps into the light.

Mike's hand—wavers.

Partially stripped, her bloodied skull nods moronically, face a crossfire of nerves. Her nose hangs flat, the torn half-mouth slack. She jerks her head aside, and both flap open, revealing the craters at their roots. A lipless grin chatters from chin to ear.

The nude moon of her left eye bulges and slits, blankly, as its lid smears itself shut.

"I—guess—this—means—you—heard—the—tape."

Mike gulps.

Adage seems to smile. Then the change grips again.

Mike staggers back, gun at knee-level, as blood sprays.

Adage's borrowed skin snaps at its seams, rucking up like a pair of old tights. She peels herself free. Beneath, the bulge of raw, red flesh. Muscles and mucous, thrust center-stage, spurt and writhe and glisten. Gristle follows, flashing taunting little hints of bone. A spine, vertebrae cracking like a whip as she moves closer. Hands, busy with tendons. Nails, still growing.

Slick, and pale, and sharp.

"Oh, Adage," Mike whispers.

"What's the matter, baby?"

Almost hear enough to touch, now.

"You're like this too, underneath," she says. "Know that? You *all* are."

Half-blind with tears, Mike brings the gun up.

"Stay away, Adage."

"Oh, but I can't. Don't you see I'm naked?"

Her hand, reaching. Claws ruffle his hair.

"Adage, please."

"You who have so much," says Adage Beck, no longer even faintly human. "Old pal, old buddy, old friend of mine. You who have so much, I pray—lend me a yard or two of hide to clothe my awful shame."

And Mike—

—fires.

SEEN

INT. APARTMENT. DAY.

RED, oddly textured, fills the screen.

> DETECTIVE CARVALHO (O.S.)
> So whatcha got for me here?

PULL BACK. The RED is revealed as a splotch of BLOOD on a rug.

> RAY WRAY (O.S.)
> Something sharp . . .

> CARVALHO (O.S.)
> (Unimpressed)
> Yeah, no shit.

We KEEP PULLING BACK, revealing more and more splotches—a definite trail, like spray from an invisible wound . . . a whole bunch of invisible wounds. Then a tail-end of CRIME-SCENE TAPE and the chalk OUTLINE of where a body used to be.

RAY (undistinguished, middle 30's) is down on his knees next to the OUTLINE, checking notes on his clipboard. He wears plastic gloves and a disposable coverall.

                        RAY
                      (Points)
    . . . thin, no edge, no blade. Kind of rounded,
    maybe an awl, or a big needle.

                      CARVALHO
    What, like some kinda mad knitter?

A NEW ANGLE establishes the rest of the room: Mass slaughter, but no bodies—just tape, chalk and blood trails.

                        RAY
    Well, I need to do more tests, obviously. But
    the closest parallel I can get you right now
    is something the size of a catheter or a
    trocar, like what they use for draining off
    fluid during an autopsy.
                      (Gets up, turns to point)
    So here's how it plays out . . .

CARVALHO turns too. He sees—

HIS P.O.V.: A QUICK CUT of an outline next to the fridge.

                      RAY (O.S.)
    Mr Riker's in the kitchen, getting himself some
    Minute Maid; Mrs Riker's checking the roast.

E.C.U. of an ORANGE JUICE CONTAINER overturned in a dried stain of juice, combined with streaks of red: Equally dry BLOOD.

                      RAY (O.S.)
    Kids are watching TV.

SOUND F/X: The CLICK of a TV dial; TV sound.

E.C.U. of the TV's flickering blue light, cast on the floor between screen and couch.

> RAY (O.S.)
> Our killer comes in through the front door,
> pretty much right behind them, and . . .

ANGLED E.C.U., almost parallel with the jamb, of the front DOOR swinging gently open. FLASH EFFECT.

MONTAGE, linked by FLASH EFFECTS: CRIME SCENE PHOTOS of each body as it was discovered.

—The freshly BLOOD-SOAKED COUCH, with RIKER CHILD ONE and RIKER CHILD TWO's bodies vaguely glimpsed, sprawled in either direction at the bottom of the frame.

—MRS RIKER's SHOE, kicked against the wall, half-submerged in a flood of BLOOD.

—MR RIKER on the kitchen floor, full on. ORANGE JUICE everywhere, hands raised and bloody, pierced eye-sockets staring in horror at his attacker.

CUT BACK to RAY and CARVALHO.

> RAY
> We've got defensive wounds, but nothing offensive—no fighting back, no evasion.
> It's like they never saw it coming.

> CARVALHO
> Drugs?

> RAY
> Not unless the kids were on the same stuff.

CARVALHO's gaze shifts to—

HIS P.O.V.:—A casual group PHOTO of the Riker family stuck up on the fridge door. They look nice, normal, happy.

TRACK OVER. On the wall, written in blood: SEE ME.

BLACK SCREEN. OVER:

> RAY (V.O.)
> Whoever it was washed off in the bathroom, afterwards. We found blood traces in the shower, but no human detritus—

INT. RESTAURANT. DAY.

RAY and his sister, LEEANNE WRAY, are sitting over their dinner.

> RAY
> —no hairs, no fibers. Like they were just sponging the blood off a coat made from rubber or vinyl, one of those plastic, uh—

> LEEANNE
> —slickers.
> (Wry)
> Nice dinner conversation, Ray.

> RAY
> Yeah, I guess. Sorry.
> (After a moment)
> You, uh . . . hear from—them?

INSERT SHOT: A family PHOTO, posed vaguely like the one in the RIKER home—except that the parents (MR and MRS WRAY, LEEANNE and RAY's father and mother) are barely looking at each other, and neither are looking at the little boy and girl (CHILD RAY and CHILD LEEANNE) posed uncomfortably at their feet.

BACK TO ANGLE ON LEEANNE, who shrugs.

                            LEEANNE

Not lately. You?

INSERT SHOT: The same PHOTO, CLOSER UP. Only CHILD RAY and CHILD LEEANNE are visible.

BACK TO ANGLE ON RAY, who shakes his head.

                            LEEANNE

Well.

INSERT SHOT: The same PHOTO, E.C.U. Only CHILD RAY and CHILD LEEANNE's eyes are visible.

                            LEEANNE (V.O.)

Not like they ever noticed we were there, anyway.

BACK TO ANGLE ON RAY, who looks uncomfortable.

                            RAY

That's kinda harsh.
                    (She raises a brow)
I mean, it's over, right? We got over it.

                            LEEANNE
                    (A dry laugh)
YOU did, baby bro. Me?
                    (Points at the waiter)
We've been here, what? Two hours? Raise your hand, he's there. Skips right over ME, though. Must be able to tell I'm not the one with the Gold Card.

                            RAY

Lee. C'mon . . .

He glances out the window, and sees—

RAY's P.O.V.—a WOMAN wearing a see-through RAINCOAT, coming towards him, walking against the grain of the crowd.

E.C.U. ON HIS EYES, locking—

E.C.U.—on hers.

NEW ANGLE. The WOMAN reacts, as though startled that he's looking at her at all. She pauses, turns, stares.

NEW ANGLE. RAY reacts, startled by HER reaction. He meets and matches her gaze, like: Yes?

> LEEANNE (O.S.)
> Ray. Ray. Heh-LO?

PULL OUT as she snaps her fingers in his face; he looks at her. She leans back, annoyed but vindicated.

> LEEANNE
> Now, THAT's what I'm talking about.

RAY glances back. Behind him—

RAY's P.O.V.—the WOMAN is gone.

INT. RAY's APARTMENT. NIGHT.

SOUND F/X: A MICROWAVE BUZZER goes off.

RAY sits at the kitchen table, eating a microwave dinner. WE HEAR the TV in the background.

> TV ANNOUNCER (V.O.)
> ... still have no explanation for the complete lack of witnesses, but maintain that forensic evidence recovered from the scenes holds a clue to the mysterious ...

LATER. RAY lies on the floor, working out, doing flys with a barbell in either hand. The TV is still on.

                    TV INTERVIEWEE (V.O.)
          ... "estrangement": A certain—alienation—
          from society and the world around them. A
          sense of being somehow, somehow ...

LATER. RAY is in the bathroom, door open. WE HEAR the sound of running water. The TV is still on.

                    TV PREACHER (V.O.)
          ... 'unseen creatures fill the air, both when
          we wake and when we sleep.' This, my friends,
          is much like how the Lord's invisible but
          constant presence ...

LATER. RAY, hair wet and wrapped in a towel, sits in front of the TV paying bills. He isn't looking at the screen, but BLUE FLICKERING LIGHT illuminates his face.

                    TV SPORTS GUY (V.O.)
          ... hoo! Buddy, that's GOTTA hurt. In
          football, meanwhile ...

A surge of blooper-clip MUSIC. RAY shuts his eyes.

CLICK. BLACK SCREEN.

E.C.U. RAY's eyes SNAP open.

NEW ANGLE. The WOMAN from the street is standing over him, still wearing her see-through RAINCOAT.

                    WOMAN
          You can SEE me.

                    RAY

What?

WOMAN
See.

INSERT SHOT, with FLASH effect: The bloody word, on the Riker kitchen wall.

WOMAN
Me.

ON RAY, with FLASH EFFECT: His eyes WIDEN. He's suddenly realized just WHERE he's heard/seen this before.

WOMAN
Out of which EYE can you see me?

RAY
(Dry mouth)
... both.

WOMAN
THAT's a pity.

A blurred MOVEMENT, just on the edge of the frame, as she— E.C.U.—brings up a big needle, like a TROCAR.

BLACK SCREEN.

SOUND F/X: We HEAR a puncturing thunk, followed by a SCREAM.

FIRST CREDIT ROLLS.

SOUND F/X: The same noise, again.

ROLL CREDITS.

TORCH SONG

You are labeled the dark or black Goddess,
the Goddess of graves, killer of man, the unholy.
At Delphi, you are known as Aphrodite on the Tomb.
—Christine Downing

Don't threaten me with love, baby."
— Billie Holiday

Sweat, fever—I woke coughing glass. Down to Lee Earle's for twelve on the dot, just him, me and the other regulars: Two any-age habitual D-and-D offenders—one male, one not—and a clutch of pyramid-scheme drones from the strip-mall office space, still loud and wired after an all-night selling jag.

Listening to Georgia Gibbs' "Kiss of Fire" on endless repeat, slowly teasing my lingering bourbon-fume haze back into a righteous full-on drunk; studying the scar tissue on my knuckles, wondering just how long I would have to keep this up before I either died from liver damage or got myself killed in a brawl. I hoped not that much longer, but suspected I hoped in vain.

The count: Four years this Valentine's, and still going.

The record, thus far unbroken: Never any more than two or so days spent sober, in between trips to the dry-out ward or the tank.

"Hit me," I told Lee Earle, tapping my glass. Got a sideways glare back: Hung-over voodoo eyes. Like he wanted to take me literal, but didn't have the guts. I slammed the bourbon, tapped it again.

"Your old partner's back in town," he said, leaning to fill 'er up.

"Lookinland. You hear about that?"

"No," I said. "I didn't."

"Well, he is."

Another swallow—it went down burning, hot and hard, straight to where I always used to think my heart was located. Before I knew better.

Lee Earle: "Did a Quantico internship, now he's mister big-shit honorary profiler, with a hard-on for cults and crazies. Pitched them some new division—same old freak-show cases you guys used to break back when. Like that rape/snuff job they found Monday on Jenner, in the vacant lot."

"Didn't hear about that, either."

He reached under the bar, threw me a copy of the *Highlight*. "Try reading the paper every once in a while, Proulx. In between drinks."

Fresh ink, smeared fingerprints. The headline, all screaming caps: BRUTAL MURDER! "TORTURED," SAYS CORONER! LOCAL BOY TO HEAD! Behind me, Georgia's sour-sweet pipes wailed on over piano-wire strings—Argentinian whore-house tango turned over-orchestrated Hollyweird torch song, the words a bad-translation joke. *If I'm a slave, then it's a slave I want to be!*

Beck's familiar face stared up at me where he knelt by the body, lifting a tarpaulin corner with his pen—a black-on-grey collage, all dots and shadows. New suit, new grey paling his short brown hair, new glasses: Plastic frames—easier to break, harder to embed. A thin white shadow of raised keloiding along the length of his occipital bone.

Don't pity me!

More bourbon, acid on a sandpaper tongue.

Don't pity me!

His dark, level eyes under dark, level brows, gaze narrow and discreet as ever. A hidden bruise.

Hadn't seen him in the flesh since the day he walked into the locker room, put his crushed and purple nose next to mine, and told me if I ever got this close to him again, he'd shoot me cold and call it self-defense. And all I could think of then, like all I could think of now: How bad I wanted to feel the sharp, new-moon ridge of his scar on my tongue; to taste and trace the damage I'd made, in the heat of the moment.

Smelling his hair, his skin. Feeling my heart swell, rib-locked, so quick and huge it made me want to cry.

Me.

I put the paper down. To Lee Earle: "This dump got a phone?"

"Not for free, it don't."

Twenty on the counter—receiver in my hand, low-grade magic. I punched the station switchboard, gambling on booze-soaked memory. Itchy flame stinging at my eyes and groin, lighting my way.

Beck's nameplate, hovering phantom in the dark behind my forehead: A blind neon pain.

* * *

"I wish you love, Detective," she whispered to me, as she went by—Mrs Silas. First name Maria, N.M.I. I looked it up in her file. Her head was bowed, hair hanging in her eyes; just a breath of a phrase on my cheek, consonants etched in bile and honey. Beck didn't even hear her.

I did. And laughed, because it didn't seem like much of a curse. At the time.

* * *

Afterwards, I went home, called it in from my own line. I.A. found me ten hours later, so long gone they could have used my blood to spike the V-Day party punch.

They brought me a letter of resignation to sign; I signed it. No charges pressed, no publicity, no pension—some deal. Better than I deserved.

They told me Beck told them I did it. I allowed as how I had.

Asked me why.

I swore to Christ I did not know.

Now: Four years later, and I know it all. Not that it helps one fuck.

* * *

"Lieutenant Beckwith Lookinland, Ritual Crimes."

"Beck."

Silence—not even breathing. Went on so long I actually started saying, into it: "It's, uh—"

"I know who it is, David."

So cold.

I bit the inside of my cheek. Told myself: *Don't say it. Do* not *say it.*

"This girl in the lot—"

"I'm not going to discuss police business with you."

"Look, I just think I might have something."

"Well, we did set up a line for tips—just a minute, I'll get you their number."

"Fine, that's how you want to play it. Here's your tip, okay? The Cyprian Temple's reopened. Down on Quentin. Off of Jenner."

"We're already looking into some leads."

"That one of them?"

No answer.

"C'mon, Beck," I said. "You know what this reminds you of."

"Talking to you reminds me of a lot of things, David."

"You gonna check it out, at least?"

Beck paused. Carefully: "You are not my partner any more, David. You aren't even a cop. This is not your case, and I am not having this conversation."

"Oh, fuck you, Beck," I snapped back. "All I want to do is help."

"And why would that be, I wonder?"

Thinking: *Do* not.

Synaptic finger-pop. Bone echo.

Anything else but that.

Electroshock crackle to the limbic region. My dick jerking up like Hitler's arm, meat-puppet on a string.

Blurting, unable to stop myself:

"Because I *love* you."

"So you keep saying," he replied, and hung up.

* * *

Four years. It was a milk run, pure career P.R.: Do your superior a solid, and move on up. Eugene Silas, career Narco snitch, twenty years departmentally connected—gave up the straight line, time after time, on anybody dumb enough to try for a crossover market in weed, pills, H. Main hobbies included whores and wife-beating, up until Mrs Silas went suddenly missing. Instant recipe for dinner party disaster, right there; shaky host, no hostess.

So: Silas called the Cap, Beck and me caught the squeal.

We met at the Silas house, traded coffee for a wedding photo two-shot—Mrs S., dark-haired and delicate in off-white with pearls, pancake makeup layered on over what looked like fresh welts.

"I ran the initial interview already," Beck told me. "No prior skips, no relatives in town. No friends—or boyfriends—he knows of, though I suspect that doesn't mean much."

"Gumshoe shitwork," I said. "Better wipe your day-planner for the next week or so."

Beck shrugged. "Maybe not."

Easy call—some meter-reader made Silas' car an hour later, parked outside the Temple. Cyprian for Cyprus, birthplace of the Greek love Goddess Aphrodite, lez poet Sappho's favorite patron. This according to Beck, who did enough degrees (Eng. Lit, Crim. Psych, Anthro) to quote me in detail more books than I ever had time to read. Like so:

Nothing is left of me each time I see you . . . tongue numbed, arms, legs melting, on fire . . .

I took a pull off my paper-bag bourbon breakfast, absorbed this. "And the moral is, thinking with your dick rots your brain."

Beck's crooked smile, the sardonic version: Oh, you big lug! "Sappho didn't have a dick *per se*, David."

"Yeah, well—whatever."

Another pull. I offered Beck the next; he passed, like I knew he would. Never saw him drink once, on the job or off.

Not even . . . later on. When I—

But anyways.

The Cyprians worshiped Love with a capital L, that catch-all cheat of a concept. Intimacy, affection, loyalty. Lust. Ideal into intent: The generative and the destructive. The spiritual lighter-flick at the heart of every secret thing.

Or, as Georgia puts it:

I touch your lips, and all at once the sparks go flying . . . .

"So they shack and fuck, and call it a religion," I said, slugging the bottle dry. "So Mrs Silas likes a little ceremony with her extracurricular cock. She's over eighteen."

"Silas wants her back—what happens after we drop her off is their business. Besides, laissez-faire only goes so far, when some cult leader's busy making bucks from whipping his followers into an erotic frenzy. Love's a pretty volatile emotion at the best of times."

"And you're brown-nosing for a rank raise. Get it straight, Beck—not everything's a favor or photo op."

Coolly: "No. Just the things that matter."

Two days before Valentine's; I Luv Eazy-Rock from every passing car window, rising candy-apple stink. Scarlet sans-serif magazine covers, blaring bad advice. TEN SEX SECRETS MEN FLIP FOR! WHAT WOMEN REALLY WANT! LONELY HEARTS ASK: "HOW WILL I KNOW?"

"Love," I said, "ain't nothing but sex misspelled. To lift a well-worn phrase."

"Why, David, I never knew; you're a genuine romantic."

"Just a realist, college boy. Strip away the fancy rhymes, it all comes down to this—nobody ever said 'I love you' for free."

. . . for though it burns me and it turns me into ashes, my whole world crashes without your kiss of fire.

* * *

I can still remember not loving Beck—not liking him even, all that much. Me, Big Dave Proulx, slow-track shithouse uniform loser. Bruiser, cunt-hound, borderline crank-junkie: Bad attitude personified. A string of formative moral clusterfucks had left me disappointed with the world, so I made up for it by toiletizing my own last chances, one by one by one. Spent my shifts getting high and wasting time, cruising for trouble in bad neighborhoods, waiting to get insulted and go ape on some (mainly) undeserving repeat offender.

Officer Beckwith Lookinland was the only one who ever trusted me to do more than lose my temper and botch my collars. A prodigy, Cap's pet pick for surrogate son: He'd done his research, heard about a couple of righteous busts I'd done Year One, wanted to know more. He chatted me up, drew me out—sat quiet with me whenever I showed up to work with the cold sweats, three days no sleep, all bed-stink and bad breath. Covered my procedural blank spots. Wouldn't leave me alone.

And after the brass implied he could basically name his own partner, he asked for me.

He rewrote me, that pretty, prissy rookie. Got me sober. Made sure I stayed sober, those times it really mattered. There was a puzzle called human evil that needed solving, and he wanted me in on it. He made detective, made sergeant, took me along for the ride. My fitness reports went up for the first time in ten years.

He was a living rebuke: An effortlessly good cop. Not that he ever saw it that way. Or ever conceived that I could have.

It poisoned me, poisoned us—what happened at the Temple, with Mrs Silas, just its most overt expression. This whispered curse from a beaten bride, this unlooked-for gift from a long-dead Goddess. This friendship I never wanted. This partnership I never prized. This . . .

 . . . *love, Detective.*

Back in the here and now, I close my eyes, pound booze. Lee Earle at my elbow—somebody else wants the phone.

Beck's wry/cold voice in my head, looping back on itself. Two versions, overlapped: Past and present; pre- vs. post-; before and after.

All my muscles knotting and humming just to hear it—my heart, my groin. This unkillable love still alive in every part of me, like cancer.

"I love you, Beck," I told him for the first and worst time, that Valentine's Day night, on the steps of his suburban house. "I'm yours, you're mine. I could never hurt you. Never."

Not 'til a few minutes later, at least.

* * *

Last call. Out onto the street, booze-burned and fever-bright, glass in my lungs again. Down to check out the Jenner lot: Blurred chalk outline, yellow tape just left lying—homicide haiku.

Some of my sources still talk to me. I used them to dummy up my own case-jacket, following Beck's semi-warm evidence trail.

The dead girl's name: McLay, Monica Ellen. 26. Good tits, bad buck teeth. Good record down at the Quentin Street Safeway—two years, night-shift floor manager. Her boss said he'd seen this guy from the Temple checking her out.

Illiterate mash notes slipped under the back door. "Afrodytee sez yr da 1 fr me." Met the guy on a bank run, told him to take a hike. Laughed hard about it later—as if.

Forensics: Cracked skull, blunt instrument; swelling and haematoma at the base of the brain—she was unconscious before it started, dead ten minutes in. Rape kit positive, post-mortem. Trauma to the outer genitalia, cauterization to the inner.

Hypothesis: Same stalker mofo from the bank approached her from behind, slugged her, dragged her to where they wouldn't be disturbed. Got busy. Then stuck an iron up inside her (soldering or curling, battery-operated) and turned it on. An open letter to the general public, corpse-written.

Not enough, just to drop her and do her the once. This skell had ambitions—total ownership. Possession, inside and out.

I'm the best you ever had, the last you ever will. I love you so much I'd kill for you, die for you. I love you too much to let you live.

You leave me, mock me, turn me down, and I'll eat your beating heart.

I knew the impulse, intimately.

Wished to—Christ Jesus, Aphrodite, who-fucking-ever—that I didn't.

* * *

Back at my place, too drunk to sleep, too late for much else. Eyes closed: The Temple.

Mrs. Silas.

Beck.

Records had the Temple owned by one Adonis Herson, born Graham M. Knowlton. No priors, nothing outstanding. Beck favored the direct route; I agreed. More chances to get into something.

Long story short—she wouldn't come. They wouldn't make her.

"We don't interfere," Herson told us. "The heart wants what it wants."

Beck shot me an eyebrow. Gently quizzical: "Didn't I hear somebody else say that?"

I snorted. "Yeah—Woody Allen, when Mia asked him why he was bonin' the kids."

Mrs. Silas and her guy, some unnamed cult member, standing arm in arm behind Herson. The rest of them in a supportive U around them: Red-robes/low-cleavage. Fresh flowers everywhere you looked, huge holiday wreaths and bouquets—massy, dripping, belled cups of fragrance, spilling sickly-sweet. Red candle shadows flickering on the walls, filtered through taped-together star displays of candy-heart lollipops. Too many smiles, *waaay* too much smug, quiet tolerance. As though they could read all the pain and rage I ran on at once, but didn't care enough to give it much cred—just had me tagged as kind of old, kind of sad, and kind of ineffectual, even with my gun bulging out the side of my jacket for everybody to see. Worth a warm and sticky slice of their sympathy, if not their full attention.

An offhand mental group hug from everyone in the room: There there, big man.

It made me so mad my teeth hurt.

Beck watching me, sidelong. My partner, looking for a cue to follow.

No probable cause. No legal grounds to do anything but leave, and tell the

Cap we blew his choice assignments—back in the shithouse for another ten years plus, this time with Beck to keep me company. All that energy and effort, gone to waste; all right for me, sure. Par for the course.

But not for him.

To Herson: "You don't interfere?"

"Never."

Well, okay.

I nodded, turned to Mrs. Silas. Said, conversationally: "So how about I let you make up your own mind, lady? 'Cause here's the options. You come home. Or this piece of beef—" I pointed out the Cyprian stud—"eats the rest of his Valentine's candy through a straw."

"David," said Beck.

I started rolling up my sleeves. "Look the other way, college boy. You wanna make Chief by thirty-five, you gotta start getting good at that."

Beck: "*Dave*, I don't—"

"Shut up, Beck," I said. And I hit Mrs. Silas' guy full tilt boogie, so hard I popped a vein in his cheek with my high school ring: Pure black/red boom, spurt, all over my nice new tie.

Mrs. Silas was tough. It took cult-boy coughing teeth through his nose, liberally slimed with bloody phlegm, before she finally stiff-legged it over. Telling Beck: "I'm ready now."

Beck, to me: "We're leaving."

A last kick to the stud, flipping him—black/red ebbing, but slow. I gave him one more stomp to the gut, just for luck. Blood on my shoes: I scraped them clean on the floor-mosaic Aphrodite's bare breasts.

To Herson: "Nice religion you got there, shitbird. Stand back, do nothing. I could get used to this."

He looked at me then, at last, full on. Light blue eyes—cerulean, they call them. Water on white stone; submerged Greek ruins.

"I'll remember you said that, Detective Proulx."

* * *

Beck made Lieutenant two months later, after they threw me off. A week of all-night drunks got me crazy enough to connect the dots—camped outside the Temple, straight-up begged Herson to take this thing off me. His only answer, just what you'd expect: He wouldn't interfere. Ever.

Mrs. Silas' curse. Mrs. Silas' call. I would have crawled ten miles on broken glass to eat her pussy all day, if I thought it'd do any good.

Except I knew, because Beck told me—Silas had already thrown her down the stairs an hour after we took her home, for talking back. Broke her little neck like a twig.

* * *

Lying here. Burning. Tonight and every right.

Beck across town, somewhere. Working, maybe—maybe doing the same. But not like me. Not for me.

I made damn sure of that.

Valentine's Day night, I woke up at 3:00 a.m., thinking: *I gotta apologize. Gotta go find Beck, and apologize for the whole Silas thing. He thinks I was out of line, and he's right; I gotta tell him. 'Cause he's my partner, my only friend. And because . . .*

. . . I love him.

It swept up on me, then and there—this painful need to kiss him till his lips were one big bruise, bite his tongue and drink his bloody spit. Slap him barely conscious, then go at him till he opened those narrow eyes wide—do him so rough he fought me back, fought me with everything he had, then keep right on and do him some more. Hurt him like I hurt. Break him down.

Show him I was his, and make him mine.

The truth, plain and simple, a razor in my heart: That's love, to me—all I know, all I'm capable of.

I could get used to this. And I guess I have, in my own way. Got used to this love, like insects swarming in and on me, everywhere at once—this love, a cage of sick shivers. This love, the stink of my own quick rot. Gangrene hot flash, indistinguishable from envy, from anger, from anguish. This Goddamn love I bear for the fine fellow officer whose head I slammed against the tiles, whose ribs I broke to hold him still, who I fucked hard up the ass till he screamed out loud, clawing and squirming, smart mouth gone dumb with pain. No lube, no finesse, no climax for anybody but me—no respect, no dignity. No mercy.

Just love, love, love.

I lay there, thinking it. Wanting it. Which was bad enough, all told.

But then I got up, drove to Beck's house. And actually did it.

* * *

Morning came, barely. Too early for Lee Earle—I leaned back against the alley wall, collar up. Caught a flashing red light from the corner of my eye: Cheap cop symbology, a jolt to the spine, reflexes obviously still in the process of dying hard. Two radio cars, one unmarked—Beck's, probably.

Ritual Crimes, parked outside the Cyprian Temple.

I followed along, made myself scarce. Saw him come out, flanked by uniforms—Herson and company hanging back at the top of the steps, a shadowed red mass. Watching.

Not interfering.

Beck gave orders, headed for his car. Then stopped, as I stepped from the shadows.

Five paces left between us, give or take. My hands cold, palms wet; heart a stroked lesion, a ticking caffeine fit.

His dark eyes turned on me for the first time in six whole years. One look, one single glance—watchful fear vs. barely-controlled hate, with only a slight procedural correctness chaser—and I was already up and running, aching to fuck or fight. Or both.

Staring him down, hair-trigger; a potential breath away from death, and just about ready to come in my pants.

Quiet: "I have a gun, David."

"Well, good. Wouldn't want you on the job without one."

He looked at me. I waited. Got no response. Took another step, tentative:

"Beck, I—"

He pivoted down, drawing quick—safety off, locked and loaded. Two-hand stance, held steady. Voice shaking, just a little bit.

"You just—stop. You . . . just stand right there."

My own hands up, empty. "Okay. See? I'm doing it. This is me, standing. See?"

"*There*, David. I *will* shoot, believe me."

"Baby, I'd probably thank you if you did."

We looked at each other again. Me still, him calmer. After a moment: "Mind if I ask some questions?"

"As long as you don't call me baby."

Glance back at the Temple—doors shut, now. A soft red light in every window.

"They got your guy in there, hidden. Claiming some kind of religious sanctuary, am I right?"

"You're right."

"Got a warrant yet?"

"It's on its way."

Conversation at its curtest. Like pulling teeth, only a lot less fun.

"You talked to Herson."

"Yes."

"So—what did he have to say? 'Bout your boy, I mean. Or is he still playing it strictly non-interference?"

Beck lowered his eyes, raised them. Gave me a stare, stretched long and level. Contemplative, almost.

"This is the last time I ever talk to you directly, David," he said finally. "Ever. Unless I'm reading you your rights."

"I know."

A sigh. "The murderer's name is Luther Louvin. He's been with them for five months. Herson said they all knew what he was going to do—knew it long before he did it. Apparently, he talked about it all the time."

"And natch, they didn't feel this meant they had to do anything to stop him."

"Herson said, and I quote: Love comes the way it comes. All its forms are equally valid."

An echo in his voice, almost familiar. Four years ago, he would have given me that crooked smile—shared insight acknowledged, the whole partner thing at work. But not now.

Never now.

Love comes the way it comes.

"But you . . . don't share that view."

"You know I don't."

The barely-veiled implication: *And both of us know why.*

Then, briskly: "I don't have a lot of time, so here's the rest. Herson only said one other thing, that if I couldn't understand why they gave Louvin shelter, then I didn't know what real love was. The kind of love that's the purest expression of who you are." A pause. "But that I would . . . and soon."

"He said that."

"That's what I said."

"I guess—" slowly—"you probably wouldn't believe me, if I told you that was a threat."

This time, Beck really did smile: All thin and straight, these days—not wry, so much, as bitter. Replying, with deceptive ease: "It wouldn't surprise me. Although, to be fair, the only person who's ever threatened me with love . . . is you, David."

Fever, rising fresh. Glass cough shattering on impact, lodging deep; black ice splinters of night air in the back of my throat, unmelted. Beck saw, and opened the car door. He sat down, gun still kept on me—one-handed, so he could turn the key. The ignition roared, caught.

But before he could shut it, I said, quickly: "Beck—I won't say 'I love you' any more, okay? 'Cause I know you don't believe me. But what I did—to you—"

"Yes?"

His dark stare, waiting for some kind of easy answer. The name of the puzzle: Human evil. The proof: His rapist ex-partner, drunk and crazy, straining to explain why he broke every bond of trust imaginable—to make it all clear and clean, somehow. Wash it away with a few choice words, if nothing else.

Trying. And failing miserably.

"Like Herson says: 'It's just . . . the way I am'."

Beck shut the car door in my face. Then rolled the window down, just a crack—enough to be heard through. And replied: "Then that's a pity, David. Because I always wanted to think you were something more."

* * *

The Cyprians say Love, capital "L", is whatever you make of it—is *you*, to the infinite. You outside of you, loving someone like you love yourself; more than, actually.

In my case, it'd have to be.

I wish you love, Detective.

Real love.

Love the way you are.

Love, my emotional brain tumor. Love, my habit, my jones. My uncontrollable urge. My will to power. Love, my unscratched itch—my addiction, with all the word entails:

Ecstasy, mania, withdrawal. My suicide in progress.

I couldn't have love soft and sweet if I tried—I know, believe me, because I have. I really have.

And suffering Christ! Just look what happened then.

* * *

Valentine's Day night, four years ago: Rang the doorbell twice, three times.

Beck answered on four. Had his pyjamas on already, 1950s slippers like my old man used to wear—sitting around the house, drinking beer till he passed out. Before he ate his gun, and we found out his pension wouldn't even cover our utility bills.

"David," Beck said, squinting out at me through the screen—more puzzled than anything else. "It's very late."

Not cold, not then. Cold would come later.

With me just nodding, moronically. Panting, so hard I could barely shape the words:

"Back there, with Mrs. Silas—that made you pretty sick, huh? Not too moral, right?"

Gently: "You're drunk, David. Go home and sleep it off."

The way his lips moved as he said it—oh, my. *Those devil lips that know so well the art of lying* . . .

Singing in my head, my groin. Georgia above the belt. Blood below, hissing—pure red/black, just like in the Temple, washing up on an endless tide.

"I did it for you," I told him, "like I always do. The stuff you won't. The dirty work, to keep you clean. Doesn't that count for anything?"

"Go *home*, David. We'll talk tomorrow."

His tongue, flickering—oh my, God damn.

And the words rising through me, voicing themselves for the very first time ever. The first, and worst, time.

"I love you, Beck. Doesn't that mean anything to you?"

And did I see a little revulsion in his eyes, perhaps? A little bit of fear, even then? Surprise, at any rate.

Repeating, simply:

"Tomorrow."

Already shutting the door, firmly, stopping just shy of an outright slam. I stuck my foot in the jamb; barely felt the impact, as it rebounded.

"No," I said. "Tonight."

My head still singing: *Give me your lips, the lips you only let me borrow* . . .

My first punch caught him where jaw meets cheek, smashing his glasses like paper: The wire-rimmed frame slicing deep, embedding itself into the flesh and sticking there, a proverbial knife through butter. I picked him up bodily, threw him inside—he went down kicking, but couldn't find enough purchase to break himself free. One hand shoved down his pyjama pants, found the elastic, ripped, groped for my fly; I kept the other over his mouth while I kneed him in the chest, winding him before he had a chance to really scream.

. . . love me tonight, and let the devil take tomorrow . . .

And when I finally got his leg up high enough to cram myself inside, all he gave was a weird little shriek of outrage—before biting down on the web of skin between my thumb and forefinger, so hard and deep it seemed to explode with a gush of capillary-fed blood.

. . . I know that I must have your kiss although it dooms me, though it consumes me . . .

Jesus, it makes me sick just to remember. Sick at how good it felt. How good it still feels. My secret love for Beck made sudden, awful flesh, through dead Mrs. Silas' gift—a torch song dream whipped high and hot, let loose to burn down the whole waking world.

Love, this candy-coated, bright red lie that killed my life.

Love, my very own personal . . .

. . . kiss of fire.

* * *

In the alley now, watching the Temple's red windows flicker; breathing deep for the last of Beck's exhaust, the only thing of his I'll ever have again. Left two uniforms on stake-out in front, but I could get by them blind, never mind just drunk. I spent a year waiting for them to resurface, another casing this dump, before I finally gave up on the idea of revenge: Long as Mrs. Silas is still dead, I'm fucked no matter what happens to Herson and the rest. As well I know. Nothing they can threaten me with anymore, them or their Goddess.

But Beck's a whole 'nother subject, even going by that bitch Aphrodite's rules—and that's where the Temple fell down, back when they taught Mrs. Silas how to work this spell of theirs on poor, dumb, shield-wearing assholes such as myself.

They took it all, everything—all except the one thing that makes me capable of doing what I'm gonna do.

A shed out back. Fuel cans, for the Temple generator. Easy to carry. Easy to set in clusters around the walls, run a trail from pile to pile. Easy to soak myself and walk on in, stinking—Herson's smelled me drunk before, though never on gas.

"Just wanted to tell you freaks you were right all along," I'll say. "'Cause the fact is, I never loved anything till you put this thing on me. Not even myself."

Singing along, silently, in the gathering red/black dark of my head:

Just like a torch, you set the soul within me burning . . . I must go on along this road of no returning . . .

After which, I think I'll give Herson a smile—give them all one, just like the day we picked up Mrs. Silas. Wide, and sweet, and waaay too happy to be anything but real bad news.

Saying: "But I do know what love is, real love. Now."

And then, right then . . .

. . . though it burns me and it turns me into ashes . . .

. . . is when I'll light the match.

THE DIARIST

Day One. Starting small. I went to your driveway, just before dawn, and picked out eighteen uneven white stones from the area falling under your car's shadow. One for every letter of your full name. Took them home, made the sign of the Cross reversed on their dusty skins in stolen gasoline—my own personal brand of unholy water. With eyes, lips, flesh between nail and finger, back of my throat all burning, breathing out fresh curse with each inverse word: Thee baptize I, Holy Ghost and Son, the Father, of Name the in.

The water was already boiling when I dropped them in. No salt necessary.

When it was all gone, I wrapped the stones in a clean dishcloth, put them back in my purse and walked six blocks down to the nearest sewage drain, which I was pretty sure would count as a river. Assuming the original recipe allowed at least some metaphoric leeway for we poor, unfortunate, city-dwelling practitioners of the Craft.

Then I went home again, and wrote this down.

* * *

Calling you. Calling you back. Leaving messages. Waiting for replies to said messages, replies that never come. Doing research, in between dialing; the same facts, mainly, barring some slight referential variations.

My books list at least thirty different methods of extracting payment from people who break their promises. At the rate I'm going, I probably could do two a day. Maybe more.

The next time you don't answer the phone, I'm going to make sure it's because you can't.

* * *

Day Two. Quartering lemons in the kitchen with my black-handled knife, each one coming apart with a sudden spurt, like acid-soaked yellow hearts. Skewering them with pins and leaving them to shrivel. I'm learning the lessons my mother never taught me, the secret lore of housewives—what a surprising amount of mischief you can actually do, without ever having to leave the kitchen.

Afterward, I scoured the cupboards beneath the sink for as many poisonous substances as I could find, took them out to the garage, tied a scarf around my face and mixed them up together in an empty bleach bottle. Added paste, two boxes' worth. Ripped up my largest pile of "disposable paper products".

It took every letter I've written to you since the breakup, all those returned-to-sender vows of eternal devotion, to contrive a passable papier-mache likeness. Which I then left to dry, already rotting in on itself, until tomorrow's bonfire.

* * *

"Depression is anger turned inward." That's what Dr. Abbott used to tell me. Or, as my mother once put it: "Depression is when you're already in mourning over a part of yourself you know you're going to have to kill."

Some 1800s-era French murderess used to call keeping a diary "writing my novel". It's a phrase I particularly like, because it implies being able to choose how your story will end.

This litany of curses. This literary stigmata.

I told you, more than once, how far I'd go for you, if you required it of me.

But I'll bet you never thought I would go this far.

* * *

Day Three. I took a photo of you and me, cut it in half. Stuck your half under the dripping kitchen faucet.

Dug up the old barbecue pit, set the head in the garage on fire, and watched it burn to goo.

As of tomorrow, I'm going to start getting a little more elaborate on your ass. Throwing out some old-style hurt your way, just like the good books say—and I quote:

Make an image in his name who you would hurt or kill, of new virgin wax; under the right armpit place a swallow's heart, and the liver under the left; hand about the neck a new needle threaded with new thread; place the hand where the foot is, and the foot where the hand is, and the head facing down; write the name of the party on its face, and on his or her ribs these words: Allif, casyl, zaze, hit, mel, meltat.

Then string it up by a thread and lightly stroke it, with a single damp finger. That slow, cool touch on your back, your side. That indefinite shiver.
Feel that sweat? Your face, moistening. In a day, it'll be wet.
In a month, it'll be gone.

* * *

You tell me you think you probably never loved me quite as much as I loved you. You tell me you did love me, but you don't any more. You tell me you don't want to hurt me. But how can I believe you?
Because if you could just wake up one day and know you didn't love me, then everything I thought was love was actually a lie. Which means everything else could be a lie, too. Everything you say now. Anything you ever said.
And how did you really think I'd feel, after you'd made your confession?
Because however little I was loved, it was always good enough for me. Back then.
Before I knew any better.

* * *

Day Four, Five, Six. Day Seven. Day Eight.
Day Nine, and counting.
Imagine for a moment, if you will, the difficulties, the sheer and simple *effort* of what I undertake for you. I mean, dough in a box on your window-sill, sure; boiling a lock of hair carefully collected from your barber's floor, no particular problem. (And did that keep you up at night? Yes? No?)
Oh, good.
But anyway: So you light a candle at midnight, and then break it with a hammer. So you light another, and bury it. Weave more hair into a bird's nest. Scrape a growing branch, and introduce the hair into it; watch, as the bark

covers it over.

Try writing swear-words on consecrated wafers and feeding them to a toad, sometimes. Try burying that, alive.

I bury bottles and vials along paths we used to walk, knowing that where your foot touches them, disease will sprout. I bury an old glove I found in the back of the closet, stiff with the dust of your absence, and wait for it to rot. Drive rusty nails into your footprints. Shove hairballs from the neighbor's cat under your porch steps.

I contemplate breaking in one morning after you've run out of the house without flushing, late for an early class, and thrusting a red-hot soldering iron into your toilet.

In a magazine ad for condoms, I found a couple who look enough like you and her to qualify, and I cut them out, tore the picture down the middle. I gave her part to the only demon I could find—that perpetually drunk and crazy guy on the corner of Church and Wellesley. The other I keep safe, inside my pillow.

It gives me dreams, which I then send to you.

I sow dragon's teeth. I seed the clouds. I plow my broken heart in secret, in silence.

See what grows.

* * *

Here is how it works, then, for those who wonder:

Magic, white or black, operates on a principle of sympathy. You make an image, identify it with the person (usually by giving it that person's name), then destroy it. Fast or slow.

Patience and impatience, running in tandem. One action wears the wall between us away. The other cauterizes it. Dulls and dims your understanding of the wound's fatal nature, so it takes that much longer for you to die.

And the other part is, the person has to know. Which is why I'm writing you this at all.

At least, that's what I tell myself.

* * *

Day Ten. Of what month? My TV's broken, and all the paper boxes I saw today were empty.

I go to bed, early or late. I get up, early or late. I open my eyes in grey darkness, a pall so dim it almost qualifies as light. The clock is just another liar, and every hour is the same.

I'm so tired.

Guess I'll just have to take a key to my palm, jagged edge down, and cut myself a whole new lifeline.

* * *

By the way: I hope she breaks your heart. I hope you break hers. And then I hope the two of you sit around thinking about it, all the time. Crying for no known reason at your place of work. Ringing in items with everyone watching. Because don't fool yourself—you did it once, you can do it again, and somebody else can do it to you.

So don't you ever, don't you ever tell yourself again you're just the nicest little boy in the world.

That's two cherries you broke on me, you weak motherfucker.

* * *

Day Eleven.

My mother called this morning. I could feel it, somewhere in my stomach, the way cats always know when it's going to rain. But I couldn't call her back, because I've forgotten where I hid the phone.

Spent the day sticking flowers full of pins and lighting black candles, letting them melt down into malleable puddles of wax. I fumigated the house with all the evil odors of Mars, with sulphur and asafoetida. Staple-gunning yet more copies of that condom ad to my walls, torn so that your face no longer points toward her. Saying:

Usor, dilapidatore, tentatore, seignatore, devoratore, concitore et seductore—all ye ministers and companions, I direct, conjure, constrain and command ye to fulfil this behest willingly, namely straightaway to consecrate this image, which is to be done by (insert name here) *in the name of* (insert name here), *and that as the face of the one is contrary to the other, so the same may never more look one upon another.*

But you don't care about all that. You don't care about anything I do.

Do you?

* * *

At 6:30 I reset my watch. I brought everything back down to zero.

I went through the house, breaking things. I was pretty systematic about it.

I went upstairs. I took off my clothes. I folded them neatly, and burned them.

I smeared myself with incense ash, and ran myself a bath.

I washed myself clean, nameless.

Soon I will take a new knife, never used before, and write your name on the inside of either wrist. An inch deep.

* * *

It's hard to write now, and I apologize for the way this letter must look. But you can console yourself with the knowledge that it will be my last.

The most effective spell of all in my catalogue involves baptizing something living in the name of the person you wish to affect, and then killing it. As the body decays, the person whose name it bears suffers a similar dissolution.

It's the oldest spell I know—the most direct. So, fittingly enough, I saved this one for last. Very pure. Very simple. If it works, I won't be around to take it off; if it doesn't work, I won't be around to find out.

Everybody wins.

* * *

I date this letter Day Twelve.

I think you will recognize the signature.

DEAD BODIES POSSESSED BY FURIOUS MOTION

I wanted to dance with the young men in town
I wanted to dance till they hunted me down.
—Susan Musgrave.

It was 1976, it was night, it was Malibu. Elder Tallbie bent over to snag herself a beer, posing for this big, dumb guy named Flynn who she had her eye on—normally straight as an equally big, equally dumb post—who thought she was a guy, and wanted her anyway. Desperately. Which was fine with her. Easier to move and act the way she wanted to, in this particular teeth 'n' tits-obsessed decade, with a sexually ambiguous glamor to hide behind; she estimated it had probably been 75 years since she'd last worn a dress on more than two consecutive occasions.

Not that she missed the sensation, exactly.

As she rose, Elder caught Flynn sneaking a sidelong glance at her ass and gave him a narrow, wicked glare in return, licking the sharp tips of her fangs.

"Hey, fag," she said. "You checkin' out my action?"

Flynn went red. "As if. Fag."

"Fag."

"Fag."

And then it was later, time-lapse fast: The moon blinking up and over, a swollen white balloon against the endless night. They lay back in the light of the dying luau pit, surrounded by drained beers. Flynn trying hard not to let any part of him touch any part of her, as Elder toyed with her last bottle, and kept her fierce gaze firmly centered on his sweaty, fire-reddened cheek.

"Want to smoke a doob, man?" Flynn finally asked, falling back on his oldest—and most reliable, hitherto—trick.

"No, Flynn. I don't.."

"'Cause it's, uh, good stuff . . . "

"No."

Bicentennial firecrackers were going off somewhere in the distance, accompanied by the hoots and hollers of drunken children. Elder shut her eyes a moment, remembering grazing through a clutch of dying redcoats near the far side of some foot-bridge in upper New York State: Choking musketfire chest-wounds, faint Cockney and Lancashire curses. Blood leaking slow from the open side of one boy soldier's neck, even as she ripped the other wide and let the overflow spill down her greedy chops, soaking her bodice, drying so thick and hard that she'd actually had to throw her clothes away, afterward. She'd drunk her fill, drunk more, then eventually stumbled back to Eudo Lemonastere, three days late for their agreed-upon rendezvous—dazed, replete, naked and stained under a British officer's discarded frock-coat, with bugs in her unbound hair from sleeping under piles of leaves on the forest floor.

And Eudo had responded by slapping her face, sickened by her lack of restraint. Called her a peasant, uneducable, one brief step up from an animal.

She grinned at the memory, even now: Pretentious Eudo, her long-suffering maker and so-called master, with his clean white hands and his dirty, dirty mind. Still playing the saintly father-figure with her, vampire Pygmalion to her mortal Galatea, even after he'd paid her parents gold for the pleasure of taking her virginity—no different from any other aristocrat—and then hadn't been able to muster enough self-control to keep from killing her while he did it.

But guilt only went so far, after all. Which was why she most often chose her own spawn as she did, from the ranks of fools and freaks—to avoid, quite frankly, the inconvenience of ever having to feel any.

Flynn, Elder could tell, wouldn't be capable of considering his options long enough to resent losing his one chance at permanent oblivion. He'd welcome the Change with open fangs: One big par-tay 'till dawn and beyond. All of the fun, with none of the fallout.

She turned on her side, studying him closely. Watched him shift uncomfortably under her eyes' weight, readjusting himself, knee half-raised to mask his growing erection, with a cute little hip-twist for emphasis—a laughably furtive movement for someone his size, just this side of a squirm.

"'Kay," he said, apparently still meditating on her bewildering refusal of free weed. "That's okay. Um. So. Well . . . "

. . . what *do* you want to do?

Elder sat up, stretched, languorous. She leaned over Flynn, towards the cooler—"discovered" it empty. Leaned down, close, a little closer, then nose to nose; Flynn's sunburned surfer's beak looming dangerously close to her own sleek, cat-snub profile. Close enough for him to smell her, and rouse further—helplessly—at the pungent scent: Woodsmoke and spices, plus a faint slaughterhouse tang of old blood.

Appalling, the unexpected stink of it, under this fresh salt air. And yet . . . intoxicating, somehow.

"*Wellll*," she repeated, drawling. "What I'd actually kinda like to do—is—to suck—"

(Flynn gasping, an incongruously tiny squeak)

"—your blood."

"Whuh . . . ?"

Elder laid her lips on his, lightly, as her palm pressed against his straining crotch. Exhaled, equally light. And felt him shudder in response, groaning—spurting into his own baggy shorts at the barest touch of her clawed hand.

A slow whine: "Ooooow, my Gohhhhdddd . . . "

"You like that, big guy?"

Flynn shuddered again, eyes rolling; she nipped at his bottom lip, just nicking it—a paper-cut thin blood-weal, a mere shaving-accident scratch—and felt him spasm in response, paralyzed. Shaking like a dog left out in the rain, hair wild, sweat suddenly everywhere, gluing his hot skin to hers; her cool, nacreous moon-tan, pale as a pearl by the white beach's reflected light.

And then Elder slid down between his legs, taking his waistband with her. Pushing his poker-stiff penis aside to find the femoral artery, biting neatly in—hearing him yelp as he came again and again, gushing up over his own incipient pot belly. The beads of sperm choking his auburn pubic thatch until they hung in clusters, like limp stars.

Elder laughed aloud to herself at the sight, coughing blood through her nose. And went back to what she was doing.

Flynn, meanwhile, just kept on coming, right up until the very minute his big, dumb heart finally stopped: An empty thud, a last, wet squeeze.

Then silence.

* * *

Afterward, Elder buried them both in the sand under a pitched-over boat, curling catlike into the slack arm of his corpse. And when the next night fell, she slapped him awake—then hiked up her little boy's bowling shirt, and gave herself a shake in front of his dazed, red new eyes.

"Hey, man," she said. "It's like, a miracle, or somethin'. Take a pull on you the once, and look what I grew."

"Huh," Flynn replied, surprisingly unsurprised.

Then, slow: "'M sorta . . . thirsty . . . "

Elder's smile widened. Sharpened.

"Yeah. I just bet you are."

Thinking: *I give you about thirty years at the most, buddy. Starting now.*

More like fifty, as it turned out. But by the time it finally came to pass, nevertheless, all she could find it in herself to feel was: *Hmm. Gee.*

Right again.

* * *

"This cadre of yours," Eudo began, disapproving, as the second millennium drew to its close outside—sitting pretty in the back of his limo, parked on the outskirts of Elder's first official all-vampire rave. "A haphazard collection of strays, detritus . . . "

Outside, Flynn shot Elder the high-sign through the limo window, then put on a serious face, and asked one of Eudo's Familiars what looked like a fairly intimate question about his mother. The Familiar, doing a passable Eudo imitation, simply ignored him.

"Our Blood is not to be passed on lightly, Elder. There are channels, levels of approval."

Elder nodded. "Same ones *you* were following, when you made me," she suggested, idly playing with the hem of her shirt-cuff.

"I do find this continual harping on the circumstances of our first meeting remarkably tedious, Elder."

"I know you do. Eudo."

Beyond Flynn, Ulrike was augmenting her usual ballet-based dance moves with a series of Faster, Pussycat!-style go-go gestures. Tall, blue-eyed, blue-haired Ulrike, wearing nothing above the waist but a cross made from bondage tape over either tiny nipple. Ulrike, formerly single-name famous, who always struck Elder as having been genetically engineered to prove, through sheer embodiment, the general public's sneaking suspicion that no one who looked like—or was—a supermodel could really be quite human.

But here was Eudo again, still making that obnoxious, *I smell something* face of his: "I can't shield you forever, Elder. The Clave demands respect for tradition. You would do better—"

"I'll do what I want, *'magistere' meo.*"

He sniffed. "As you say."

"That's right." Elder opened the limo door, stood up—snapped her fingers at the Familiar, who passed her her cane; Flynn came running at the sound, grinning. Throwing back, to Eudo, over a feel-it-in-your-chest-loud rush of sound: "*Exactly* as I fuckin' say."

So don't let the coffin-lid hit you in the ass on your way out, motherfucker.

* * *

Later, she peeled Ulrike's crosses away—delicately, using only her blunt lower teeth—while Ulrike moaned in soft appreciation. Behind them, Flynn busied himself with the fourth occupant of their communal bed (some wannabe Familiar too pathetic to distinguish a valid invitation to the dance from yet another potentially fatal milking), baby-birding blood straight from the jugular back and forth to both women via long, exploratory, open-mouthed kisses. Ulrike, not normally interested in anyone born with more equipment than herself, tolerated this only because she wanted the hit; each successive draught made her shiver in Elder's arms, clutching, arching.

Elder, meanwhile, lay back on Flynn's heaving barrel chest, letting his sloppy worship drizzle crimson down the length of her naked torso. She felt him stiffen and hunch against her, heard his vestigal parody of breath grow ragged, while their shared victim's own breathing dimmed and clogged to a wet death-rattle. And wondered why this entire process—pleasant as it had one seemed, when she was still as young as Flynn or Ulrike—now made her feel far more bored than sated.

Thinking: *Things have to change.* And knowing full well that they would, eventually—no matter *what* she did.

Or . . . didn't do.

She turned her head in the hollow of Flynn's throat, and whispered—into his convulsing jawline—

"So: Big guy—"

"Uh."

"That scientist you were telling me about? One who works for NASA?"

Murky, mouth full: " . . . Uhuh . . . "

"I want you to invite him by—tomorrow, next night, maybe. The uptown graze." Snapping her claws against his cheek, sharply: "You hear me, Flynn?"

" . . . sure."

"Say it like you mean it, then. Just for my own personal peace of mind."

Flynn wheezed, whimpered; Ulrike, hovering on the raw edge of climax herself, made time to force a last bark of laughter at his obvious distress. And then they were hugging each other, instinctively, bone-crack hard, crushing Elder fast between them—their mutual convulsions sending their victim's corpse sliding to the floor beside the bed, limp and pale, drained to nameless anonymity.

Already forgotten.

"I mean it, man," Flynn whispered, finally, his sticky mouth glued to Elder's ear. And fell immediately asleep.

"Quel moron," Ulrike muttered, face-down in Elder's lap. Then: "If you really want something *done*, you know, you can always send me."

Elder just shrugged. And kept on stroking her "daughter's" spiky blue hair, until the blood-daze overcame Ulrike as well.

Thus freed from her spawn's distracting attentions, Elder lay looking up at the mirrored ceiling of her bedroom for the rest of the day, choosing to forgo her usual diurnal hibernation period in favor of thought rather than rest—something neither Flynn nor Ulrike would ever consider doing, even sheltered from the sun as they all were, here behind the penthouse's triple-layered steel shutters.

Bed-bound, Elder studied her own reflection at length, scanning in vain for any subtle hint of change. Everything was exactly as she remembered it, however: Her clean-lined jaw and flat cheekbones, the thick, roan fall of her hair. The thin scar bisecting one eyebrow, where the village priest's ring had cut it open with a backhanded slap after she'd blurted out that—with his dark locks and sorrowful eyes—the image of Christ crucified looked just like those Savages she'd seen trading furs down at the Post. The curve of her profile, incongruously elegant; a courtesan's nose, Eudo used to say, accidentally misplaced onto the face of a feral child.

Elder opened her narrow eyes wide, lips curling back, fangs extending:

Her ancient's stare, androgynous and blank, an empty blue-green like teal touched with milk.

Well, she had to admit, Eudo did have one thing right—her story, sad as it might seem in retrospect (to her, at least), really was nothing new. Every night, the vampire nation increased exponentially just because some Old Guard-member found a piece of prey pretty enough to want to keep around forever. Yet these same parasite aristocrats remained, as a class, almost constitutionally incapable of realizing that no one could stay a toy for more than one lifetime.

Eudo, for example, had wanted first a quick meal, then a catspaw, a curiosity gained on his tour of the Americas—a real, unlive wild Colonial girl to dress up and show off, to play with and teach to sing, to dance, to read and write and make herself entertaining. And for fifty long years, at least, Elder had been utterly content to feed on his livestock and act the chosen whore for his delight: Ash-gal at the shindy, as her relatives' later Western descendants would have put it, by the colorful early 1850's.

To a point, though. Only to a point. And no—fucking—further.

Poor Eudo. It really couldn't have been *too* amusing, for a creature so ancient he craved amusement in almost the same immediate, desperate way he craved blood, to look into his pet's eyes—one night, in an endless string of nights—and suddenly see an equal staring back at him. Like a dancing dog, a preaching hen, a singing rose: Depressingly, confusingly, terrifyingly improbable.

And yet . . .

. . . that's what happens, isn't it? She thought, with a certain contemptuous impatience—restless, reckless, heartless as ever, by poor Eudo's wounded estimation. *When your children grow up, I mean.*

Though, as God knew (or didn't, depending on who you asked), she sometimes did wish hers *would*—just to add even some small hint of variety to the well-established pattern.

Eudo again, sniffing, at her mind's ear: *Fools. Freaks. Flesh-drunk addicts. Cannon fodder.*

Oh, yes. All that, and far, far less.

But herein lay the difference: Only choosing spawn who came with clearly-marked expiry dates was the safest and most certain way Elder'd yet found to make sure they'd burn out long before you ever had to drive them away, or kill them. Which, in its turn, all but guaranteed you'd never again have to spend even a moment of your eternal life alone . . .

. . . unless you wanted to.

* * *

Tomorrow, next night: Upstairs, where a floor-full of 'Nought-i.e. nightcrawlers jigged and jumped, taking turns posing for each other while Elder watched, sipping her usual blood-and-tonic mixer, overcranked still center of their pathetically stop-motion world. And taking a certain secret pleasure in the knowledge that, all the while, a similarly stylish set of vampire younglings were going mosh-wild in the Tank beneath her feet, nipping and howling at each other as they jockeyed to get first bite at whatever tapped-out ex-Familiar the handlers threw in on top of them next. Flipping back and forth to deejays scratching 300 BPM, frenzied with white noise madness mixed far too fast for mere humans to hear, let alone follow . . . doing sept-, oct-, nonotuple twists in mid-air, upright and mid-step again before they even hit the ground . . .

Now, that was a fuckin' *party*, like this was just work under a different name: Nothing less than necessary, but definitely nothing more. Waiting, barely patient, on Flynn to sweet-talk the NASA guy through her front door and into her clutches—Elder could hear them clearly, music notwithstanding, and it didn't sound like any known version of a sure thing, as yet.

"You *know* it, G. She's, like, sooo totally hot for you—tellin' me just the other day how she wanted to meet you, dude. No lie."

"And what's her name, again?"

"Elder, man. Like the sign says."

Waste of time, unless the geek in question was even squarer than he look from where she stood. Which was—well—

—always possible.

Another sip, tiny hemoglobin hit sparking bright across her palate and up behind her eyes, making her already-pixilated pupils go click, bang, zoom. And starting to smile in spite of herself, with a brief black-light flash of teeth; studying her mark a little more closely from across the crowd room, and seeing a big, black man in a big, black, button-down suit, too-careful attempts at "hipness" screaming out from his mini-dreaded scalp on down. Straightening those press conference-ready little steel-rimmed specs as he repeated, slowly:

"So . . . she's 'hot'. For *me*."

Weighing the word, with its single unlikely syllable, as carefully as if it were some unfamiliar new scientific term. While Flynn laughed out loud like the big, sloppy-cute dolt he still was, almost forty years after Elder'd sucked him to death on the woodsmoke-scented Malibu sands. And assured Mr Suit right on back, with a twinkle in his red-tinged eyes—

"Oh yeah, seriously. And Elder? She, I mean, she's . . . "

. . . the fuckin' living *end*.

Later, in Elder's private elevator—Tank-bound, with the scientist (his name had proved to be Darnell) still playing it strictly on the wide-eyed tip: Poor, boring, office-bred me, cut hopelessly adrift against the likes of exotic, downtown-dangerous you. Unlucky for him, in context, that it was only a stance; his self-delusion meant the shock of being turned would be severe, no matter how Elder chose to do it—fast or slow, sidelong or straight-on. Gentle, reassuring. Or, maybe—

—not.

"I don't suppose I'm up to the kind of conversation you're used to," Scientist Darnell allowed. To which Elder replied, without pretense at preamble:

"Actually, I was hoping you could enlighten me about something. You're going to be using string theory on the new G-Class Interplanetary, right?"

" . . . right."

"And how does that work, exactly?"

Darnell double-took; Elder just watched, waiting. Then started her smile sharpening, just a bit, as she saw him really *see* her for the first real time—assess her the way he'd judge any other unknown quantity, plunge past the "obvious" distractions of her pale, fragile, human veneer to solve for x. And get the barest hint, here and there, of some far older, less recognizable equation.

"That . . . would take a *really* long time to explain," he said, at last.

The elevator touched ground, clicked in. Elder leaned to key her access code, pumping out a whiff of vampire perfume to make Darnell shiver: Morgue-cold, pheromone-choked. A black rose's poisoned pollen.

"Really," she repeated. And showed him her fangs.

Tightness in the chest. Tightness at the fly. And Elder's glacial meltwater gaze, suddenly impossible to elude. Her little hand on his, claws sliding flick-quick to puncture his pulse on one bright flash of pain, one hot gout painting both their palms arterial red as he shuddered and jerked ridiculously in place, too caught even to gasp.

Six feet plus of gym-sleek bulk, all straining muscle and hammering, hemorrhaging tissue. But Elder already had him bent back over her knee by the throat, off-center-helpless as a child: Draining him quick and hard, and watching the Tank's apparently "empty" dance-floor fill up with gyrating bodies through his dimming eyes as the change took effect, rocketing him irreversibly towards immortality. And feeling the Tank's sound-system set her solar plexus spinning like some B-Movie mad scientist's hoary Hypno-Wheel, a different beat spiraling outward through every knotted, venom-flooded limb—while three centuries' worth of musical interplay clicked simultaneously by inside her head, lines piled one upon the other, like archaeological layers—

She's sold her rod, she's sold her reel
She's sold her only spinning-wheel
To buy her lad a sword of steel—
Her Johnny, who's gone for a soldier . . .
O believe me, if all those endearing young charms
That I gaze on so fondly today
Were to melt in an hour and fleet in my arms . . .
Gimme a pigsfoot and a bottle of beer
Get me gay, I don't care
Get all your razors and your guns
We gonna be wrasslin when the wagon comes . . .
It's got a backbeat, you can't lose it
Any old way you choose it . . .
No matter where you come from, no matter what you done
you got six million ways to die, choose one . . .

Surrounded by a circle of its sniggering soon-to-be peers, Scientist Darnell's dry husk folded up on itself like an old cocoon; his pulse slowed, stuttered, stopped. The younglings around him high-fived each other, cheered, and threw in at the bar to buy him a worthwhile first post-death drink, whenever his reborn cells chose to wake him back the fuck up.

Out on the Tank floor, meanwhile, Elder spun and sang, chin-slick with the last of Darnell's blood. Her mind returning, automatically—as it usually did, in such ecstatic moments—to the "secret" plan which had dictated his forcible conversion in the first place: Not exactly inaccessible to whoever wanted to hear about its particulars for quite some time now, though she did like to think it still both complex and unique . . .

. . . and Eudo's reaction alone, when she'd first explained it to him, had been more than enough to confirm *that* impression.

* * *

"Flynn's in with some half-closeted vamp fetishist down at NASA," she'd told him, as they sat together in Eudo's idling car—shield discreetly up, muffling their voices from the Familiar chauffeur's prying, half-mortal ears. "According to him, they're gearing up to build themselves a Terrestrial Planet-Finder space telescope sometime during the next fifteen years, and launch it into Jupiter's orbit. It'll locate G-Class planets—that's Earth-sized worlds, with oxygen in their atmospheres—and then send pre-loaded probes on reconnaissance planetfalls, to scout 'em out."

"And so?"

"And *so*, I'm gonna be on one of those probes, when the Planet-Finder fires it off. A hundred and twenty extra pounds of weight, all wrapped up in an information-gathering marker pod strapped to the undercarriage. They fit me with a softwire package that relays a fake telemetry back to Mission Control on Earth, I put myself into hibernation for most of the journey . . . "

"What is this science fiction nonsense?"

"It's progress, you fuckin' relic. Evolution."

"An elaborate and expensive way to commit suicide."

Elder snorted, twirling her cane impatiently; thought about how fast the blade inside would razor that sneer from Eudo's ex-monk face, if only she'd let herself let it. Then stepped down hard on that particular impulse, and snapped back—

"Way *I* see it, sport, we're all dead already. So who gives a big, fat, staving-off-creeping-mortification-of-the-flesh-through-drinking-hot-fresh-human-blood fuh—"

Breaking in, dismissively: "I *know* how it is that you 'see it', Elder."

"Oh, I'm very sure that you think you do."

Eudo half-turned, favoring her with that look—the same one whose merest lowering hint had once been enough to pin her to her seat with fear and embarrassment, turn her insides to flame and her knees to water, render her instantly and automatically desperate to fall at his feet and do whatever it might take to make him happy again. But it'd been a good two hundred years since she'd felt either any of the above, or any need to conceal her feelings on the subject from the man-shaped thing who'd made and trained her: Her demon lover, her awful father. Her former master, still fuming over the mere fact of his pretty plaything's self-emancipation, even though it'd been years on years on *years* since the lack of his approval had had even the slightest possible effect on anything she did, or didn't do.

"They think it'll take about a century to reach full colonization," Elder continued, "patiently". "'Cause they'd need a compact power-source like an antimatter engine, and that takes a real conceptual breakthrough; hard to concentrate on, when you're still havin' to worry about petty little stuff like death and taxes. So Flynn brings Mr Man by, I turn him and throw him back . . . this time next year, half of NASA's gonna be working 24/7 to find the next potential Earth.2, on nothing but a liquid diet."

"The Clave would never approve such a venture."

"Like I need their approval. For anything."

"Elder . . . " he began, then paused. And began again a moment after, with a strange—almost new, somehow—note in his voice: "This world is all we have, child. We must either live in it as it is, or change what little we can—and live with the consequences of those changes, afterward. There's nothing more *to* do, however much we may . . . occasionally . . . wish there were."

And there was the Clave's party line, in a proverbial nutshell: Traditionalist, exclusionist, literally conservative. All about having to preserve the vampire world's "ancient, secret culture" at all and any cost, while conveniently forgetting that none of them actually *had* a culture to preserve, *per se*—just a bunch of fairly disgusting personal habits they'd somehow raised, over the millennia, to the status of (un)Holy Writ.

A calcified nightside parody of social structure run by those who deified the past to the point of glossing over how bad it had really been, back when they were still numerous enough to be feared, or their prey still knew enough to remember how to kill them. How they'd frozen stiff under the iron earth in cheap coffins, been poisoned like rats, hunted down and herded screaming from their catacombs to explode in the sunlight, tortured and scarred and burned at the fucking stake . . .

No, you've somehow skipped right on over all that, she thought. *Because you don't change, even living forever. You just—endure.*

But those who forget the past are doomed to repeat it. As you, Eudo—should definitely know.

"So *dixit me, magistere*," she asked, her tone kept strictly conversational. "The world *did* turn out to be flat after all, right? And that Don Cristobal de Colon guy . . . he just fall off the edge, or what?"

Man, where *was* I born, anyway?

A thousand years of ebb and flow, empire-rise and -set, with nothing happening that hadn't already happened a million times before. And then, three hundred years back—just around the time of Elder's own Re-birth, strange to say—a critical mass of ideas, exploding outward. So many new devices. Curiosity like a viral cluster, an ever-spreading plague, increasing exponentially.

Three hundred years of change, of nearly constant forward motion. But if studying history had taught her anything, it was that momentum always peaked and dropped, the same way that milk left to sit always curdled. That people always forgot how good they had it, comparatively speaking, because the most recent generation—these twentieth- to twenty-first-century vampires, for example, with their routinely endless, intrinsic sense of entitlement—rarely understood exactly what drawbacks they'd been lucky to avoid having to deal with, in the first place.

"You grew up with television, Flynn," she'd snarled at him, once, when his various inanities finally grew too immediate to ignore. "You grew up with indoor heating, refrigeration, medical care, the Bomb. When I was alive, there weren't even roads. I went barefoot for seventeen years. Couldn't read. Didn't know there were *continents*. I wanted to take a crap, I'd up my skirts and squat in the streets. I never saw myself in a mirror, 'till after I was already dead."

And Flynn had nodded, lip pooched out, trying his level best to understand. Even though his best would never be good enough, no matter how much of his supposedly eternal life he spent trying to upgrade it.

But: That *look*, or its near cousin. The new note peeling away in a repressed, teeth-grinding growl, like old skin shedding. Eudo, struggling for control he'd lost long before this conversation started—but soldiering gamely on, nevertheless. As though he still had . . . faith . . . that he could eventually make her see things his way.

"If you threaten everything we've struggled so long to build, the Clave will be forced to intervene. Your cadre will suffer—not that you care, I suppose. But you . . . " A pause. "They can have you exiled. Or even killed."

A shrug. "They can try."

Eudo stared down, studying the floor. Then said, quieter:

"I loved you, Elder. Does that mean nothing?"

To which Elder laughed out loud, right in his downcast face. And returned, with total simplicity—

"Doesn't it?"

* * *

Poor Eudo, still mourning the cold and sudden undeath of his long-lost dream-dolly. Because it had all been just so much easier, back then, hadn't it? So much more . . . fun.

Though—not quite for both of them, as Elder recalled.

(But then again, she certainly did still like to play with *her* toys, whenever there was nothing better to do.)

Still, it was only natural—as natural as anything vampiric could claim itself: Time-tested, the proven formula. Youngling to ancient, they'd all been in the same position, once or twice upon an age. Eudo too. Someone had probably dressed him up, steered him 'round, told him where to go and made him say thank you for the privilege; back before the Crusades, before the Flood. Perhaps he'd "loved" *that* person, too. Or told himself he did.

Always assuming, that was—

—he'd actually had any choice in the matter.

Truth was, though . . . the truth was, *this* had been what Eudo had seen in her eyes, that day. The prescient shadow of this same impossible ambition glowing like lingering atomic residue, like a skeleton of dead light. Stars in her eyes, deep-buried, waiting to burn up and flare anew.

And wondering, at the same time—was it really so very hard to understand, the idea that she just wanted to go as far as she could possibly go? To pit herself against the void like an exercise in sheer willpower, the same way that all these dead bodies around her kept on acting as though they were still alive: Dancing, flirting, fucking, killing, just because they wanted to. Because . . . they *could*.

Hunger, after all, could only take you so far, no further. And there were so many appetites to choose from, once you allowed yourself to think outside the biosphere's blue and fragile box—hungers which might prove to extend far beyond the agreed-upon version of reality, beyond the basic reach of flesh and blood itself.

Things were born in chaos, and they ended in chaos. And the only thing between chaos and chaos was velocity. So the only reason to go backwards, in Elder's eyes—

—was because you'd already reached the end.

Of everything.

* * *

Fast-forward: Fast, faster, fastest. And then it was 2020 or thereabouts, yet more years having passed the same way they always did, quick as insects—hatching and molting, metamorphosing, mating and laying and dying in a single blink of that long-ago swollen Malibu moon. Three o'clock A.M. in what still stood of anti-pollution activist-bombed downtown Toronto, with Ulrike, Flynn and Elder marching straight into the fabled silk-hung heart of the Empress' Noodle house itself, where Grandmother Yau Yan-er was rumored to be hosting a members-only Clave meeting somewhere upstairs. But since her restaurant had been traditionally recognized as neutral ground since the turn of the (last) century, the Dragon-born Lady could well afford to do exactly what she obviously chose to, instead: Make herself conspicuous by her absence, lurking in the opium-scented shadows with her thousand-year-old hands deep inside her brocade sleeves, while Elder used the quote-unquote "anonymous" invitation she'd received earlier that evening—a strangely familiar Mandarin chop, imprinted in scrupulously virus-clean blood on a gilt-edged piece of silk-thread parchment—to get by that persistent knot of ghosts guarding the banquet room's lacquer-red front door.

The sound of her cane against the inlaid parquet floor caught Eudo in mid-rant; he turned, wholly taken aback by such effrontery. Projecting, even from this distance—

Iesu Christo, these AMERICANS. So uncompromising. So insolent. So damned, damnably . . . proactive.

Yeah, well. Welcome to the New World, Fossil-Man.

To Elder's own mild surprise, fifteen years of monitoring and vague, threat-laden menace had elapsed before Eudo's Familiars finally took direct action. They'd started at the top, naturally enough; begun with Darnell, oldest of her NASA moles, whose ashes were (even now) blowing free in the lingering compression vortex created when his lab had gone up in smoke. But the rest of the team had already scattered according to drill, vowing to join Elder later—assuming, always, that she actually survived this meeting—at their alternate launch-site. A resentful bunch even by most vampire youngling standards, though gradually won over by the one-two combination suckerpunch of Darnell's infectious enthusiasm and Elder's undeniable logic: Having a "live" viewer on board the probe *would* be invaluable, in terms of potential information-gathering . . . especially one for whom the idea of a life-support system, under most circumstances, was a strictly optional luxury.

Flynn took west flank position, Ulrike the east. Elder leant on her cane between them, smiling a bit at the thought of how the red-tinged light of the paper lanterns must be making interesting patterns on her sleek, bald, shaved-for-liftoff scalp.

"Gentlemen, ladies," she said, bowing slightly. Then: "Eudo."

"You see?" Eudo demanded, of no one in particular. "She has no respect, no loyalty . . . "

"Not for *you*, no."

Stung, Eudo managed what looked like a legitimate blush; must've really fed well, to be able to pull *that* off.

" . . . she . . . " He began again, with slightly shakier momentum. "Surely you can see how she doesn't think she owes—us—"

(me)

"—anything."

(*I LOVED you, Elder.*)

But: No. *I* loved *you*. Once.

(Once.)

Elder gave Eudo what was meant to be a last direct glance, cool teal to milky blue. And replied—

"Eudo . . . you did me a disservice when we first met, as we both know, even if you'll never be man enough to admit it." Raising her voice, then, to drown out his automatic protestation: "But I'm reconciled to that, I truly am. I don't even care enough to want to kill you over it anymore. So—do yourself a favor, monk—"

"—and don't *make* her," Ulrike chimed in.

Flynn: "Yeah, man."

(What *she* said.)

Eudo paused, struck momentarily speechless, throat working like he still needed to gasp for air. Elder raised a brow at the spectacle, and asked the nearest Clave-member—she thought his name might be Eater Of Found Things, the one whose low forehead and facial scarring rumor branded him as a possible genuine Missing Link, turned mid-Ice Age by something still older, wiser and even more ruthless—

"I mean, Eudo didn't tell you he just found out about this, did he? 'Cause I made sure to tell him first, the minute I got the idea."

Old friends that we are, and all.

But: "Yes," the gold-laden Yoruba matriarch seated across from the Eater said, dryly. "So we read, in your memo."

"What?" Eudo blurted.

"The memo I sent 'em, magistere. One 'Rike got that hacker-grrrl she Biblically knows to mass-mail, under *your* sigil."

"Whah . . . " A cough, not-so-neatly slurring from one word to another in mid-syllable. " . . . when?"

The Eater, in his creaky, ice-burnt voice: "Last week."

Long before you called this meeting to order, or ran your mouth about how I was gonna bring down a new Inquisition on each and every one of us by doing something whose most likely only casualty—if and when any one of a three-page long list of predicted SNAFUs occurs—would be me, and me alone. Long before the Clave just sat there and let you act like you had 'em all in your figurative back pocket, let you *presume* to speak for a coven of vampires whose youngest member (aside from yourself) was either personally present when that Jewish prophet of yours had his moment of doubt and shame, or heard about it first-hand from somebody who was.

My memo. The one that begins: Since you all like history so much, let's take the *real* long view. Imagine the Earth rendered uninhabitable even for us, probably in only a few more hundred years—a dead body marking off millennia, waiting to be engulfed by the sun when it goes nova. Vampires with no alternate food-sources, forced to turn on each other; a Dark Age longer than all previous Dark Ages put together, with chaos and boredom reigning supreme, and the Red Death holding sway over all.

(Unless.)

Unless, unless, unless.

Because: I can offer them what you would never think to, *magistere*; tempt them with an easy way out, lie to them with the truth. *I* can buy their approval by tempting them with a reason—however improbable—

—to *hope*.

Elder risked yet another next-to-"last" peek at Eudo, who seemed caught between synapses—realizing, slowly but surely, how completely the tide of opinion had finally turned against him. He shook himself, half-pivoting her way; she showed him her back, decisively: Just another open insult in a long, long line of the same, nights without end, amen . . .

. . . which was how she—*she*!—somehow managed to miss the exact moment when Eudo's vaunted composure snapped like tinsel, propelling him forward; claws out to knuckle-length, eye-teeth hooked almost double, like a cobra's. Leaping for her with all the accumulated rage of a mentor scorned one too many times, only to find Flynn (of all people)—

—*but who else, really? Not Ulrike, not LIKELY*—

—instantly, automatically, idiotically in his way.

At which Eudo hissed, drove his right-hand index and ring-fingers through Flynn's eyes, his thumb through Flynn's nose—like a particularly gory bowling accident—and ripped Flynn's shaggy head neatly *off*, with one curt upward motion.

Flynn's ashes broke over Elder as she turned: A hot grey wave, burning her eyes, filling her mouth; she coughed them out again, plunging her cane straight through Eudo's shoulder-joint. Eudo's arm fell almost instantly severed, Flynn's skull still stuck fast to his fist, both crumbling to mingled dust on contact with the floor.

"El—" Eudo began. Elder kicked him in the jaw, round-house, and jumped as he spun. Knee to the small of his back, fingers sliding fast down his spine to rip through on either side, grabbing for the floating ribs—

Raising him, hugging him, cracking him. Drawing his beating lungs out through the holes her hands had made, wet as embryonic wings, while the rest of the Clave just watched, impassive.

"You know what the Vikings called this, don't you, my monk?" She whispered, in Eudo's agonized ear. "The blood-eagle. Nasty way to die, last I heard; nasty way to *live*, 'specially if you live forever."

So I guess you better get one of your Familiars to push 'em back in for you, before you heal this way.

"I'll still be here," Eudo hacked, bow-bent in uncontrollable spasm—no air left, without his lungs, to generate a voice anyone but another vampire could hear. "When you come back. Here . . . to watch you *crawl*."

"Doubt it," Elder replied. And dropped him.

Somewhere in the shadows behind them, she heard Grandmother Yau clap her hidden hands just once—a gentle sound, yet more than enough to send her ghosts scurrying off en masse in search of a dustpan, a bucket, a mop. Good help being always hard to find, as the old mantra went, and thus better ruled with an iron hand than a kind word, whether alive or dead. Or undead.

Grit under her heels as she moved towards Ulrike, now: Part of Eudo's detritus, grinding even finer beneath her shoes' soles? Part of Flynn's?

Not that it really mattered, Elder supposed.

Taking her dumbfounded "daughter's" hands in hers, meanwhile. And assuring her, aloud: "I leave you in charge, after the launch."

An open-mouthed kiss, flavored with their mutual "elder"'s blood; Ulrike received it eagerly, as Elder had always known she would. Sighing in anticipation: Oh, power, at last. At *last*.

Ambitious little toy, Elder thought. And smiled, to herself, at the observation's very . . . familiarity.

"We'll wait," Ulrike promised her, lying badly. "Your name will live forever."

Elder smiled again. "Just act according to your nature, 'Rike," she replied, mildly. "And I'll be satisfied."

Then she stepped through the ashes which had once been Flynn—part of him, at least—

—and was gone.

* * *

Plasma stores wouldn't last long, and after that, sleep would be the best option—the least painful, in the long run.

Until then, though, she planned on keeping her eyes . . . open.

And now, looking down, what did she feel, exactly—seeing the long drop lengthen, then Earth pull away below her? That frail blue shell, dimming to a sliver; homesickness, a kind of nostalgia, coring her with a quick and intimate pain. And in her mind's eye, superimposed, a barefoot girl slogging upward along the dirt track outside of New Amsterdam, hem-deep in mud, and a carriage stopping—a door opening. The gape on her own silly bumpkin face, half-remembered, half-imagined, heartbreakingly empty of experience.

And no, she wanted to cry out, through time's veil: *No, don't trust, don't take that man's smooth, pale, clean hand. Go back, go back—live out your little life, breed and die. Do nothing. BE nothing. Go nowhere. Lie easy in the earth, until you ARE earth.*

But Eudo was always so calm and comely, in his suit of lace. And she, in her innocence, always accepted his offer.

Things were as they were. They couldn't be otherwise. And Elder, knowing this, sat back on her heels in the ship's pod; alone once more, without even her own long-gone ghost left to keep her company.

Up and out, and out, and out. Further and further, from star to shining star—manifest destiny made ever more manifest. She was the Tricentennial Woman . . . *Quad*ricentennial? Not that such distinctions mattered much, either now or for much longer . . .

(Acceleration alone would see to that, in the end.)

America's child. The Revolutionary. The one for whom there were no borders, no traditions—to whom no one, and nothing, applied anymore.

So catch me if you can, you effete techno-illiterates—you self-obsessed history-whores masturbating over your glyphs, your archives, your ruined, buried monuments.

I'm leaving, on a jet plane. Don't know if I'll be back again.

(Ever, ever, ever.)

Maybe she would go out into darkness and find nothing there at all—nothing but emptiness, endless starvation, an infinite sentence of unslaked hunger. Or freedom from the cycle, even at any cost—the tyranny of vulgar desire, of pleasure and pursuit: Wanting, having, consuming, wanting again. Slash and burn and waste.

Or maybe she would find herself sitting by the side of some different sea on some different world, under the potentially far less harsh light of a some very different sun. Maybe she'd cut her palm on some alien rock, drop a few pulses of her own infected blood into the warm, saline tide . . . and stay there as long as it took, to see what might grow to sentience from the impetus.

If you only wait long enough, Elder thought, *then whatever you can conceive of, no matter how improbable, must surely—eventually—become possible.*

"Man," Flynn had begun, once, while stoned on some fellow stoner's blood—blissing out on the concept of space-travel, then glitching over its logical consequences, "you ever come back, the whole Earth could be gone, it could be just that long. We might not even *be* here anymore."

"'As Venus dives into the sun . . .'"

"Yeah. Yeah! That's what I'm sayin', man."

And: But everything I knew already is gone, Flynn, she remembered almost replying. The whole structure of my universe, changed beyond comprehension. Cars, electricity, recorded music; fast food, open all night. I died damned, and live on in a world where science kicked the Holy Ghost's sorry spectral ass too long ago to mention.

So what should I miss? What should I cry over leaving behind? I have—literally—nothing left to lose.

(Not even you.)

Good thing Flynn died when he did, she thought, with a sudden stab. *HE would have missed me, after. He was just that dumb.*

But—

Elder raised the filtering visor of her helmet, cautiously—for who knew what radiation lurked out there, what stray wandering portion of the ultraviolet spectrum? And space would be a particularly bad place to cook and drift in.

She looked out on the great wheel of constellations, the endless hub: Stars whose dead light washed over her, whose positions she was already beginning to watch alter. Whose hidden faces she would view from every angle, before the arc of her passage finally brought her home again.

A long trip, and a hungry one. Blood of every sort, on every sort of world. A universe of unmapped loneliness and potential prey. A forever-distant horizon—no borders to cross, no boundaries to push. Just on, on, on, on, on.

The stars, turning. The constellations, splitting and reforming into new animals, new myths. New monsters.

Rivers of gas and dust and heat. Cradles of light, already cooking up new worlds for her to drain.

Elder's ship, like Elder's corpse—a viral net, animated forever by its own disease. A universe of dead bodies . . .

. . . possessed by furious motion.

AFTERWORD Q &A

DISCLAIMER:

Though framed as a (hopefully amusing) Q and A session with the disembodied voices inside my own head, the following afterword deals mainly with the ins and outs of my creative "process." Those of you who like this sort of thing may find this the sort of thing that you like, while everyone else may well find it excruciating or disillusioning, or both. If you happen to fall into the latter category then thank you, goodnight, and please do keep an eye out for my next collection of short stories, *The Worm in Every Heart* (October, 2003), also from Prime Books.

And now, without further ado—

Q (grinning nervously): "So, like—where do you get your ideas?"

A (grinning evilly): Well, since you ask . . .

I first got the germ for "Kissing Carrion" back in 1993, when I was still in the most formative possible stages of what would eventually become my career: Writing stringer articles for *eye Weekly* magazine on every subject under the sun, dodging calls from the government about back taxes relating to my last year at Ryerson, placing stories here and there for copies, telling people I was a writer, feeling like the world's biggest minimum wage-earning, unqualified, futureless loser. I'd just quit my job as Vibrator Room floor attendant at Lovecraft, Toronto's most upscale sex shop, where the virulent combination of having an eighty-percent employee discount but no significant other to share the spoils with had already begun to screw with my ideas about "healthy" sexuality; I also spent a fair amount of time listening to early Nine Inch Nails while reading underground comics and 'zines, simultaneously jealous and admiring of their creators' capacity to self-publish material which seemed to come straight from the same vein of icky, suppurating, intensely private darkness I was becoming somewhat afraid to tap in myself.

I began developing "Kissing Carrion" for an editor who wanted stories that were genuinely vicious rather than darkly Romantic, which had been my stock in trade up 'till then. The turning point came when I discovered an article in one of said 'zines about those wacky folks down at Survival Research Laboratories (whose self-destructive industrial antics would later inspire NIN's "Happiness In Slavery" video), which lead me to rent their performance tapes from Suspect Video—I was particularly struck by the infamous "rabbot," a rotting bunny corpse hooked up to a system of rods and pistons and technical what-have-you which puppetted it around, making it parade itself back and forth until it started to fall apart. Mix well with the Pixies, and Pat Calavera's Bone Machine was born. Ray and his fixations, meanwhile, evolved from both the confessions of Scottish serial killer Dennis Nilssen and the real-life female necrophile who inspired Lynn Stopkewich's film *Kissed*. But things soon slid to a halt, as they often do with me, and the story lay fallow for years... I had vague ideas of submitting it for a zombie anthology like John Skipp and Craig Spector's *The Book Of The Dead*, which is how the whole "triangle between a man, a woman and a corpse splits apart when the corpse objects to the arrangement" theme came into play.

Still and all, it took 'till 2000 for me to finally realize that the narrative perspective should come from Mr Stinky, rather than Pat or Ray. A deadline was proffered by Ellen Datlow, for which I'll be eternally grateful, even though the story itself didn't turn out to meet her needs for the anthology in question. And the rest is history.

Q: "That's a long time between idea and product. Is this kind of extensive percolation *normal* for you?"

A: "Normal"—no, not probably. Is anything?

My mind is a mulch-heap, deep and sticky; things pile up and, once they've piled, often need time to ferment. Some times the result is more explosive than others. I've written stories at a white heat, in a matter of hypnogogically-charged hours, and ended up shaking and babbling to myself while watching the walls bend. The more *likely* version of the process, however, reads the way it does above . . . a gestation period of almost a decade, with lots and lots of intermediary drafts, rejigging and thematic side-steps before I finally hit my stride and push through those last precious pages. Like the hoary old standby of brain-as-nautilus, I spiral slowly, non-linearly outwards, or inwards. Or—usually—

—downwards.

"Keepsake" clocks in at the very bottom of said spiral. It was written during one of my (more) depressive periods, which—as my husband will attest—I'm still prone to; the details about lying in bed and marking off the day by "TV time" came out of that, while my descriptions of what it's like to be on the sparkler-side of a PMS-induced migraine are also, unfortunately, ripped whole and beating from real life experience. Rohise and Renny Gault, meanwhile, evolved in equal part from a wonderful photo of Quentin Tarantino and Juliette Lewis eye-fucking each other for a *Details* magazine article about their performances in *From Dusk 'Till Dawn* and some musings I once wrote down about the innate oddity of having siblings, as a concept—I'm an only child, as are most of my friends, aside from the two who happen to be identical twins, and as the old truism states (truism because it's *true*), what you find exotic is almost always what you're personally unfamiliar with.

Plus, I've always been far more *Near Dark* than *Interview With The Vampire* in terms of my ideas on vampirism—less "predators' predators, killing angels feeding on us from above, lie back and wait with a beating heart," more "dead people too angry to lie down and rot." So I wanted to riff on the basic trope in such a way as to make it both potentially plausible and utterly unglamorous. I'd like to believe I succeeded.

"Keepsake" went straight to Wayne Edwards, editor/publisher of the now-defunct *Palace Corbie* magazine, because he'd been bugging me for stuff that was "more extreme." He put it in #7 (Merrimack Books, ed. Wayne Edwards), then eventually reprinted it in *The Best Of Palace Corbie* (Stone Dragon Press, ed. Wayne Edwards). Finally, this story has the dubious honor of having apparently grossed out enough (male) Showtime execs to make sure that I did *not* end up with one more sale to *The Hunger* under my belt for 1998—they were *right with it* up to a certain scene, and then . . . well. I think you'll probably be able to spot the point of exit, if you try hard enough.

Q: "Were you always like this?"

A: Oh, baby: Bet your ass.

I started writing when I was maybe eight or so. My first love was science fiction, but that died pretty quickly after I realized that (aside from certain types of biology) I had little or no interest in science per se. By twelve I was reading Stephen King and writing monster stories to match—pastiches that definitely lent "No Darkness But Ours" (first published for no money down in City Alternative High School's 1987 yearbook), which now frankly reads like the teaser to some King-esque novel, more than a little of its overall inspiration. But the rot started earlier on, I suspect; back when I was ten, I was already writing stuff like the wonderfully-titled "Gore In The Woods," a sad tale of gratuitous supernatural torture which contains these immortal lines:

It hurt more as the [eerie, glowing green] worms began eating through the muscle wall and burrowed into his stomach. Then he could feel them slipping into his intestines and up his esophagus towards his mouth. Others burrowed into his veins and began drinking his blood as they slithered towards his brains. "This is it", he thought. "This is the end", as one of the worms finally reached his heart. And it was.

This collection contains three of the oldest stories I still have floating around: "No Darkness . . . " "Mouthful Of Pins"—my first true fiction sale (to *Northern Frights 2*, Mosaic Press, ed. Don Hutchison)—and "Skin City," published initially in *Grue #16* (Hell's Kitchen Productions, Inc., ed. Peggy Nadramia) before being reprinted in *A Crimson Kind Of Evil* (Obelesk Press, ed. S.G. Johnson). And while I think they've held up fairly well, I've certainly already spent a fair amount of the time since I wrote them trying to figure out why I'm so apparently compelled to revisit the themes of emotional isolation, sexual obsession, supernatural transcendence, repetitive patterns of loss and violence . . . the death of love, the love of death, the darkness which comes just before—and after—every night's dreaming.

The only vague sort of conclusion I've reached, however, is that when it comes right down to it, the reason I've come to respect horror above almost every other form of literature is that its considerations simply seem more *honest* than those of any other genre. Through horror, we force ourselves to explore the things too much fantasy tries its best to avoid, to escape, to deny: The skull beneath the skin, the inescapable and unsettling knowledge that while some of us may indeed die sooner and in more inventive or spectacular ways, all of us will—eventually—travel the exact same ghost-road on our way to whatever lies beyond the undeniable fact of physical dissolution.

Seed becomes matter, matter becomes decay, energy moves unquantifiably forward; entropy in action, or maybe something more. But all we have to go on, or can create in the interim, is a shadow-puppet theater version of our own fears, our own desires... our own slim, yet unextinguishable, hopes in the face of apparent hopelessness.

Oh yeah: That, and the eerie, glowing green, blood-drinking worms. 'Cause they're just *cool*.

Q: "A lot of these stories are pretty explicit, like boobie/penis-type explicit. Do you just think about sex all the time?"

A: Thankfully not, especially the way that sex usually turns up in this particular context. There was a period during the mid-1990's when "erotic horror" was momentarily all the rage, though, which happened to neatly coincide with my first few invitations to participate in genuine *paying* anthologies—the *Hot Blood* era, as I like to call it, when body-parts and blood were juggled to produce an effect which was supposed to be equal parts titillation and terrification. This was a good market... indeed, it occasionally seemed, the only market. I wanted in. 'Nuff said.

Of course, the urge which lay behind this trend has never really gone away, since sex and death still form a primal, if subliminal, link in most people's minds. Nevertheless, because such stories' potential content tends to be somewhat limited, the plain fact is that these pieces often end up with a kind of "porno pacing" first popularized by books like John Clelland's *Fanny Hill*; you slow time to a crawl, poring over every possible detail, to disguise the fact that nothing really *happens* for pages and pages except what, in your average screenplay, would probably just read like this: "They have wild, passionate sex."

"Rose-Sick" (c. 1996) was written for one such anthology, *Seductive Specters* (Masquerade Books, ed. Amarantha Knight). I vaguely remember deciding on erotic asphyxiation as the motor of choice behind my plot mainly because of a slightly disturbing encounter I'd had—while taking part in one of those inevitable midnight panels on Sex & Death for some convention the year before—with a fan who seemed to be totally obsessed by the subject. I also seem to recall soon becoming really, really bored by the literal mechanics of making sure the horror-to-"erotic" quotient stayed balanced; at least one draft I initially submitted came back with the comment that it needed "about a hundred more words of sex," prompting me to fantasize about just adding the words "hot" and "wet" to every other sentence. I.e.: *You walk down the hot, wet corridor into the hot, wet room. It's hot in there—hot, and wet.*

(*And DARK.*)

Still, it's not like this didn't pay off, eventually. Doing "Rose-Sick" for Amarantha led to her asking me to submit to another, similar anthology, which meant I got very familiar with the subgenre's specifications, very fast ... and since erotic horror was the stock in trade of *The Hunger*, it all worked out. "Skeleton Bitch" (first published in *Palace Corbie* #5, Merrimack Books, ed. Wayne Edwards), written around the same time, definitely seemed to benefit from my having already had a bit of practice at being exactly as explicit as I needed to be; I'm also kind of proud of having been able to slip my real-life, Lovecraft-gained sex toy expertise in there, right near the end.

Q: "In some of these more explicit stories, you're writing from the perspective of being a man—a *gay* man. What's that about?"

A: Aside from it supposedly being part and parcel of being a writer that you get to pretend you're anybody you want to, as long as you do it convincingly ... ?

I'll readily admit that I've always been fascinated with man-to-man sexual tension, so much so that it counts as (one of) my personal kink(s), along with those nasty little recurrent consent, power disparity and moral ambiguity issues. Maybe it comes out of having gotten most of your childhood sex ed from *Penthouse Letters* rather than *Yellow Silk*, and thus not recognizing a lot of yourself in those giggly, garter belt-wearing female meat puppets with the always-available array of holes which populate most popuLAR porn—an innate impulse to identify with the do-er rather than the do-ee.

Or maybe it's just that lure of the alien again, the spectacle of watching guys interact with each other on a supremely violent or oddly vulnerable level. My favorite TV show IS *OZ*, after all—*Homicide: Life On The Street* creator Tom Fontana's operatic/realistic six-season pay-TV evisceration of the prison system—just like my favorite characters *on OZ* are Tobias Beecher (the upper-middle-class rage addict with bad to no impulse control) on the one hand, and Vern Schillinger (the White Supremacist rapist with serious family issues) on the other. Which—along with Edward Norton's performance in *American History X*, plus some re-reading of various texts on

Viking culture and berserker shamanism—certainly did feed into the writing of "Bear-Shirt," first published in *Queer Fear* (Arsenal Pulp Press, ed. Michael Rowe); I wanted to take a good, hard look at a particularly icky yet attractive subset of my own fetishes, a lingering Anglo-Saxon pull towards those who share my propensity for "blood in the face."

Which is not, obviously (though this can never be made *too* obvious), that I'm hugely sympathetic towards people like Karl Speller; not *hugely*. Small-ly. Like I'm sympathetic to a whole host of other, equally fucked up people . . . so far, at least, as to want to write either about them or from their point of view. People like Dave Proulx, for example, main character of "Torch Song" (first published in *Transversions #8/9*, ed. Dale Sproule and Sally McBride)—a fairly overt homage to *L.A. Confidential* author James Ellroy, especially in his *White Jazz* mode, with a sidebar of bitch-slap for all those who grew up thinking Aphrodite was a *nice* Goddess just because she's the patron mythodaimon of "love." Love being, after all, such a very many-splendored thing: The black end of the spectrum, along with the red.

Or vice-versa.

Q: "Most people say you should 'write what you know.' Do you agree?"

A: In a way, yes. With certain qualifications.

Let's take the case of "Hidebound," for example—first published in *Transversions #5* (ed. Dale Sproule and Sally McBride), then optioned for adaptation by *The Hunger* (the resultant episode aired during the show's 1998 season). Now, I'm very fond of this one, even though I had no (official) input into its screenplay adaptation—primarily since it has dry-voiced, perpetually unimpressable, blessedly full-figured Brooke Smith (probably best known as "the girl down the well" in *Silence Of The Lambs*) playing main character "Lee," better known as "Gemma with a slight dye-job and far more obvious ass-kicking capabilities." But "Hidebound" is also rife with autobiographical elements—liberal use of details gleaned from several sites I worked as a security guard, "Lee's" painful break-up with her fiancé forming a continual subplot to the considerably more dramatic pseudo-werewolf foreground, etc.

So: Do these elements add or detract, in the end? Or, considering most readers who don't know me can't possibly know what's "based on a true story" and what's not unless I tell them, do they even matter?

I don't really think you can ever *avoid* putting bits of yourself into original characters; obviously, some turn out more "you" than others, but the "you" parts will always be the parts that make things *work*, essentially. They're the parts that resonate. And it took me a very long time to accept this fact, because it sounded so much in my mind like that "Why don't you write what you *know*?" thing Mom always used to say to me, and I always used to resent so bitterly: I write fantasy, I don't write reality. But the fantasy spirals off from reality, and it's that little core of "real" that makes the fake that much better, more original, more rooted in some sense of a larger, understandable reality—that makes the impossible more possible, in other words.

The older I get, the more I realize that the reason I wasn't able to finish some earlier projects had less to do with a lack of invention than with a lack of emotional *understanding* which can only come from actual, physical, real-life experience. Inevitably—when I revisit abandoned stories, screenplays, whatever—I find that the true fault lay in an inability to see exactly why and how the things I somehow knew had to happen would, or could, happen: The subconscious, synaptic connections between instinct and impulse, action and reaction, which take actual human beings years to untangle.

So often, we rarely understand our own motivations except in hindsight—and things only become more complex, less black and white, the further we move away from them. In other words, the events themselves don't change, only the way we perceive those events . . . and the way we perceive them only changes because *we* change enough to recognize the distance between who we are now, and who we once were.

All of which is utterly essential, to my mind, when trying to create a realistic, resonant character. Because if your characters can't be at least as marginally self-aware as you yourself are, then what's the point of writing them at all? The more detailed and realistic the character, the more the reader—a detailed, realistic character him/herself—can identify with them, developing an empathy for their situation and problems which goes far beyond the easy evocation of shallow sympathy most simplistic stereotypes evoke.

Weirdly, the more specific a detail, the better it travels; people somehow know that it's *just* distinctive enough to ring "true". Which is why, in the end, you should never be afraid to "write what you know". . . even if your mother once told you to.

"Hidebound," partially based on my break-up with one fiancé, was written during my break-up with another. A year after the episode premiered, my second fiancé ran into me at a party and boasted about how his Dad, watching late-night TV, had been appalled to realize that this scenario about a woman making sure her ex got ripped apart by supernatural beasts (the patented *"whammo!"* ending, added in translation for maximum Hollywood North effect) was based on something I wrote. "'No, no, that's about Gemma's *other* ex,'" my second fiancé told me he'd assured my former prospective father-in-law, then laughed: Pretty funny, eh? Oh yeah, I agreed—adding: "And the *really* funny part is, I actually just sold them the one that's about *you*." (That'd be "The Diarist," first published in *Transversions* #7 [ed. Dale Sproule and Sally McBride]; the episode based on *it* aired during *The Hunger*'s 1999 season, shot from a teleplay written by yours truly).

Another "writ[ing] what you know"-type trend I've stumbled across recently in my work is the deliberate evocation of script format, as in "Folly" (written for the official 2001 World Fantasy Con CD/ROM, ed. Nancy Kilpatrick, on a theme of "Ghosts & Gaslight"), "Job 37" (first published in *Dark Terrors 6*, ed. Stephen Jones and David Sutton, from Gollancz) and "Seen" (first published in *The Narrow World* Chapbook for World Horror Con 2001, ed. Stephen J. Barringer, Quantum Theology Publications). On the one hand, I teach screenwriting for a living these days, and format really counts; the biggest struggle, for most of my students, is simply having to accept the fact that what they're writing is basically more a list of suggestions than any kind of holy writ—a blueprint for a coalition of other artists to enlarge upon, over which you have little or no control after the first draft is sold. On the other, this means that getting your point across is a real exercise in directness *and* subtlety . . . and since I often think I overwrite anyways, in terms of trying to render the sensual "reality" of a given situation as exactly as possible (I remember once reading a section of Caitlin R. Kiernan's *Low Red Moon* 'blog in which she lamented having spent approximately half a day trying to get one of her characters to cross a room and flick off a light switch, and thinking: *Yeah, that's about the size of it*), having to occasionally keep everything strictly "off-stage" is good for me.

Or so I explain it to myself.

In terms of inspiration, meanwhile, "Seen" is related to an old Irish fairytale about a midwife called upon to deliver a fairy baby retold in Georgess McHarque's *The Impossible People*, while "Folly" owes a roughly equal debt to *The Legend Of Hell House* (with Roddy McDowell!) and an article on cthonic rituals in ancient Greece I read in an issue of *Archaeology* magazine, or somewhere similar. "Job 37" is the result of an interview read in *Harper*'s magazine, extensive web-searches on crime-scene clean-up, and probably too many episodes of *CSI: Crime Scene Investigations.*

Q: "How come so few of your main characters are nice, likeable people?"

A: Are most people "nice" or "likeable," generally? I know *I*'m not. Are you?

It's funny. On the one hand, I'm increasingly willing to admit that being a hero is probably ten times harder than being a villain, in much the same way that the Dark Side of the Force always beckons twice as hard and seductively as the . . . Um . . . Not-Dark Side; anger, hatred and fear are such *easy* emotions to evoke, after all, just as compassion, balance and hope are such incredibly difficult ones to sustain. But admiration only takes me so far: In the final analysis, it really *is* always a bad-ass that makes (this) girl's heart beat faster. I like slippery people, difficult people, self-justifying people—people with issues, yo—and thus the characters I choose for my protagonists usually end up fitting that particular bill.

"Blood Makes Noise," first published in *Transversions #11* (ed. Dale Sproule and Sally McBride), evolved because I started thinking vaguely about how cowards rationalize their own behavior—is "the fate worse than death," whatever it may be, *really* all that worse (especially if you're scared shitless of dying)? Regis Book himself, meanwhile, owes an equal debt to Alex Krycek from *The X-Files*—I *was* at Ad Astra, Toronto's biggest yearly multifandom geek romp, when I got the initial idea—and the conspiracy rants of Dead Kennedys frontman Jello Biafra; many details about deep sea life come from William J. Broad's *The Universe Below,* amongst other sources.

And speaking of Ad Astra . . . "Pretend That We're Dead," first e-published in *The Three-Lobed Burning Eye #7* (ed. Andrew S. Fuller), is the direct byproduct of a Shared World Project developed by myself, Sandra Kasturi and Jason Taniguchi for the 1998 version of said convention. I'd therefore like to acknowledge their input into this piece, thank them for their support and friendship generally, and gently bug them to fix up and submit the stuff *they* wrote that year within what we came to call the Toronto: The Infestation universe.

Q: "Okay. What next?"

A: Aw, you know. Same old same old.

I've been writing—and publishing, amazingly enough—short stories for about fifteen years now: Won an award and carved out a bit of a name for myself, just like I once made the equivalent of a whole year's salary with a single sale (my own script adaptation of the story "Bottle Of Smoke," for [you guessed it] *The Hunger*)—which probably, if I dare say so myself, isn't something a lot of other people can claim to have done. People tell me the next logical evolutionary step is to write a novel, and I believe them; this collection, along with another one I have coming out from Prime Books pretty soon, is sort of designed to help hothouse what last few short stories I still have lurking around on my hard drive to ripeness and fruition, so they'll stop interfering with that all-important process. I guess we'll find out if it works.

Which brings us neatly to the last story here: "Dead Bodies Possessed By Furious Motion," first published in *The Narrow World* chapbook (ed. Stephen J. Barringer, Quantum Theology Publications). I see it as a return to my roots, somewhat . . . pseudo-science fiction, liberally larded with those anti-Rice vampirism theories I talked about earlier. A bit thick on the metaphor rather than the logic, but I'll freely admit I love Elder and her febrile world dearly; it's maybe two-thirds the visual sense and style of Stephen Norrington's *Blade* mixed with Mike Mignola's *Hellboy*, but the rest of it is mine, I tells ya . . . *alllll* mine.

(Oh, and watch for at least one of these characters to pop back up in *The Worm* . . . as well as making a not-so-cameo appearance in that book I'm already currently laboring on; no, no hints. It's so much more *fun* that way.)

At any rate. The leap into the long, cold dark, with only hunger for your friend and guide: A good note to end on, don't you think? And so, farewell. Thanks for listening.

You've been a most gracious—and attentive—audience.

About the Author

Born in London, England and raised in Toronto, Canada, Gemma Files' horror and dark fantasy fiction has appeared in magazines like *TransVersions*, *Palace Corbie* and *The Three-Lobed Burning Eye*, as well as in anthologies like **Northern Frights, Queer Fear I** and **II, The Year's Best Fantasy And Horror 13**, and **The Mammoth Book Of Vampire Stories By Women**. Her story "The Emperor's Old Bones" won an International Horror Guild award for Best Short Fiction of 1999. She is happily married to upcoming high fantasy and science fiction writer Stephen J. Barringer, has tattoos, a pet snake and very thin skin, and is currently hard at work on a first novel.

Files left Ryerson University with a B.A.A. in Magazine Journalism, eventually spending eight years as a freelance film critic. For her most recent reviews, check issues of *Underworlds* and *Rue Morgue* magazines or at http://www.thechiaroscuro.com, where she co-writes "Gemma & Mike's Movie Throw-Down" with fellow award-winning horror author/critic Michael Marano.

Over the 1998/1999 seasons, five of Files' short stories were adapted into episodes—two from scripts she wrote herself—of **The Hunger**, a half-hour anthology TV series produced by Tony and Ridley Scott for Showtime. Currently, Files draws her primary paycheque from the International Academy of Design and Technology (Toronto branch), where she teaches courses on scriptwriting for short films and TV, film history and Canadian film history. You can order her dark fantasy novella Narukh: Chaos Engine online, at http://members.tripod.com/gemma_files/

PERMISSION AND ACKNOWLEDGMENTS

"Introduction," copyright © 2003 by Caitlin R. Kiernan.

"Kissing Carrion," copyright © 2003 by Gemma Files, originally published here for the first time.

"Keepsake," copyright © 1995 by Gemma Files, first published in *Palace Corbie* #7.

"Rose-Sick," copyright © 1996 by Gemma Files, first published in *Seductive Spectres*.

"Blood Makes Noise," copyright © 1998 by Gemma Files, first published in *Transversions* #11.

"Skeleton Bitch," copyright © 1994 by Gemma Files, first published in *Palace Corbie* #5.

"Folly," copyright © 2001 by Gemma Files, first published on the *World Fantasy Convention 2001 CD-Rom*.

"Mouthful Of Pins," copyright © 1994 by Gemma Files, first published in *Northern Frights 2*.

"Pretend That We're Dead," copyright © 2000 by Gemma Files, first published in the ezine *Three-Lobed Burning Eye* #7.

"No Darkness But Ours," copyright © 2001 by Gemma Files, first published in the ezine *Twilight Showcase*.

"Job 37," copyright © 2002 by Gemma Files, first published in *Dark Terrors 6*.

"Bear-Shirt," copyright © 2000 by Gemma Files, first published in *Queer Fear*.

"Hidebound," copyright © 1997 by Gemma Files, first published in *Transversions* #5.

"Skin City," copyright © 1995 by Gemma Files, first published in *A Kind of*

Crimson Evil, a chapbook from *Obelesk Press*.

"Seen," copyright © 2001 by Gemma Files, first published in *The Narrow World*, a chapbook from *Quantum Theology Publications*.

"Torch Song," copyright © 1998 by Gemma Files, first published in *Transversions #8/9, Spring/Summer issue*.

"The Diarist," copyright © 1997 by Gemma Files, first published in *Transversions #7*.

"Dead Bodies Possessed By Furious Motion," copyright © 2001 by Gemma Files, first published in *The Narrow World*, a chapbook from *Quantum Theology Publications*.

"Afterword," copyright © 2003 by Gemma Files.

Printed in the United States
1009000001BA